The Hollisters' Brothers Homecoming

The Hollisters' Brothers Homecoming

Edited by LEZLI ROBYN

CAEZIK
ROMANCE
ARC MANOR
ROCKVILLE, MARYLAND

SHAHID MAHMUD
PUBLISHER

www.CaezikRomance.com

The Sheriff Trap copyright © 2024 by **Anna J. Stewart**
Where the Heart Is copyright © 2024 by **Kayla Perrin**
A Place to Belong copyright © 2024 by **Melinda Curtis**
Claiming the Soldier's Heart copyright © 2024 by **Cari Lynn Webb**
Epilogue copyright © 2024 by **Cari Lynn Webb**

ISBN: 978-1-64710-061-2

First Edition. First Printing. July 2024.
1 2 3 4 5 6 7 8 9 10

CAEZIK
ROMANCE

An imprint of Arc Manor LLC
www.CaezikRomance.com

Contents

Contents

The Sheriff Trap

by Anna J Stewart

1

"Nothing I love more than playing phone tag with my globe-trotting brothers," Sheriff Seth Hollister muttered as he pocketed his phone after leaving yet another voice mail. One would think, with their father getting remarried in just a few weeks, Van and Jarod could give him some peace of mind regarding their attendance.

"Morning, Sheriff!"

"Good morning, Lindie," Seth Hollister greeted the little girl with a chuckle as she skipped down the center aisle of Sea Glass Bay's Town Market. Lindie's pigtails bobbed behind her as she zipped in and around the craft tables and straight into the arms of the paint-spattered woman sorting through supplies. He could almost hear the squeal of contentment from both Lindie and her stepmother, Claire, and the sight brought a smile to his lips.

Seth's affection for his hometown never ceased to amaze or entertain him, even if his job sometimes strained his patience. Small town antics. Small town drama. Small town perfection. Family issues paled in comparison to the sea wafting through the Sunday morning breeze even as the church tower bell began to chime. *Nope. Definitely nothing to complain about.*

"Dad, I know I screwed up last night, but I don't need you escorting me through town to apologize to Serena."

Ah. Seth took a deep, patience-steeling breath. Now he remembered. "Oh, I think I do." He glanced at his fifteen-year-old son and, even through the fog of frustration, wondered when Matty had grown up. Hadn't it just been yesterday that he'd run behind his gangly little boy, holding onto the back of his training-wheels-free bike, insisting he wouldn't let his son fall? Now here he was escorting his almost-grown son to the Wide Awake Café where, not only would he be buying the kid a double shot espresso, but also bearing witness as Matty issued the appropriate apology due the owner. "I know this whole dating thing is new for all of us, but you were late getting Kimberly home last night and no doubt stressed her mother out. The least you owe her is an apology."

Matty grumbled something under his breath. Seth stopped walking and pinned Matty with *the look.* "I'm sorry. I didn't quite hear you."

"Morning, Sheriff!" Clancy Zimmerman zipped by on his shiny blue bike, his backwards baseball cap declaring his undying devotion to the 49ers.

"Morning, Clancy. *Whoa!* Hang on, Mrs. Arlis." He darted across the aisle and caught the corner of the distracted woman's pop-up canopy before it popped free.

"Thanks, Sheriff." Connie Arlis, arms filled with jars of her famous local honey, sighed in relief.

"Well?" With the tent secure, Seth didn't miss a beat where Matty was concerned. "Did you say something?"

"No, sir."

Matty scrunched his mouth in a way that reminded Seth so much of Matty's mother he almost grinned. Matty had gotten Seth's dark brown hair and eyes, but those dimples, and that just waiting to burst free spirit? That was all Matty's mother.

On mornings like this, however, he was reminded of the challenges of being a single father, especially to a teenager. Not that Opal would have considered Matty's transgressions cause for concern. Seth's high-school girlfriend had always had a loose relationship with rules and expectations, which explained why she'd taken off on a life of adventure rather than staying in Sea Glass Bay to raise Matty.

"I'll apologize to Serena and promise it won't happen again," Matty assured him.

"Excellent plan." Seth pushed his hand against the back of Matty's head, their coded sign for undying affection. Matty snort laughed and pretended to shake off his father's hold, but Seth snaked his arm around his neck and hung on.

How had his parents done it, Seth wondered? Taking in not only Seth (at the ripe old age of thirteen), but three other challenging boys? Somehow Seth and his adoptive brothers—Vin, Jarod, and Axel—had been given everything their jaded and wounded hearts could have ever hoped or asked for. More importantly, they'd been granted a stability Seth had been able to cling to when his own son was born.

A son who would be on his own in the blink of an eye. Seth had prepared himself for many things over the years, but that might be what would finally do him in. Matty had his eyes set on Los Angeles and a film writing career, which meant Seth had to take advantage of every second he still had with him.

Even if some of those seconds were spent doing uncomfortable things.

As the weekend market continued to open behind them—the stretch of road containing the main thoroughfare of shops, eateries, and various scenic walking paths down to and around the beach—Seth found himself filled with the gratitude he embraced every day. A gratitude that gifted him with the patience of a saint when it came to dealing with the more colorful characters dwelling in the small, west coast, ocean-side town. Putting on his uniform of khaki slacks, shirt, and tan baseball cap embroidered with the initials for the Sea Glass Bay Police every morning reaffirmed he'd found where he belonged. A place he, unlike most of his brothers, had chosen to make his permanent home.

He smelled Wide Awake Café before he saw it. That tantalizing, stomach-tempting, caffeine-promising aroma that jump-started his mornings.

"Dad, really." Matty slowed his pace, shoved his hands into his front pockets, an action he took whenever he really didn't want to do something. "I can do this on my own."

"Consider me verification of that fact." The red and white stenciled lettering on the window of the café promised a selection of cold and hot beverages and some of the best homemade pastries in a hundred-mile radius. Seth pulled open the door, ushered Matty inside.

"Daaa-ad."

Seth partially surrendered, gestured to one of the round tables in the corner by the window. "I'll wait over there. Oh, and I'll take a medium triple shot espresso." He blinked in mock innocence at his son's reaction. "What? You got paid this week, didn't you?"

"Yeah, yeah," Matty mumbled again and shifted his tall, lanky form toward the front counter.

Seth left him alone, glancing around the small café that was nearly filled to capacity. Tables were comfortably separated, smaller round ones for up to two people, larger rectangular ones for larger groups, and a higher counter with a row of bar stools lined the far wall where customers could plug in their computers or recharge their phones.

The aroma of cinnamon and hot butter coated the air, along with the bitter hints of coffee spiked with imported chocolate. In the five years Wide Awake had been open, Seth had rarely missed a morning cup.

"Morning, Sheriff." Garbriel Abernathe peeked over the top of the Sunday paper and peered at Seth over his thin rimmed glasses. "You going to have a talk with Cecily today about that danged cat of hers? Mangy critter was out all night caterwauling and looking for a date. Howled outside my bedroom window so loud I couldn't hear my TV."

"Cecily and Ranger are on my agenda," Seth assured the man who had been old when Seth had been Matty's age.

"Good to know," Gabriel said. "Got my invite last week to your dad's big pre-wedding shindig. Going to be quite the bachelor party, isn't it?"

"So I hear." Seth offered a quick smile and moved toward the still empty table. If he wasn't addressing town issues, he was fielding comments and questions about his father's upcoming nuptials to Gail Butler. With less than a month to go before the big day, Seth had finally come to terms with the fact his father was getting remarried.

Well, mostly.

Maybe it was just the idea of a *bachelor* party that didn't sit well with him. His father wasn't a bachelor. He was a widow and had been for the past two years. Calling Clay Hollister a bachelor felt like kicking dirt on Leda Hollister's grave.

The pang of grief that accompanied thoughts of Leda Hollister struck low and deep. How he missed popping around the house for a late morning coffee and catch-up. What he wouldn't give to see her kind, steady face smiling up at him in pride and affection or find her working in her arboretum of a backyard, a pitcher of her special brewed iced-tea sitting on the metal table for anyone who might pass by. Seth could never have imagined the void losing her would leave. Or that years later that the void had yet to fill. He could count on one hand the number of things he truly longed for. Top of the list?

His arms and heart ached for one more hug from his mom.

Seth shifted the chair to keep his back to the wall and tried not to watch the activity at the front counter of the café. Because he couldn't help himself, he caught Matty glance over his shoulder. Wide-eyed panic had set in.

"On my way, kid," Seth muttered under his breath. He set his cap on the table to hold the place and made his way to his son. "Hi, Serena." He flashed what he hoped was his best peacemaker smile even as he ignored that ridiculous chest clenching he felt whenever he was in the vicinity of the café owner. "Did Matty apologize for Kimberly missing her curfew last night?"

"He did." Serena's bright blue eyes danced with amusement. "I'm betting in a few years he'll be almost as eloquent as his father."

Seth felt the color rise in his cheeks. As usual, Serena Covington had her thick blonde hair tied back from her face. Her worn jeans had his fingers flexing against the temptation to explore those curves of hers. The shirt beneath the logo-emblazoned apron was the color of the blue sea glass he'd been collecting since he was a boy. They'd known each other for years; had danced around each other for even more years, as life always seemed to be overflowing. But these days …. These days Seth was thinking about another kind of dance.

"Yeah, well." He cleared his throat, ignoring the amused glint in his son's eyes. "I'm teaching him everything I can. Honestly, it will not happen again."

"Oh, I know." Serena jerked a thumb toward the back where a miniature, younger version of her zipped past with an armload of baking sheets.

The teen glanced over, eyes wide, and nearly bashed into the wall before she caught herself.

"Kimberly and I have already discussed it. If you are going to bring her home late," she added to Matty, "just make sure one of you calls or texts, okay?"

"That won't be necessary," Seth insisted. Matty and Kimberly wouldn't be seeing much of each other anymore. This apology was only the beginning of Seth's plan. Matty was far too young to be this serious about anyone. His son had his education to think about. His education and his future. Both were things Seth had dismissed at Matty's age, hence Matty's arrival when Seth was only sixteen.

Seth was more than happy with the way his life had turned out. But he was not going to let Matty forget not only the plans, but the dreams he had for his future. Dreams so large they couldn't be contained in Sea Glass Bay. "Did you order?"

"Yeah. They're brewing up now. I'll just—" Matty pointed to the pickup counter. "Again, I'm sorry, Serena."

"And again, apology accepted." Serena glanced at Seth once Matty moved away. "Did you want something else?"

Some*thing*? No. Some*one* …? Lord. He'd been hanging out with Sully Vaughn too much. Watching his friend's relationship with Claire Bishop blossom into wedded bliss had left Seth feeling the forgotten pangs of … well, loneliness. No doubt that was what resulted in Seth's unwitting focus that kept circling back to the pretty, single-mother café owner.

"Do you have a minute?" Seth asked her.

"Sure. Caitlyn?" Serena motioned for one of her employees to take over. "Let me grab your coffee and I'll come around."

"Great, thanks." He eyed Matty, who was leaning so far over the counter to wave at Kimberly he lost his footing and knocked over the cups of stirrers. Seth rolled his eyes. What was it about teenage boys that they went straight-up stupid at this age?

Serena came out of the back with a tray holding two cups and a small paper bag of promise. She stopped long enough to tease Matty and inform him his drink was coming up next before she gestured for Seth to follow her out the back door.

"Busy morning." She set the tray down on a sea-glass mosaic table in the private garden that served as her employee's break and eating area. "Nice to have an excuse for a break. Sit. Drink. Eat." She plopped the bag in front of him. "Your favorite. Just out of the oven."

"Chocolate orange scones?" He felt like an idiot for sounding like Matty on Christmas morning, but he ripped open the bag in the exact same fashion. "They're heaven on a plate. Or in my case, a napkin." He sipped his coffee first then bit into the flaky biscuit-like treat. With a sigh, he sat back. "You are magic."

"Seeing that expression on your face makes waking up at 3 a.m. to cook worth it." Her smile, when he looked at her, could chase storm clouds away. "So what's on your mind?"

"Right." He wiped his mouth, considered his words. "Matty and Kimberly. I'm concerned they're seeing too much of each other."

Serena inclined her head, her assessing gaze making him want to squirm. "Reluctantly, I'm going to have to agree."

"Yeah?" He hadn't meant to sound quite so surprised.

"Yeah. Kimberly failed a math test last week. And a history exam the week before. Both were taken on days after she'd spent the previous night *studying* with Matty."

"That's not good." Seth frowned. "I'm sorry. I didn't know."

"No reason for you to." Serena shrugged. "She's my daughter. She knows what her responsibilities are, and she knows I'm disappointed that she's not putting the appropriate things first."

Seth almost melted. He laughed, shook his head. "I am so relieved to hear you say that. I thought for sure I was going to have a fight on my hands trying to convince you to help me."

"Help you what?" Serena asked, clearly confused.

"Help me break them up. Now"—he took another bite of scone and glug of coffee—"where do you think we should start?"

"Well?"

Matty Hollister jumped then glared over his shoulder at Kimberly.

Her pixie face and pert little nose honed in as she peeked around the edge of the door into the garden. Her long blonde hair was braided down her back and tiny dots of pink sea glass sparkled on her ears. But her eyes were filled with the same mischievous determination percolating through Matty.

"Well what?"

"Is it working?" She grabbed hold of his arm, rose up on her tiptoes to look over his shoulder. "They're getting along, right? They're smiling. And laughing."

"Oh, they're getting along." Even better than Matty had hoped. An unexpected flash of uncertainty shot through him. They were doing the right thing, weren't they? Since his grandmother had died, Matty had begun to pay more attention to his father, to his life and how—other than Matty—he really didn't have anything except his job. He needed someone, someone who would make him laugh, someone who would challenge him. Someone who could make his father light up the way his Grandpa Clay lit up around Gail. "I think my dad's had enough of my behavior by now. He has to be looking for ways to bust us up."

"Awesome." Kimberly giggled, then snorted.

"Nice." He shifted to give her more room. "Hopefully it'll be worth you tanking your GPA for this."

"Hey!" Kimberly smacked him on the arm. "We agreed. We each have to risk something in order for this to pay off."

"Yeah, yeah." He blew out a breath. "Man, I really hope this works. With my grandpa getting married next month and me looking at early college admission, I really need my dad taken care of."

"My mom's his perfect match," Kimberly confirmed. "They've been flirting for years. It's about time someone made them do something about it."

"Well, step one's complete at least." Matty stepped back and closed the door. "I guess the next one's up to me. You're sure you're ready for this?"

"Doubly sure," Kimberly said with an oddly evil grin. "Let's get to work."

2

"*You* want to break up our kids." Serena Covington sat back and stared at the town sheriff, wondering how such a good-looking, kind-hearted man could be so utterly and completely clueless. "Are you out of your mind?" Seth's frown had her realizing that yes, he might just be. "Do you not remember what happens when you tell a kid not to do something? That's all they want to do."

"That's not entirely … true." But Seth's frown deepened. "I mean, yeah, generally, but that's only if you're unprepared. We just have to keep on top of things. Come up with ways to counter their reactions. Find distractions for them."

"Remind me again"—Serena tilted her head—"how old were you and Matty's mom when you had him?"

That wiped the humor off his face.

"I'm just saying." She held up her hands. "And I speak from my own experience. My parents did everything they could including dead-bolting my door to keep me away from Kimberly's father. See this scar?" She pointed to the faded, jagged mark on her left forearm. "I got this falling out of the tree outside my second story window when I made a break for it."

"Ouch." Seth's expression softened. "That's some grim determination."

"Maybe now that we're both over thirty it's difficult to remember just how potent those teenage hormones can be." She hoped he saw the warning in her eyes. As much as she wanted Kimberly to shift her focus away from Matty Hollister, she knew how futile the fight could be. "How many conversations did your parents have with you about Opal?"

He cringed. "So many that my brothers code named those talks 'Defcon T'."

"I rest my case." She crossed her legs, folded her hands in her lap.

"But in the end my parents trusted me to make my own decisions," Seth added. "It was Opal's parents who forbid me to see her."

"And hence … Matty." She had to admit, Seth really was kinda cute when he was flummoxed.

"All right." His laugh made her lips twitch. "Point made. There are a few differences here," he said. "Matty's been taught all about sex. And responsibility."

"Like you weren't." Serena snorted. "Your mother worked as a part-time school nurse and your father was the sheriff. Don't tell me they didn't give you all the details. Forbidden fruit is all the more delicious," Serena went on when he shrugged. "You lucked out whereas in my case, the aftertaste remains bitter. At least Opal pops back into town now and again to see her son. Jackson lasted a whole six months before he took off. All these years later I'm still waiting for that first child support check."

"I could help with that if you want." His instant shift to law enforcement mentality surprisingly came across as comforting. "You could file with the courts for back payment."

"Sweet of you." It was, actually, but Serena wasn't so hard up for cash she needed to hunt down Kimberly's father. At least not yet. "I'm doing just fine without him. But we're getting off topic. This is about Matty and Kimberly. I think a compromise might be in order. We let them keep seeing each other, but on our timetable. Weekends only. No school night study sessions and no text messaging after eleven."

"Ten," Seth countered. "Heck, I'd be happy with nine. That kid's going to have to have his thumbs replaced before he's twenty at this rate."

"It's a generational mutation," Serena agreed. "We old folks will have to suffer the effects of carpal tunnel well into our dotage. So—can we agree not to Montague them at this point?"

Seth chuckled. "Montague. Nice."

"Life's serious enough without freaking out over the little stuff," she told him. "I like Matty, Seth. And in a lot of ways, I think he's been good for Kimberly. From what I hear he's a lot like you were at that age."

"Oh, he's not nearly as challenging, believe me," Seth countered.

"That's not what I mean. And yes, I've heard the stories. I know you were considered …"

"Difficult?"

"A handful," she corrected him. "All you Hollister boys were. Wasn't it you who got suspended for hotwiring the high school principal's car and taking it for a ride?"

"That was Axel." Seth grinned. "I got suspended for stuffing Steve Plunket into his gym locker."

"Oh, that's right." Serena's heart did a little flip. "Caterina Walford told me about that at one of our wine parties. Steve had been bullying her because of her weight, and you turned around and invited her to the school dance right there in front of half the school."

"Yeah, well." Seth shrugged. "It seemed like the right thing to do at the time. And Caterina's a great dancer."

She loved that shade of pink on his cheeks. "See? A good guy. Just like your son. How could I not want Kimberly to date someone like him?"

"I appreciate that." Seth polished off his scone and picked up his coffee. "Now that we've got this somewhat settled, I need to get to work. I have a cat in unseasonal heat that I need to corral and an owner to give a talking to. The sheriff's job is never done. I'll see you tomorrow morning for coffee. Thanks again for the scone."

"You're welcome." She watched him leave and, not for the first time, found herself looking forward to tomorrow. How different her life would have been if her teenage self had fallen for Seth Hollister instead of bad boy Jackson Temple?

She wouldn't have wound up alone, that was for sure.

Getting pregnant at sixteen didn't exactly make for an easy life; nor had getting thrown out by her parents who saw Serena's pregnancy as the final straw to her rather active and rebellious teenage years. Thankfully, both her grandmothers had stepped in, joined forces, and, a few years after Kimberly was born, moved them all to Sea Glass Bay where they gave Serena all the emotional and financial support she needed. They'd devoted their time to making certain Serena not only finished high school, but also earned her degree in food management and gave her the startup funds for Wide Awake.

Now it was Serena's turn to take care of them.

Too bad she was beginning to feel like an abject failure in that department. Between the business and the mortgage and a teenager who would be college bound soon …

Sometimes she felt like a hamster on a runaway wheel.

Worrying about Kimberly's social life was just one more thing to add to her pile of responsibilities. A pile that, if she wasn't careful, was going to come crashing down on her head.

"But that's a worry for another time," Serena told herself as she headed back inside to work. Definitely another time.

Because Cecily Perkins's house was only a few doors down from his parents', and because Seth had spent the last half hour repairing Cecily's back screen door in an attempt to corral her wayward cat, during which he'd talked himself hoarse trying to convince her to have the animal spayed, he found himself heading for the comfort of home.

Not his two-bedroom cottage on the other side of town, but the two-story saltbox that had, from the moment he arrived, provided safety, perspective, and love.

The exterior may have changed, but what was housed inside had not. The white picket fence had been replaced twice over the years. The home repainted a bright sunshine yellow with white trim and shutters. The porch planks were as squeaky as ever but, as the four Hollister brothers had learned shortly after arrival, acted as an alarm system indicating incoming teenage boys.

The flowering and blooming bushes were exploding into pre-summer abundance, encouraged not only by the gardener his father had hired shortly after Leda's death, but also Leda's spirit. One couldn't step foot on Hollister property without feeling her presence. Maybe it was that, Seth thought as he unlatched the gate and stepped onto the cobblestone path, maybe it was Leda who drew him here today.

The matching For Sale signs stopped him for a moment. It shouldn't have surprised him. He'd been informed of his father's plans months ago. His stepmother-to-be had moved out of her house next door months before and, once it sold, they'd look for a new place in Sea Glass Bay before putting the house he'd grown up in on the market.

Strange to even contemplate, Seth thought. Gail Butler had been their neighbor for as long as Seth could remember. She'd been his mother's best friend; they'd gone to nursing school together. Shortly after Gail's husband filed for divorce, Leda had been diagnosed with an aggressive form of ovarian cancer. Gail had taken a leave of absence to help care for her best friend and, in the final days, been a Godsend for their father. Much like Leda's garden, Clay and Gail's friendship eventually blossomed into something new. Something unexpected.

Seeing the For Sale sign on Gail's house felt like an odd rite of passage that would put an end to the life they'd all known before, and hopefully, lead to a renewed future.

No sooner did Seth's foot hit one of those squeaky porch boards than he heard footsteps on the other side of the door.

"Morning, Seth." Clay toasted him with his mug of steaming coffee as he pushed open the screen door.

His father was quite possibly the only person on the planet who could still make Seth feel like a kid. At six-foot-six, Clay Hollister stood a good four inches taller than Seth and maintained the healthy physique of the thirty-year law enforcement professional more than five years after his retirement. His dark blond hair was caught in that heading-to-gray-but-not-quite-there stage. "Gail's just finishing up a fresh batch of bagel bread," Clay said. "You want in?"

"Ah, no, thanks." Seth removed his cap, tucked it into the back pocket of his pants and followed his father down the short photograph laden hallway into the spacious kitchen. "Good morning, Gail."

"Seth, hello." Gail Butler slammed her fist into the bowl of dough sitting on the counter and aimed a welcoming dark-eyed gaze in his direction. "There's a fresh pot of coffee brewing."

"I just had some at Wide Awake. Any more caffeine and I won't need a patrol car to zip around town."

"Don't stand on ceremony," Clay ordered. "You have time to sit for a bit or is this just a walk by?"

"I can stay a while." Seth sat in his usual chair across from his father. The Lazy Susan in the center of the table held a selection of coffee additions, Leda's antique butter bell, and a jar of Gail's homemade lemon marmalade. It all felt so ... normal. He knew not all the Hollister brothers were on board with the wedding, but when all was said and done, Gail had given Clay back his spark. And that, Seth acknowledged, would have made Leda incredibly happy. "Thought I'd stop by and see if you needed any help with the wedding arrangements."

"I'm leaving all that up to the bride," Clay said. "Gail?"

"Everything's coming along just fine as far as I know." Gail draped a towel over her bowl. "The wedding planner is overseeing all the deliveries to the island. She's promised me I only need to pick out a dress and show up."

"Good, good." Seth couldn't help but feel relieved. The offer had been more to do with obligation than capability. He didn't know the first thing about weddings. "Your party's all set, I take it?" he asked his father. "Gabriel Abernathy got his invitation."

Clay's brows lifted as he set his mug on the table. "Nothing special. Just getting together at Tank's for some drinks and food."

"Make sure they keep the red label scotch out of play." Axel, his hair damp from what Seth assumed was a shower, wandered into the kitchen. "Morning. Hey, Seth. What are you doing here?"

"I've got the same question." Seth shot a confused look at his father, who only shrugged as Axel filled a mug with coffee and took a seat at the table.

"I got Gail's car done early so I dropped it off." He took a long drink. "Grabbed a shower while I was here."

"You want some eggs?" Gail set the carton of milk on the table.

"No, thanks, Gail. Coffee's fine."

"Some toast then," she countered and got him a plate. "Put something in your stomach."

"Thanks." Axel scarfed down half a slice then reached for the marmalade. "What's new with you?" he asked Seth.

Seth hesitated. "Matty's dating Kimberly Covington." Was it wrong for him to wish Matty had never discovered the opposite sex?

"Oh, she's a sweet girl," Gail said. After washing her hands, she let down her shoulder-length dark hair. "I see her in the café helping her mother all the time. Your Matty's a good choice for her."

"Thanks." Despite his misgivings about the relationship, pride ballooned in his chest. "Dad, when Opal and I were dating—"

"Ah, the good old days." Axel smirked into his coffee and earned a kick from Seth under the table.

"I was thinking about all those talks you and Mom gave me about cooling things down, taking things slow. Did you …?" Seth plunged in before he lost his nerve. "Did you and Mom ever talk about trying to break us up?"

"It came up." Clay nodded solemnly. "I thought you were too young to get tied down to one girl. Your mother seemed to think keeping you two apart would only push you together more." A small smile curved his lips and he glanced at Gail. "One thing about Hollister men. When we fall, we fall hard. Things turned out all right in the end. You made us grandparents a bit earlier than we'd planned, but he was a blessing. That boy just lit up Leda like the North Star."

Seth smiled despite the pang of grief hitting dead center of his chest. "Sometimes I think Opal's parents really robbed themselves of something special."

"Opal's parents are asses," Gail said, and Axel snort laughed. "Sorry." She held up her hand, her eyes wide as if surprised she'd spoken out loud. "Family history and all. None of my business."

"No," Seth said when she started to stand. "Please. I'd appreciate your input, Gail."

Gail blinked in surprise, then—when Clay reached up and took her hand—she sat in the chair Leda would have occupied. "Well, I'm happy to lend my two cents."

"You knew Opal's parents?" Seth asked.

"Before they moved away. And before you ask, I'll tell you I think their disapproval of you had more to do with them losing control of a girl they'd already lost than you specifically. The tighter they tried to hold on to Opal, the quicker she slipped away. You were right there waiting to break her fall. She needed that. Needed someone." Gail shook her head. "Opal was a puzzle to them. They never understood her, and she certainly didn't understand them."

"That probably explains why she was so terrified about being a parent," Clay said. "You did right by her, Seth. You gave her what her parents couldn't, a choice in how to live her life. What's all this about? You worried about Matty and Kimberly going down that same path?"

"*Pffffth.*" Gail waved off that idea with a laugh. "Not going to happen."

"I wouldn't be so sure." Seth grumbled. "They're becoming inseparable."

"Well, wedging them apart isn't going to stop that," Clay warned him. "Now I don't know Kimberly that well, but Matty's got a good head on his shoulders. I wouldn't worry too much. Let it ride out."

"You sound like Serena," Seth told them.

"Serena?" Clay's expression was too innocent. "Kimberly's mother? You talked to her about this?"

Seth shot a look at his brother just in time to stop him from commenting. Seth's long-standing crush on their local café owner was anything but a secret among the family. "I kind of needed to."

"So now you're on the opposite end of this teenage relationship situation then."

"Looks that way." But maybe Serena—and his father and Gail—had a point. Maybe he was overthinking this and not giving Matty or Kimberly enough credit. Maybe backing off, giving them a chance to readjust their priorities, get their grades and study habits back under control, would do more good than lowering the boom.

"Not that anyone asked me," Axel tossed in. "But nothing makes a woman more appealing than a bit of—"

"Forbidden fruit?" Seth cut him off. "Yeah, Serena said that, too."

"Smart woman," Axel said and picked up his mug. "I need to head in to the shop. Thanks for the shower. Dad. Gail."

Seth waited until he heard Axel close the front door before he looked back at his father. "Everything okay with him?"

"I've learned not to ask," Clay said and earned a disapproving cluck of Gail's tongue. "If he needs something, he'll tell one of us."

Seth wasn't so sure. It wasn't a secret that Axel had never felt as if he completely belonged. It must have hurt to be the only Hollister boy Leda and Clay hadn't officially adopted.

"You Hollister men," Gail chided. "Takes a crowbar, a pair of pliers, and a stick of dynamite to get any of you to talk about anything. Well, except maybe Seth," she offered with a quick grin. "Don't worry about your brother. He'll come around. You all always do." She cleared away Axel's plate.

"Thanks for the coffee," Seth said. "And for the advice about Matty and Kimberly."

"Door's always open." Clay rose to refill his coffee. "You hear from Van or Jared lately?"

"I called Jared earlier." He purposely avoided admitting he hadn't actually spoken to him. "And I talked with Van last week." Discussing Van was like walking across a field of landmines. Of all the Hollister boys, Van was the one most out of touch with the family. Serving in a special division of the military that kept him on the move didn't make for tight or reliable family ties. The lack of communication certainly didn't go over well with Clay. It never had, especially when Leda had been ill. "He was heading out on assignment, but he wanted to say he got your email about the wedding."

"How nice he let someone know." Clay kept his back to Seth, but there was no hiding the disappointment in his father's voice. "Did he happen to mention if he plans to grace us with his presence?"

Seth glanced at Gail and for once, he found her expression unreadable. "He'll be here if he can."

"Or he's found an excuse not to be," Clay said. "I haven't forgotten he never came to see your mother. Couldn't be bothered—"

"Clay, don't." Gail's voice softened. "This is difficult for them. Leda—"

"Would want Dad to be happy." Sensing Gail needed reassurance, Seth offered her a warm smile. "You've made him happy, Gail. My brothers are blockheads at the best of times, but they'll see for themselves when they get here. And they will get here."

His father turned and, over the top of Gail's head, shot Seth such a look of gratitude, Seth's heart trembled.

"I appreciate that, Seth." Gail's smile was tight. "I don't want there to be any animosity around this day. I want it to be a celebration. A new beginning for all of us. More than anything, I want us to be a family."

"We already are," Seth told her. "Jared and Van will come around. And if they take too long, I've got a couple of holding cells down at the station they're all too familiar with." He flashed Gail a smile and squeezed her hand before standing. "It'll all be fine. I promise."

His father followed him to the door, caught him by the shoulder before he stepped outside. "I know I don't say a lot about this." He waited until Seth faced him before continuing. "You're a good father, Seth. But you're an even better man."

Seth swallowed hard. Clay Hollister wasn't known for his loquacious compliments or emotional, verbal purges. Despite that, Seth had always felt his father was proud of him, but hearing the words was an entirely different experience. One he wasn't entirely sure how to process. Or respond to.

"I had an excellent role model." Seth pulled his cap out of his pocket and settled it on his head. "Don't worry about Van and Jared, Dad. It'll be okay. I'll make sure of it."

3

"Ha! I've got you now, you no-good, double crossing ... take that you ugly-ass troll!"

From her makeshift office in the dining room, Serena pushed away from the table and tossed her pen onto the keyboard of her laptop where she'd been working on the café's books. "I am going to lose what's left of my mind," she muttered as Kimberly swooped through the kitchen's swinging door.

"I've got this, Mom. Gigi!" Kimberly yelled as the volume on the TV increased. "Gigi, dinner's almost ready!"

"Can't stop now." A cavalcade of explosions and clanging swords echoed through the house. "Got a horde of barbarians on my six and I need ... hey!"

Blessed silence erupted and as Serena leaned back in her chair, she spotted her daughter holding the plug to the video game console in one hand.

"Gigi, it's time to eat. You can finish your game after dinner."

"Half my team will be in bed by then. I'm not hungry. Gimmie that." The seventy-six-year-old former welder attempted to snatch back the controller that Kimberly set out of reach on the hearth. "Kimberly Buffy Covington, now you mind your elders!"

"I am minding them. Lu said dinner's ready and I'm more scared of her than I am of you." After announcing her other grandmother's status update, Kimberly leaned over and kissed her great-grand-mother's cheek. "She made your favorite. Now grab your walker and let's head into the kitchen."

"Thank you," Serena mouthed when Kimberly returned to the dining room.

"What on earth were you thinking when I was born?" Kimberly demanded not for the first time. "Buffy? Really? Just how did you think that name would stand the test of time?"

"Your head was bigger than a cantaloupe and my epidural didn't work," Serena said to a cringing Kimberly. "Trust me. I wasn't thinking about anything other than *get out*."

"Ugh. Mom. TMI." Kimberly started tidying up the stack of household bills.

"Buffy was Gigi's choice." One of the biggest benefits of parenthood was embarrassing her teenager and she took advantage of every opportunity. "It was your bad luck she'd been binge watching season five that week."

"Count your blessings, little one," Gigi hollered as she made her way down the hall. "If it had been season six, your middle name might have been Spike! Now there's a vampire worth taking a tumble for."

"Clearly TMI is a family trait." Kimberly muttered.

"Considering you've dived into the potential realm of nocturnal activity with Matty Hollister," Serena said. "There's no such thing as TMI in this house. Get used to it."

Her daughter's face went bright red. "Not funny, Mom."

"No," Serena agreed as she thought back on her conversation with Sheriff Hollister. "It's definitely not. Go help Gigi into the kitchen. I'll be there in a few minutes."

Kimberly headed out, then turned. "Is everything okay, Mom?"

"Huh?" Serena blinked, then, seeing concern that didn't belong on any fifteen-year-old's face, quickly smiled. "Everything's fine. And even if it wasn't"—Serena stood, walked over to her daughter and brushed a kiss across her forehead—"there's nothing for you to worry about. Stop trying to take on adult problems, kiddo. You'll have to soon enough."

"You work too hard," Kimberly muttered. "You should have some fun."

"I've had my fun." She pivoted Kimberly around and gave her a gentle push. "Now scoot."

Before her daughter or her grandmothers got too nosy, Serena ended her game of musical credit cards for the evening, gathered up her paperwork, and carried it up to her bedroom. The last thing she needed was Gigi or Lu getting a peek at the straining household finances. When Gigi's medical bills had started coming in, she'd had to extend the café's hours, but she wasn't going to stay ahead of things much longer.

Since moving to Sea Glass Bay more than a decade before, she'd called the bedroom off the kitchen her own. But after Gigi's stroke last year they'd exchanged rooms so Gigi wouldn't have to traverse the stairs. It also gave Serena an added daily workout as she lugged her out-of-shape rear upstairs. Because working ten hours a day at the café wasn't exercise enough.

When Serena returned to the kitchen, she found Gigi settled in at the table, Kimberly filling up Gigi's glass of grape juice and Grandma T's famous chicken enchiladas steaming and waiting. Serena leaned over, took a deep breath. "Smells amazing, Lu."

"I cut back on the jalapenos this time, just in case." Tallulah Romero, her long silver hair braided into a rope down her back, stuck her thumb in Gigi's direction. Paint flecks the color of a West coast sunset dotted her fingers, a testament to the new series of paintings she'd begun last month. Lu had made a modest living for years as an artist and, since their move to Sea Glass Bay, had been expanding her following to include one of the local galleries that had offered her a private show later in the year.

She'd married—and divorced—four husbands, while Gigi had never remarried after losing her one and only. Her grandmothers were as different as two women could get, but they shared a heart-stopping capacity for love.

As masterful as Tallulah was with a brush and canvas, she was, thankfully, even better in the kitchen. "Better safe than sorry with the spice," Lu said under her breath.

"Nothing wrong with my ears." Gigi held up her fork in a menacing threat. "You make that red rice, too?"

"Getting it now." Lu returned to the stove.

Serena pulled the half-filled bottle of wine out of the fridge and poured a glass for herself and Lu. "Kimberly, you know the rules. No phone at the table."

"Yeah, I know." But she kept tapping away anyway. "This'll just take a second."

"It's that Hollister boy, isn't it?" Gigi asked, then angled a look at Serena. "How come the little one's got a better social agenda than you?"

Kimberly smirked.

"I mean it, Kimberly," Serena said. "Second warning. One more and you'll lose it for the next week."

"You won't take my phone away," Kimberly countered without looking up. "You know I need it."

"Necessities can be altered. Just imagine all the years we existed before cell phones." Serena held out her hand.

"Fine." Kimberly sighed over dramatically and handed over her cell. Serena set it on the back counter out of reach. "But—"

"One more word," Serena warned and held up her finger. "Just one."

Kimberly pressed her lips tight and held out her plate as Lu sat down. No sooner had Serena picked up her fork, than the doorbell rang.

"You have got to be kidding me," Serena muttered.

"I'll get it." Gigi made to get out of her chair, but Serena waved her back down.

"I will get the door. You all eat." Her stomach rumbled in protest as she headed down the hall and, after pulling the curtain aside, opened the door. Her eyes widened. "Seth." She smoothed a hand down her hair. Of course at the end of the day she looked, or at least felt like she looked, like something the cat horked up. "Hi. What brings you by?"

"Sorry to bother you at home."

"No, it's fine. Is everything okay?"

"We had a call about a disturbance behind the café. I tried to call—"

"Oh! My cell." She patted her back pocket. "I could have sworn I had it with me. Do you need me to come down?"

"No. I checked it out. Didn't see anything odd, but I thought you should be aware when you go in in the morning. Let me know if there's anything amiss."

"Okay, thanks." There must be something about a man in uniform under moonlight that added to his appeal because she suddenly felt as if she'd gone a bit dreamy eyed. "There're a couple of stray cats that hang around. I think Kimberly's been feeding them on the sly."

"That could be it. Um, also …" He shoved his hands in his pockets and rocked back on his heels. "Since I'm here, I'll tell you, I've decided to take your advice about Matty and Kimberly."

"Oh? What changed your mind?"

"I'm not sure I changed my mind," he hedged. "But someone might have pointed out I was overreacting and that we should just let things play out for a bit. With those restrictions we talked about."

Her lips twitched.

"Mom! I need—oh, hi, Sheriff Hollister." Kimberly, her dinner plate in one hand, held out Serena's phone. "You left this in the kitchen."

"Thanks. Where are you going?"

"I got a text from Janine. It was our emergency code. I need to call her back."

"After dinner," Serena said.

"But, Mom—"

"Emergency?" Seth shot to attention. "Anything I can help with?"

"Doubtful," Serena muttered. "Janine's idea of an emergency is over plucking her eyebrows."

"Ha-ha," Kimberly said. "Freddie broke up with her. She's in a state, Mom. I need to be there for her."

Her daughter knew her well enough that she knew Serena wouldn't make a scene in front of the sheriff. "Fine. Just clear it with Lu before—"

"Already did. Oh, hey, you should stay for dinner, Sheriff. Lu made plenty." Kimberly shot her mother a grin before she darted upstairs. "Night, Mom."

Serena's cheeks went fire hot, but when she looked at Seth, he was grinning. "If you don't have plans for dinner, you're welcome to stay."

"You sure?"

"It's Lu's enchiladas. You tell me."

"My mother spent years trying to get that recipe," Seth said. "Matty's at basketball practice and I was just going to reheat leftovers."

Serena's insides did that odd little dance that was becoming synonymous with Seth's company. "Well we can't have that. Come on in." She waved him inside and closed the door.

"Ms. Lu, that was delicious." Seth shoved his plate away and sat back in his chair. It had been a good while since he'd sat down to an actual family meal. "I'm going to have to run an extra mile in the morning to pay for it though."

"I drink tea on the front porch around seven," Gigi announced as she reached for her walker. "Feel free to run past anytime. Us old ladies like a nice view."

Serena gasped. "Gigi, for crying out loud."

Seth chuckled as Serena's face went bright red.

"One of the best parts of my job," Gigi went on. "Lots of fine-looking men in my line of work." She wagged what was left of her eyebrows and cackled. "Made for some entertaining days. And nights. Not that any of them held a candle to my Elliot."

"Someone put me out of my misery," Serena moaned.

"You have plans for the rest of the night, Hattie?" Seth asked when Serena looked as if she was going to melt under the table.

"Call me Gigi," Hattie ordered as she shoved herself to her feet. "Everyone who matters does. And I do indeed. I have a hot date with a troll."

"Is that a metaphor for something I don't want to know about?" Seth asked.

"World of Warcraft," Serena said with a sigh. "The doctors suggested she needed to work on her eye hand coordination and might have mentioned online video games as therapy."

"Woman racked up two hundred bucks in special features before we caught onto her." Lu shook her head as she reached for Seth's plate. "Now she battles hordes and armies of darkness into the wee hours."

"Let me help with that," Seth offered, but Serena's other grandmother waved him back down.

"Guests don't clear or clean," Lu announced. "After you've had three meals at this table, we'll talk. In the meantime, sit."

"Yes, ma'am."

Serena poured them both some coffee as Lu sliced up what looked like homemade strawberry pie.

"Where are you going?" Serena asked when Lu picked up two plates and started to leave.

"I'm on Gigi duty tonight, remember?" Lu blinked too-innocent eyes at the two of them. "I'll take care of the dishes later. You two just relax and chat."

"Gigi duty?" Seth asked.

Serena's smile didn't quite reach her eyes. "Since her stroke, nighttime can get a bit weird. Most of the time she's okay, but she's been known to get out of bed and wander."

"Wander the house, right?"

"Not always." Serena shrugged, and it was then he noticed the exhaustion creeping onto her face. "A few nights ago I came downstairs and her bed was empty, the front door was open. I drove around for a half hour until I found her waiting at the bus stop three blocks away. She thought she was late for work." Serena tried to look amused. "She hasn't worked since long before we moved here. Her memories are getting jumbled."

"I had no idea this was going on." Seth drank some of his coffee, then cut into his slice of dessert. "You could have called me."

Serena arched a brow. "I had it handled. I got her into the car, talked her out of her confusion. We've put a new lock on the doors for nighttime, ones she can't reach. And Lu and I take turns keeping an ear out at night. Baby monitors aren't just for infants, you know."

"Still." Seth couldn't gobble his pie fast enough. It was clear who Serena got her baking talent from. "That's what I'm here for. To help with things like this."

"Asking for help isn't my strong suit. In my experience, it's pretty much a setup for disappointment."

"I might take that as a challenge. If you ever want to take the chance, call me."

She leaned her chin in her hand and batted her lashes at him. "Is this what they call law enforcement flirting?"

It didn't even cross his mind to lie. "Would it be a problem if it is?" Before Serena could answer, his phone buzzed. "Saved by the bell," he teased, then frowned when he saw Matty's coach's name on his screen. "Sorry." He clicked to accept. "Gavin? Everything okay?"

It took less than a minute for Seth's blood pressure to spike. When he hung up, he immediately dialed his son's cell. "Matty cut out of practice early without permission."

"I take it that's not usual?"

"Considering he's trying to get a basketball scholarship to college? No. He's not answering. I'm sorry." He stood up, mentally caught between trying to figure out where his son might be, and reminding himself Matty was a smart and usually responsible kid. "I need to go."

"Of course. Is there anything I can do?"

Seth glanced up the stairs as the sounds of overactive video games blasted from the living room. "I'm not sure where to start looking. Maybe Kimberly …?"

"On it." Serena ran up the stairs and was knocking on her daughter's door when Seth joined her. "Kimberly? She probably has those stupid headphones of hers on." She knocked again, and when she didn't get a response, she opened the door. Three steps inside, she froze. "I don't believe this," she muttered.

Seth stepped in behind her, barely had time to take in the bedside lamp-lit room decorated in photographs, concert tour posters, and beautiful, colorful pictures she'd clearly drawn herself, before he noticed the open bedroom window and slightly billowing curtains.

Kimberly was nowhere to be seen.

"Wherever they are, the good news is I'm betting they're together." It was the only positive thing he could think to say at the moment.

"She'd better be enjoying herself because once she's back in this house she'll be lucky to leave it again before she's twenty." She swung around and nearly bashed into him. "What are you waiting for? Let's go."

"You're not coming with me." Seth stepped in front of her when she attempted to dart around him. "You should stay here in case she calls."

"On what?" Serena's hand shot out and she pointed at the cell phone lying on the unmade bed. "She didn't take her phone. I'm either going with you or on my own. Take your pick."

It wasn't a decision he needed to debate. "With me, it is. Let's go."

4

"*S*omewhere in the universe they're singing the Karma song." Serena sat at attention in the passenger's seat of Seth's patrol SUV, her eyes scanning the sunset-tinged streets of Sea Glass Bay for a sign of her and Seth's children. Except fifteen wasn't exactly a child. Fifteen meant Kimberly had crossed over into dangerous tides. Tides Serena had waded through herself.

"I don't think I'm familiar with that tune," Seth tapped on his dashboard screen that connected to his phone. "Care to hum a few bars?"

"Trust me you don't want me to sing. Suffice it to say, I'm getting massive payback for my active teenage years. She lied to me." Serena's disbelief slipped into anger. "She freaking lied to me."

"It happens."

"Not with my child it doesn't," Serena snapped. "We have a deal. No matter what, the truth comes first. Always."

"That seems ... unrealistic," Seth observed as he took a left toward the main thoroughfare and headed toward the beach highway.

"Maybe you're used to Matty lying to you, but Kimberly doesn't. Or at least she didn't before—what in the hell are you doing with that thing? Keep your eyes on the road!"

"I installed a tracking app on Matty's phone when I bought it." A few more taps of the screen and a red dot blinked on. "Yeah, okay. He's at Deep Sea."

"You installed a tracking app on your son's phone?" Serena gaped as Seth flipped off his lights and eased off the gas. "Isn't that—?"

"The word you're looking for is smart."

She glared in doubt.

"Before Dad hired me as one of his deputies, he sent me to train with a friend of his with the SFPD," Seth said. "Believe me, I saw enough during that time to learn there are some chances you don't take. Even in a small town like Sea Glass Bay. Care to finish what you were saying before?"

"Before about what?" Serena's brain had fogged over, and she had the feeling she wouldn't think clearly again until she had Kimberly in her sights.

"You said Kimberly didn't lie before. Before what?"

Even in the dark, when Serena looked over at Seth, she saw his jaw clench almost as hard as her stomach did. "Nothing. It doesn't matter."

"You were going to say she didn't lie before she started going out with Matty."

She shrugged. "It's the truth."

"You know what's also the truth? Matty didn't cut out on his basketball practices before Kimberly was in the picture."

"You're saying my daughter's the bad influence?"

"I'm saying maybe stop blaming my boy exclusively. I think there's more than enough responsibility for them to share."

Seth's continued calm raked against Serena's nerves. He had a point. Blaming one kid over the other wasn't going to get them anywhere. Obviously she missed something somewhere in regard to her daughter's behavior. Between the café and Gigi and keeping the household above water and … and and and …

Serena took a deep breath. The last thing she wanted to admit was what should've been the most important focus of her life had somehow slipped through pressure-induced cracks.

Serena crossed her arms over her chest and counted the unending minutes until Seth pulled into the parking lot. Deep Sea Diner, the Sea Glass Bay staple, was known for its double fried onion rings, seafood sliders, and over the top shakes. Normally just the idea of the place made Serena smile and crave carbs. This time she was ready to jump out of the car the instant he set the parking brake.

"Hang on." Seth caught her arm, tugged her back, and she closed the door.

"What?"

"Look. Just look at them."

He turned off the engine, pointed to the crowded diner and their two teenagers sitting in one of the window booths. Serena rolled her eyes, huffed out a breath and purposely stared. But it took her a moment to actually see.

Kimberly was slurping on an oversized strawberry shake, the same shake she'd been ordering since they first arrived in Sea Glass Bay. It had taken years for her to be able to finish one, but the challenge had become a family tradition. As the sun set, her daughter was laughing, along with Matty, who was scarfing down French Fries at record speed.

They were happy. More importantly, they were safe.

"They're good kids, Serena," Seth said. "We're lucky. We both know how tough that age is and the mistakes that can be made. But we've raised them to know the pitfalls of our past. When all is said and done, they're good kids and we need to remember that."

"Stop making sense," Serena grumbled as her anger abated in favor of relief. "I want to stay mad."

"As do I." He flashed her a look that had her shivering. "Matty's going to find out just how mad I am, but I'm thinking maybe we should have a little fun first."

"What kind of fun?"

"This kind."

It happened so fast Serena didn't have time to blink. Or think. In the confines of the car, somehow Seth managed to wrap her in his arms so completely she had no compulsion to refuse his kiss. When his mouth came down on hers, she gasped in a breath and found herself gripping his jacket in her fists to draw him closer.

His kiss was magic. Not only in the way he staked a claim, but how he put his entire being into it. Even if she'd had the ability to search her memory, she'd never have recalled ever feeling like this. As if they were two untethered beings who had finally, after years of floating around, found their perfect landing spot.

"I'm confused," she murmured against his mouth when he released her. "Was that for our benefit or theirs?"

Seth smiled, that twinkle in his eye sparking that long-dormant ember of emotion she'd locked away for more than fifteen years. "I'll cover my bases and say both. Can you see them?"

Without turning her head, Serena shifted her gaze out the windshield. Sure enough, Kimberly was gaping out the window while Matty seemed to be having a choking fit.

"I would imagine"—Seth lowered his voice to the point the sound made her stomach dance—"seeing their respective parents making out in the sheriff's car might just ruin their escapade of an evening."

"You think?" Serena laughed.

"I know. My parents used to do this all the time. Neck in the car," he explained at Serena's wide-eyed look. "My mom used to joke it was the only place they ever had any privacy. Took me and my brothers a good few years to realize what a good thing it was to have parents who were crazy about each other." He lifted his hand, stroked a finger down the side of her face. "All that said, I think maybe we need to re-evaluate our plans for letting things play out naturally between our kids."

Serena sat back, telling herself she didn't feel oddly alone without his arms around her. It was, she realized, the nicest way anyone had ever told her she was wrong. "A re-evaluation sounds in order. That doesn't mean I'm admitting I was wrong."

"Perish the thought," Seth said far too seriously.

"You should probably be careful, Sheriff Charming," Serena warned and smiled as Seth's brows rose. "You could come across as far too good to be true. Next thing you'll tell me is you're a master wizard in World of Warcraft."

"Not a wizard," Seth assured her as they pushed open their doors. "But I'm a level ninety-seven demon hunter."

"God help me," Serena muttered to herself as she slid out of the car. "He might just be perfect after all."

"I think they know," Kimberly mock whispered hours later.

"About what?" Matty narrowed his eyes and leaned closer to his laptop screen. "I think they know we're setting them up. Why else would they have been so nice when they found us at Deep Sea?"

"Nah." Matty shook his head, but it was a good question. "They were nice because we were in public and neither of our parents are into making a scene."

"You could have fooled me," Kimberly muttered.

It wasn't the first time Matty had chatted with Kimberly online well after midnight, but it was the first time she was doing so without any lights on. "Is your power out or something?"

"No," Kimberly practically whispered. "Thanks to your phase two, I'm on restriction. Whenever my mother and I are in the same location, she has possession of my phone. And, considering I'm only to go to school, the café, and home, we're *always* going to be in the same location. The only reason I have my laptop is because I need it for schoolwork."

"Sorry." Matty cringed. "This will all be worth it. I promise."

"It better be," Kimberly grumbled. "It's getting weird. I mean, I know they're not old like Gigi and Lu old, but they looked utterly ridiculous out there in that patrol car."

What Kimberly thought ridiculous, Matty considered promising.

"What did your dad say when you two were alone?" she asked.

"Not much," Matty admitted. "He got called out to Mrs. Filbert's in the middle of my lecture, so I'm safe until breakfast." Or, if he managed to get up early and hightail it out of the house, dinner. "I think we can at least say we're on the right track. They must really like each other if they're making out in his car."

"In front of half of the town's gossips," Kimberly groaned. "Everyone at school is going to hear about this."

"So what if they do?" Wasn't that what they wanted? For their parents to be a couple?

"So? Next thing you know they'll think we're dating."

"So what?" Matty gave his best dismissive shrug. "Isn't that what we want people to think?"

"Think it through, Matty. If our parents hook up, it'll be like we're siblings or something."

Matty blinked. Maybe he hadn't thought this all the way through. "I guess I hadn't thought of that." Matty gnawed on the inside of his cheek. "So we need another plan. Maybe—"

"Kimberly Covington! That better not be Matty Hollister you're talking to and if it is, you have five seconds to hang up and Go. To. Bed!"

Matty winced as Serena's uncharacteristically irritated voice reached his ears. "We'll talk at school tomorrow. You have third period free, right?"

"Yeah." She sounded less than thrilled at the evening's results. "I'll meet you in the biography section in the library."

"Definitely. Kimberly?"

"Yeah?"

"It'll all be okay, I promise. I promise."

"For the first time I think maybe you're the only one who believes that. Night, Matty."

"Yeah." Matty was staring at a blank screen. "Good night."

5

"*W*ord has it you and Serena Covington were hot and heavy in Deep Sea's parking lot Sunday night."

It wasn't unusual for Deputy Jessie Raspar to perch on the edge of Seth's desk and sip her coffee over some new town information. It was, however, the first time Seth was the topic of said information. Not that he'd had much time to think about it the past few days.

Considering he was going on less than three hours of sleep for the past few nights thanks to being down a deputy and the summer heat bringing out the mischievous side of residents, he'd bet good money the only thing keeping him conscious was that unending kick of adrenaline that surged whenever he thought about his world-tilting kiss with Serena. Heck, he felt accomplished being able to string a sentence together.

"Whose word?" Seth tried to focus on the nuisance report Mrs. Filbert insisted on filing after she called the other night to report a prowler in her backyard workshop. The old woman's taxidermy hobby was something of a town legend and, as kids reached a certain age, the peer-pressure enhanced dares to check out the old woman's borderline creepy crafting supplies workshop increased substantially.

When Jessie didn't respond, he glanced up in time to see the twenty-three-year-old deputy hide her smirk behind her Wide

Awake coffee cup. "Well, I heard it from Kevin Drummond who apparently heard it from Poppy Sotherby who—"

"Who no doubt heard about it from any one of a dozen people at Deep Sea. Got it." So maybe he'd listened to the naughty devil sitting on his shoulder rather than the do-gooder angel who had him buttoning up his uniform every morning.

Something about Serena Covington just cut right through whatever practical reason he possessed and had less logical parts of him ... acting. "For the record"—and because he knew Jessie couldn't wait to be the latest cog in the small-town game of telephone that Sea Glass Bay excelled at playing—he said, "I like Serena. And it appears it's mutual. And when two people like each other—"

"They share a very special hug that causes little tadpoles of human beings to be born." Jessie grinned and split her round face into a ray of sunshine.

"Okay, that's just ... weird." Nonetheless, Seth found himself chuckling. "Don't you have patrol this morning?"

"Yeah, yeah." Jessie sighed. "Anything in particular I need to be on the lookout for?"

"Possibly a stuffed possum," Seth said. "Mrs. Filbert couldn't be certain, but she thinks she's missing one."

"She thinks?" Jessie shuddered. "*Gah.* Don't even tell me the rest."

"Oh, Barty and Paul Evers are fighting over their fence line again. You might want to do a drive by, make sure there's brotherly peace on Helmet Shell Way. Oh, and Jessie?" he added when she headed to her desk to gather up her sidearm, badge, and jacket. "You run into trouble with those two, you give me a call, yeah? I know you think you can handle it, but they each outweigh you by about a hundred pounds. Don't chance it."

"My powers of persuasion are infinite," Jessie said proudly as she inched up her chin so she stood her full five-foot-four height. "But I hear you. With Howie finishing up his training course in Sacramento, we can't afford to be down another deputy."

"Exactly." Seth gave her a nod of approval. "Be safe."

"You, too." Jessie had no sooner pulled open the door than she stood back to let his brother in. "Morning, Axel."

"Hiya, Jess. Morning, Seth."

"Axel." Seth gathered up a stack of folders to refile. "What's up? You look wiped out."

Axel dropped into the chair across from Seth and crossed an ankle over one knee. "I've been manning the tow line the last couple of nights. Boss gave me the rest of the day off to catch up on my sleep. Why is it cars always seem to die around 2 a.m.?"

"I'd say for the entertainment value, but that would only be for me," Seth grinned. When his brother didn't respond, Seth set his papers aside. "What's wrong?"

"Nothing, really. I was just thinking." Axel scratched a finger against a hole in the knee of his jeans. "This whole wedding thing with Dad and Gail. You're really okay with it?"

"I really am." Seth rested his hands on his desk. "Why?"

Axel shrugged. "I don't know. I was talking to Jared last night and—"

"Ah." Seth tried not to feel irritated that Jared had called Axel rather than returning Seth's call. "Let me guess. Our brother's having doubts. Figured as much since he hasn't sent us his travel itinerary yet."

Axel cringed as if bracing for impact. "I'm not sure he's coming to the wedding."

Seth blinked. "Excuse me?"

Axel held up his hands. "Don't quote me on it, I'm just saying he didn't say anything about coming, so I assumed—"

"You better have assumed incorrectly." Seth dug around on his desk for his cell. "I promised Dad and Gail that all of us would be there. And for the record," he added at his brother's wince as he tapped Jared's number on his phone, "we will *all* be in attendance—attitudes, doubts, and reservations stifled, stowed, and kept to ourselves. Dad's getting this day come hell or high water and, for the record, there will be no hell. Or high water. Not from you. And not from our wayward siblings."

"Pretty much what I told Jared." Axel nodded. "And you don't have to worry about me. I'm on your side with this whole thing. I'm just saying, Jared might take some convincing."

"Oh, I'll convince him all right." He lifted the phone, then stopped when Axel stood up and headed to the door. "Hey."

"Yeah?" Axel turned, and for an instant, Seth saw the defiant, insecure kid he'd been when Leda and Clay had first brought him home from detention. "Thanks for the heads-up."

"You bet. You, ah, free for lunch?"

"I can be." Seth frowned. "I thought you were going home to sleep."

"Sleep's for weaklings," Axel smiled. "Besides, word is there might be some entertainment value for me by popping into the café. You know, to visit your make-out companion."

Seth rolled his eyes. "Get out of here, you moron."

Axel laughed, a sound that had Seth's lips twitching. "Guess I waited too long to make a move. That's one fine woman."

"Serena would have stomped him like a bug," Seth muttered as the door closed. Fifteen minutes later, unable to fight the urge to follow his brother, he grabbed his cap and headed down the street to the café.

I need to talk to you. Privately.

Seth's text had Serena's face warming as she quickly shoved her cell into her apron pocket. "Morning, Ms. Pritchard." She greeted one of her regulars with a pink-cheeked smile. "Your usual?"

"Yes, please." At barely five feet, Eloise Pritchard blinked through her goldfish round glasses in a way that reminded Serena of any number of animated characters. The never-going-to-retire librarian wore one of her ankle-length flowered dresses that threatened to trip her neon pink Croc-encased feet. "And throw in whatever you grandmothers enjoy best," Eloise added in her fifty-year smoker voice. "I'm on my way over for our weekly Mah-Jong game."

"As long as it isn't Bunco," Serena teased as she bagged up two of her oversized lemon crunch blueberry muffins along with Ms. Pritchard's peach pie turnover. "Last time I almost had to call the sheriff on the lot of you."

"That's only because Alice Farrington added too much tequila to our margaritas." Ms. Pritchard waved off her concern. "But if you're looking for a reason to call the sheriff …"

Serena merely smiled and finished the order. Ms. Pritchard hadn't been the first to mention Sheriff Seth Hollister in the last few days and she certainly wouldn't be the last. One would have thought Sea Glass Bay had nothing else to talk about other than her and Seth making out in his SUV in a parking lot. Lord, it was like reliving her less than stellar high school experience. "You be sure to let Lu and Gigi know I'll be home at my usual time."

"We'll get our gentlemen callers out of the house before you arrive," Ms. Pritchard joked. Or at least Serena hoped she was joking as the old woman carried the cardboard tray out the door.

Serena's phone buzzed again. She would have ignored it except she heard Seth's voice bidding farewell to Ms. Pritchard as he held the door for her. He stopped just inside the café, waggled his cell phone in the air, and pointed to the back door before he headed back.

"I've got the line." Caitlyn gave Serena a gentle nudge and a not-so-subtle wink. "You're due for a break, right?"

"Lord, not you, too."

"Try everyone," Caitlyn teased. "Go on. I'm caught up with the baking for now."

"Thanks. I'll just …" She grabbed a paper cup and poured Seth's occasional afternoon pick-me-up, then, because she wasn't jittery enough, poured one for herself. "Be back in a bit."

"Take your time," Caitlyn sang as she rang up the next customer.

"You are a goddess," Seth practically groaned as he accepted his coffee then motioned for her to sit. "I've had an idea."

"I hope this one's better than the two of us making out in your car," Serena said with more humor than she felt. "I haven't missed the days of being town gossip."

"If they weren't gossiping about us, it would be someone else," Seth observed. "Or heaven forbid, our kids."

"Speaking of our kids, they're still breaking the rules," Serena told him. "I heard them talking last night."

"There's no cutting them completely off technology," Seth said. "And I thought you were the one who was against stopping them from seeing each other."

"I was. I am," she added, even though she wasn't so sure anymore. Things were getting too complicated and messy, and Serena didn't like either. "I'm more concerned about Kimberly's behavior surrounding her seeing Matty than her actually dating

39

your son. I don't abide lying, Seth. Not in anyone, but especially not in my child."

"I'm not going to argue that point. Which brings me to my idea."

"Can't wait to hear it." Being around Seth Hollister had shifted from being fun and tempting to being uncertain and irritated. Uncertain because she didn't know what the heck was coming down the road and irritated because she now knew her fantasies about kissing the good sheriff hadn't come close to the reality of the event.

She'd been tempted by unrealistic expectations in the past and it shifted her life completely off course. Now that she had found her way, she wasn't enjoying the prospect of having it run off the rails again. What she needed to do was cut things off now. Just ... go back to serving him his morning coffee and occasional chocolate orange scone.

"If you're having second thoughts—"

"No," Serena said a bit too quickly. "I think it's clear we need to pull these two back into reality. If they're going to continue to see one another, then we need to be firm about our expectations and their ... restrictions." Serena scrubbed a hand over her eyes. "Why is it that I can just imagine my parents having this same discussion about me back in the day?"

Seth touched her wrist. "Life's a circle. Everything comes back around at some point."

"I really hope you're wrong. So"—she pulled her hand free and picked up her coffee—"what's your idea?"

"Considering how utterly mortified they were the other night, I think we need to up the stakes. What do you think about a double date?"

Serena choked on her coffee, nearly snorting it out of her nose. "You want to take me on a double date with our kids?"

"Uh-huh." Seth's grin did what it always did. It drew out her own, even around the disbelief and surprise. "I'm thinking Lollapa-Pizza? Dinner, the arcade. Maybe a couple of games of bowling. We can skip the roller-skating. I think those days are behind me."

"Be still my heart," Serena teased. "It sounds so utterly romantic."

"And public," Seth added. "Neither Kimberly nor Matty seemed particularly entertained by that."

"Ah." Serena finally caught on. "This is a let's-embarrass-our-kids-away-from-each-other-by-pretending-to-date kind of lesson."

"It doesn't have to be pretend." Seth tugged her hand away from her face to thread his fingers through hers. "I like spending time with you, Serena. The other night, even with our offspring-induced complications, was fun. And I'd like to see what other fun we might have together."

Her breath caught in her throat as he drew her hand toward him, lifted it to his lips and brushed his mouth across the back of her knuckles. "That's not fair, Romeo." She couldn't think when he touched her. Why couldn't she think?

"I know." His grin widened. "What do you say? Tomorrow night? Matty and I will pick you two up around seven?"

"A date on a school night?" she asked dubiously.

"Is that a yes?"

It should be a no. Everything about Seth Hollister should be a big, screaming no. She didn't have room in her life for romance right now. She had responsibilities, a business to run and employees to pay, a mortgage to stay ahead of and bills ... and then there was Kimberly and ... and and and.

When was she going to stop paying attention to the ands and just ... live?

"Well?" Seth urged and tightened his hold on her fingers.

"What the heck," Serena surrendered and hoped she wasn't making another huge mistake. "It's a date."

6

"This is so not how I anticipated my foray into dating life going."

"I know." Seth didn't know what he was happier about. That it was finally time to put his plan of dating Serena Covington into motion, or the utter discomfort said date was causing his son. As they walked up the path to Serena's front door, Seth slung his arm around his son's shoulders and gave his hair a good tousle. "Gotta learn to go with the flow, kid."

"Dad, come on." Matty swiped his hands through his too-long hair and managed to tidy it up again. "Wouldn't it make sense for you and Serena to go on a date on your own? Why drag the two of us with you?"

"Excellent question." One that took longer for his son to ask than Seth had anticipated. "A couple of reasons. One, group dates take some of the pressure off."

"Pressure to do what?" Matty asked suspiciously.

"Two," Seth continued as if his son hadn't spoken. "And this you already know—what your date orders on her pizza is a surefire way to tell just how compatible you might be."

"You're giving them the pineapple test?"

"It's a Hollister family tradition," Seth reminded him. "Say it with me, kid. Pineapple—"

"Pineapple has no place on a pizza."

"Exactly. And any other opinion is a relationship killer," Seth said. "And three is perhaps the most important." They walked up the porch stairs, and Seth rang the doorbell before he straightened Matty's collar then his own. "Neither Serena nor I plan to let the two of you out of our sights for the next few weeks, and seeing as I don't plan to wait that long to take Serena out on a date, this is my only alternative." The locks snapped open. "Hello, Gigi." Seth stepped inside and took the older woman's hands in his. "You look ravishing this evening."

"You devil," Gigi said on a cackle and beamed up at him. "You can charm the fuzz off a caterpillar. You come to take my girl out for some fun?"

"Both your girls," Seth corrected. "Matty, you've met Gigi before, haven't you?"

"Hello, Ms. Covington. It's nice to see you again." Matty gave an odd and somewhat awkward bow.

"Charm runs in the Hollister family, I see." Gigi sighed. "Just as handsome as your father. And it's Hattie, young man. Or Gigi. Come in and wait for the girls to make their entrance. I was just about to level up and if I'm AFK for much longer, my team will boot me."

"Hello, Seth. Matty." Lu glided down the stairs and followed them into the living room. "Serena and Kimberly will be right down."

"Thanks." Seth caught Matty's wide-eyed stare at the television.

"You play WoW?" Matty pointed at the screen then looked to Gigi. "You're Thundara of Ashcroft?"

"Lord help me, there's another one," Lu muttered and, shaking her head, began to tidy up.

"That's me." Gigi dropped into her chair and picked up her controller. "You play?"

"Some," Matty said.

"Please." Seth rolled his eyes. "I almost had to take out a second mortgage on the house to pay for your game time."

"Haha," Matty said with a quick glare. "I'm Golonar the Brave."

Gigi narrowed her eyes. "You are not."

"I am! We've gone on quests together."

43

Gigi's entire face brightened, and she sat up straighter. "You're pretty good. Sorry about hacking off your arm when we were caught in the Caves—"

"No, no. That was fine. One of the healers got me back in shape. I had no idea—"

Seth felt rather than heard Serena descending the stairs. He turned as she rounded the banister. She wore a simple turquoise blue wrap-around dress and kill-him-now strappy sandals that made her legs look ten miles long. But it was her hair that had his hands clenching to resist. She had it down and it was longer, thicker, and wavier than he'd realized, tumbling down and around her shoulders like a cascade of gold.

"Wow." If this was a charade of a date, he couldn't wait for the real thing.

Amusement glinted in her eyes. "You never disappoint, do you, Seth?" She stepped closer, rested her hand against his chest. "I was definitely thinking the same thing. Kimberly?" She kept her gaze on Seth as she spoke. "Aren't you going to say hello to your date?"

"How can I when he only has eyes for my grandmother?" Kimberly mumbled as she walked past them. "Nightmare scenario, take one. Hey, Matty."

"Oh, hey, Kimberly." Matty glanced at her, then did a double take and straightened. "Wow."

Seth silently groaned. There was no mistaking that glint in his son's eyes. It was the same look Seth felt certain was painted on his own face when Serena stepped in front of him. "We are so screwed," he whispered to himself, then realized in one stomach-dropping moment he wasn't talking just about Kimberly and Matty. He hadn't even been on a date with Serena yet and he was done for. His father had warned him. Multiple times and, in one of his more talkative moments, Clay Hollister had warned him. When Hollister men fell, they fell hard.

And Seth had definitely landed with a decisive thud right at Serena's feet.

Thank goodness she couldn't read minds otherwise she probably wouldn't have been so enthusiastic about ushering the kids out the front door, leaving Seth to trail slowly across the threshold into no turning back territory.

"So. Pizza." Seated beside her daughter and across from Matty and Seth, Serena opened Lollapa-Pizza's menu. The family-style eatery had become a downtown Sea Glass Bay institution and had served multiple generations of residents. What had once been a small mom-and-pop hole in the wall had expanded to encompass multiple buildings on either side, allowing for various entertainment attractions within the brick-and-mortar structure. Almost every kid who grew up here had been thrown a rite-of-passage birthday party in one of the private rooms at some point. The indoor roller rink had gained popularity with its throwback nights, and the collection of amusement park-inspired games and activities provided endless opportunities to win tacky, mostly neon-colored prizes and stuffed animals. Personally, Serena had an affinity for the old-school arcade that could be heard even above the din of classic 80's jukebox music. Well, the arcade and the delectable, hand-tossed pizza. No cardboard, throw it in the microwave pizza in this place. Lollapa-Pizza was all about the slice. "What shall it be? Personal or table size?"

"Table," Matty said without hesitation. "Kimberly, what do you like on yours?"

"Pineapple for sure," Kimberly announced and erased all happiness from both Hollister men's faces. "A pizza just isn't complete without it, right, Mom?"

"Couldn't agree more." Serena nodded as the dangerous glint in Seth's eyes faded behind panic. "Pizza prudes are the worst, don't you think? Imagine thinking less of someone because they put fruit on their pizza. It's a food group for goodness sake."

"And it's full of Vitamin C," Kimberly added.

She'd never seen anyone swallow so visibly before and she wondered if Seth and Matty realized how identically devastated they both looked. She shifted her gaze to Kimberly who had ducked down in the booth so she was hidden behind her oversized menu. Her daughter was laughing to the point Serena couldn't pretend any longer.

45

"Okay, Kimberly's going to hurt herself. Relax, boys." Serena tucked her menu under her chin as their server delivered waters and took their drink orders. "Pineapple belongs on many things, most especially in an upside-down cake, but it definitely doesn't belong anywhere on or near a pizza."

"Oh, thank God." Matty practically sagged onto the table.

"That was just mean," Seth said as his eyes flashed. "Well played, but mean. Just for that I'm going to have to kick your butt at air hockey after dinner."

"Bring it on, Sheriff Hollister," Serena challenged. "Bring it on."

Whatever strange ice had formed around the foursome on their way to dinner effectively cracked, allowing them to order a loaded pizza with little disagreement.

While waiting for their food, Seth took a long drink of beer, set his glass aside, and folded his hands on the table. "While we're all in a good mood—"

"Uh-oh." Matty's mouth twisted. "That's code for buckle up. He's about to get serious."

"Then I suggest you do just that," Seth said without missing a beat. "Serena and I have each addressed the other night's shenanigans—"

"Shenanigans?" Kimberly's eyes went wide. "Sorry," she instantly apologized at Serena's glare. "I thought maybe we'd ended up in an episode of Leave it to Beaver."

"Leave it to what?" Matty's brow furrowed.

Kimberly rolled her eyes. "You are so uneducated."

"After the events of the other night," Seth steered the conversation back on track. "Serena and I thought the four of us should sit down and discuss how things are going to proceed. There will not be a repeat of either of you sneaking out, do you understand? If something requires you to leave the house by any other means than the front door, then it is the wrong thing to do."

"Agreed," Serena said. "Let's chalk this one time up to a learning curve and that you've been sufficiently educated."

"Fine," Kimberly mumbled.

"Understood," Matty agreed.

Serena took a deep breath. "Your father and I have decided we won't stand in the way of you two seeing each other."

"You won't?" Kimberly's filled with surprise.

"That's great!" Matty's gaze flew to Kimberly's.

"It is?" Kimberly quickly bit her lip and slid into the corner of her seat.

"Coming between two people who care about each other isn't something we want to do," Seth said. "But we are going to set some rules in place, and we expect the two of you to follow."

"With dating comes responsibility," Serena told them. "You don't get to chuck the rest of your life out the window because you want to spend all your time together."

"And that translates to what exactly?" Matty asked as Kimberly swirled her paper straw in her soda and appeared to purposely avoid looking at anyone.

"Your education is your number one priority. Both of you," Serena said with a marked look at Matty. "There will be no more shirking off studying or blowing off tests or basketball practice so the two of you can hang out. You want to hang out? You can do so on the weekends after you've lived up to your obligations and when your work schedules allow. When Seth and I are convinced you're both back on track and when your grades have significantly recovered, we'll talk about letting you two study together again."

"Sounds perfectly reasonable to me," Seth nodded. "And before you attempt to argue, might I remind you that you broke our trust the other night by sneaking out. That's not something that's easily or quickly rebuilt."

"What about the two of you?" Kimberly asked.

"What about us?" Seth asked.

"Isn't it going to be kind of weird," Kimberly said. "You two dating and us two ..." She flailed a hand between her and Matty.

"Hang on. Back up." Matty frowned. "This isn't some weird plot you two hatched up to say you aren't going to try to break us up, but actually you are trying by making us spend all our free time with you?"

Serena grinned at Seth. "Now there's an idea?"

Kimberly muttered something under her breath but before Serena could address the comment, their order arrived. Their server set the eighteen-inch round tray on the weighted down coffee can in the middle of the table. Basil and garlic-infused steam wafted into the air as they ate, but most of the conversation that followed was between Serena and Seth.

By the time all four hollered Uncle and Matty finished off the last of the oversized pie, Kimberly asked if she and Matty could be excused.

"It's a school night, remember," Serena said as she scooted out of the booth to let her daughter out. "We're heading home by nine-thirty."

"I know." Kimberly didn't wait for Matty and quickly darted around the other tables and out of sight.

"She's not happy." Serena watched Matty follow, then glanced back at Seth. "You get the feeling we made a mistake?"

"Looks like a possibility." Seth frowned. "You feeling as crappy about that as I am?"

"Definitely a possibility," Serena said, then realized the two of them were alone for the first time. It was now or never. "Seth, I think maybe we should talk."

"Uh-oh." Seth flashed a teasing smile, but it vanished almost the instant it appeared. "That sounds like one of those serious talks no one wants to have."

Guilt edged its way around the pizza. She swirled her straw in her drink, and only then realized she and her daughter shared the same coping mechanism. "I like you Seth. I like you a lot."

"Same."

"But …"

"But what?" Seth reached out, caught her hand. "Serena, we both know there's something between us. What are you so afraid of?"

She snatched her hand free, inched up her chin. "I'm not afraid."

"Then what is it? What's standing in our way? We're friends. That's always a good foundation for a relationship—"

"Relationship?" Serena half gasped. "Seth, my life is insane. Beyond insane. Between the café and my grandmothers … ." She flailed a moment, trying to pull her thoughts together. This wasn't going at all like she'd planned. She'd just wanted to make a clean break before their emotions got too tangled together to separate. "I can't take on anything else, Seth. Dating someone seriously—heck, dating anyone at all—just feels like one too many things. We've asked our kids to be adults, to put their education and committed work hours first." She took a deep breath. "I think we should do the same."

"We've asked our kids to be responsible," Seth corrected as he pulled his nearly empty beer glass close. "We also have the opportunity to set an example as to how a relationship can be. I want to see you again, Serena. I want to keep seeing you. I think—no, I *know*—there's something special here. We just have to meet each other halfway. We just have to take the chance."

She wanted to. Oh, how she wanted to believe that things could be so simple. That they would perfectly fit into each other's lives. But she knew better. She had far too much on her already full plate and enough experience behind her to know it wasn't worth taking the risk. She didn't have the time or energy to devote to starting a relationship.

Even with someone like Seth Hollister.

Seth's gaze broke from hers, shifting to the side as his eyes filled with concern. "Something's wrong."

"What? With wh—Kimberly?"

Her daughter hurried over, tears streaming down her cheeks. "Mom, I want to go home. Can we go home, please?"

"What's wrong? Yes, of course we can." Serena grabbed their purses and scooted out of the booth. "I'm sorry, Seth." They both knew she was apologizing for more than leaving their date early. She dug into her bag for her wallet.

"Tonight's on me." Seth stood up, reached into his back pocket. "We'll drive you." Kimberly shot Serena such a look of panic that Serena shook her head.

"No, Seth. It's not far to walk and I think the fresh air will do us both good. Thank you for dinner."

"But it's—" Seth stood anyway.

"We'll be fine, Seth." Her tone sharpened. She didn't need him, she told herself. She didn't need anyone. But since spending time with Seth, she began to wonder if that was true.

"All right." He gave her a cool nod. "Please call me when you get home."

"That's not necessary," Serena said.

"That's coming from the sheriff," Seth said, "not your date. Let me know you two got home okay or I'll come looking for you."

He would, too. Because that's the kind of man he was.

"I'll text you when we get home."

"Mom, please." Kimberly had her arms wrapped around her waist as tears flooded her eyes.

"Okay, we're going." Serena tucked Kimberly in under her arm and held her close as they headed out of the restaurant.

7

"I guess that could have gone better." Matty slunk into the booth across from Seth, his face a mishmash of confusion, disbelief, and more than a little pain.

"For both of us." He signaled the waitress and ordered some coffee. "You want another soda?" Matty shrugged. Seth nodded to their server. "Want to tell me what happened?"

"Not really." Matty plucked a napkin out of the dispenser and began shredding it. "There's a lot you wouldn't want to hear."

"That doesn't make me curious at all." Seth waited until their drinks were delivered before continuing. "Would it help if for the next few minutes you thought of me as a friend and not your father?"

Matty's shrug was halfhearted. "Maybe."

"Give it a shot." He doctored his coffee, sipped, and felt a pang of longing for Serena's delicate barista touch. "I'll give you immunity for the next"—he glanced at his watch—"thirty minutes. Whatever you don't think you can tell me, the floor is yours."

"We lied. To you and Serena." Matty visibly swallowed. "Kimberly and I weren't really dating."

Seth blinked. He heard the words but didn't come close to understanding their context. "Explain please."

"It was just a plan. A plot really. To get you and Kimberly's mom together. So you wouldn't be, you know, lonely anymore. We thought

51

if the two of you had to join forces against us, you'd finally realize you liked each other, and the rest would just … happen."

"I see." Forget coffee. Seth needed a straight shot of whiskey. Instead of being angry or irritated, he found himself feeling oddly grateful. "Good plan. It worked. For a time."

Matty frowned and continued to turn his napkin into confetti as Seth made a mental note to up their server's tip.

"What happened with Kimberly?"

Even in the dim light of the restaurant, Matty's cheeks went red. "I kissed her. I thought she wanted me to. And she kissed me back, until she stopped. I … don't know what happened," he plowed on, thankfully preventing Seth from commenting. "I mean, we've been friends for years. Just friends." The confusion on his son's face kicked Seth in the heart. "Then tonight, I don't know. She looked … everything felt … different. So when she wanted to talk to me alone, I guess I thought maybe she was feeling the same way and I …" He sighed. "I was wrong. She doesn't like me that way, and now I've lost one of my best friends. That's what I get for manipulating you and Serena."

Seth's heart hurt for his son. Was there anything worse than a first heartbreak?

"What's happening between you and Kimberly isn't some cosmic payback for sneakiness," Seth said in what he hoped was a calming tone. "It's called being a teenager. You took a chance, Matty. We both did."

"And it's not working out for either of us."

"Does look that way, doesn't it?" Seth took a deep breath. "I'm sorry about you and Kimberly."

"You are?" Matty's doubt was evident. "I thought you'd be relieved. If we aren't seeing each other, you can stop worrying I'm going to get her pregnant and ruin both our lives."

"Is that what you think? That having you ruined my life?" Seth pushed his coffee away and leaned his arms on the table. "Matty, you are the best thing I've ever done. There hasn't been a single day I haven't loved being your father. Do I wish I'd been older when I had you?" He shrugged. "There's no point in wondering because it didn't happen. I certainly never intended to make you feel as if you were a mistake, because you were not."

"You didn't. You don't. Maybe I was just assuming." Matty glugged down his soda. "Can we be done now? Tonight's been one seriously huge suck fest. Can you go back to being my dad?"

"Fact check, kid." Seth signaled for their check. "I never stopped. And I never will."

"I said I wanted to go home, Mom." Kimberly tightened her arms around her waist. "I'm freezing."

"We'll head home in a bit." Serena stopped at the edge of the stone entrance to the beach and toed out of her shoes. "I think we both might be looking for a bit of peace. And there's no bigger place of peace than that." She looked out into the ocean, tried not to lose herself in the crashing waves tumbling up to play with the sand. "Come on. It's been a while since we dipped our feet in."

"I don't want to. I just want to—"

"Go home." Serena sighed. "I'm sorry, Kimberly, but I'm not going to let you run away and hide from whatever's going on. You're old enough to start learning how to cope with things in a positive way. Burying yourself in bed and waiting for the world to right itself isn't going to work anymore."

"What do you know about it?"

Much more than you could possibly imagine. "I know that facing your problems makes you stronger."

"Is that what you're doing with Seth? Facing your problems? I heard what you were saying to him, Mom." Kimberly's gaze turned accusing. "You aren't going to see him anymore. Why?"

"Because ..." Serena struggled to find the right words. "Because it's complicated and I don't think it's any of your—"

"Matty and I set you up. You and Seth," she clarified as if Serena didn't understand. "We pretended to date so the two of you would be forced to be together to try to break us up."

"You ... pretended?" Serena frowned. "But that doesn't make any sense."

"Why not?"

"Because I saw the two of you together at Deep Sea. You were happy. You, I don't know ... you two seemed to fit."

"We're friends." Kimberly's voice wavered as Serena drew her down to sit on the edge of the stone wall. "Or we were until tonight. Oh, Mom." The tears pooled again, and she covered her face with her hands. "I think I messed everything up."

"Okay." Serena wrapped her arm around Kimberly's shoulder and drew her close. "Okay, baby. It's okay. Tell me what happened with Matty."

"He kissed me!"

Whatever Serena had been anticipating, it certainly wasn't that. "You say that as if it should explain everything." Serena rocked her gently. "Did you not want him to kiss you?"

"Yes. No—I don't know." Her words were muffled against the front of Serena's now tear-soaked dress. "I've thought about it. I mean, why wouldn't I? But I like things the way they are. He's my best friend, Mom. I don't want to lose that. I need a friend more than I need a boyfriend."

"Oh, baby." Serena let out a soft laugh. "You have no idea how happy I am to hear that."

"Big surprise." Kimberly sat up and scrubbed her fingers under her eyes. "You didn't want us together in the first place."

"That's not true," Serena told her. "All right, it's not entirely true. Dating is a good thing, even at your age. But …" She took a deep breath. "I made the mistake of losing myself in someone else at your age, Kimberly. I didn't take the time I needed to figure out who I was before I dived into something that changed my life forever. That doesn't mean you can't date Matty or anyone else. I just want you to be sure of who you are before you become part of a couple. Does that make sense?"

Kimberly nodded. "Except we weren't dating."

"Weren't you?" Serena inclined her head. "Relationships begin in all sorts of ways and if you ask me, a solid friendship is the best foundation to start with. Do you care about Matty?"

Kimberly looked pained. "Yes. But …"

"But what?"

"I'm scared, Mom. What if it doesn't work out? What if we try dating and it's horrible and then we break up and we still have to see each other and—"

"And," Serena cut in. "And. And. And."

"Huh?" Kimberly scrunched her nose in that way she had whenever she didn't understand.

"There's always an and that'll stand in the way of something important. Believe me, I know. Being with someone, putting yourself at risk, it's hard. And it's scary." She stopped, felt her heart skip a beat. "So scary that sometimes we sabotage things purposely because it's easier than taking a chance."

Kimberly nodded. "It is easier. But then you end up hurting the other person and that's the last thing I wanted to do to Matty."

And it was the last thing she wanted to do to Seth.

"You know what we need to do?" Serena said.

"You mean besides walking barefoot in the tide?" Kimberly asked as she slipped off her shoes.

"We need to stop being scared." She'd spent so many years being overly cautious, it was time to break that final chain loose. "How about you and I make a pact? You'll talk to Matty and tell him everything you've told me and I'll—" She took a deep breath. "I'll give things with Sheriff Seth another shot."

"Yeah?" Kimberly's eyes twinkled. "You really like him that much?"

"I do. I really do." And she had just the idea to prove it to him. "If it's all right with you."

"It is," Kimberly said and held out her hand to seal the deal. "I like him a lot. And bonus: he can play video games with Gigi."

Serena tugged her onto the sand and down toward the water. "Definitely a bonus."

"No, that's fine, Dustin. I'll put in a call to the ferry service and make sure they know to expect the caterer a few hours earlier than planned." Seth rolled his eyes and pointed a finger at his phone as Deputy Jessie grinned. "No, it's okay that you called me instead of Gail. I don't want her worrying about anything wedding related. Just make everything appear effortless, even if it isn't. Yeah. Right. Bye."

"Wedding chaos," Jessie teased. "Bet you never thought you'd be caught up in the big event."

"You'd win that bet by a mile," Seth agreed. Between the tent and the caterer and the party rentals, half of Sea Glass Bay was going to be transported to the island before everything was done.

"Looks like a full house this morning." Deputy Jessie Respar aimed a suspicious look at Seth as they made their way through the town market. "Seems busier than usual."

"Earlier than usual, too." Seth couldn't remember the last time he'd seen the town market this full this soon on a Saturday morning. "Is there some special event we weren't told about?"

Jessie shrugged. "Maybe. You want coffee? I want coffee. I need coffee." She smacked a hand against his arm and picked up speed.

Seth hung back. For once he wasn't in any particular rush to hit Wide Awake. Serena's "we're home safe and sound" text had come later than expected, but at least it had come. He'd only responded with an emotionless thumbs up as he didn't think there was anything left to say. He wasn't the kind of man to push a woman into doing anything they didn't want to do, and Serena had made it pretty clear last night she did not want to pursue anything resembling a relationship between them.

It had helped, a little, talking to Matty. Knowing he'd raised his son to be the kind of person who knew when he'd screwed up and wanted to do anything he could to fix it took some of the sting of his own failure to coax Serena out of her comfort zone. He just needed to get over it. He just needed to get back to them being friends and having her brew his morning coffee and bake his favorite …

The line for Wide Awake was out the door of the café. And it wasn't even really a line, more like a crowd waiting for a sale to start. Finding his father and Gail in the crowd, along with Axel, had Seth pulling out his phone to see if he'd missed an emergency call.

"What's going on?" He stepped in behind Jessie, who had her nose pressed against the window. "Dad?" he called over the heads of a number of waiting customers.

"Best check with Serena," Clay told him. "Something about her not being open for coffee yet."

"It's nearly eight o'clock." Not liking the sound of things, Seth pushed his way through the crowd, and into the café. Was she all right? Had there been an accident? He rose up on tiptoe only to find Serena's employees, Kimberly included, standing behind the counter practically at attention.

" 'Bout time you got here," Gabriel Abernathe grumbled from his wall-side table. "That girl says she's closed until further notice."

"Closed? What on earth is going on … Serena?" Seth raised his voice over the din as he made his way up to the counter. "Kimberly, where's your mother?"

"I'm right here." Serena appeared with a filled pastry tray in her hands. "Good morning, Seth." Her smile had the same effect it always did on him, and he felt himself warming from the inside. "I've been waiting for you."

"You have?" He blinked. "Why?"

"Because we need to finish our conversation from last night. Just one more second!" She called when the crowd began clamoring for their morning jolt of caffeine and sugar. "I wanted to make this official."

"Make what official?" And why did he sound like a deranged, clueless parrot? "Serena, this mob's about to revolt … Matty? What are you doing here?" He stared as his son emerged from the kitchen to stand beside Kimberly. He stared in relieved disbelief as their hands linked and they smiled.

"Okay, everyone here?" Serena came up to the counter, leaned over and cocked her finger at him. "Come here, Sheriff Charming."

Hesitant, but always happy to do a beautiful woman's bidding, he walked to the counter. "For a woman who hates being the subject of gossip, you're about to get a feature in the town paper."

"After this, I expect to be on the front page." She reached out both hands, caught his face in her palms and pressed her lips to his. The cheers and laughter that erupted had him smiling against her mouth.

"There's no getting rid of me now," he murmured against her lips. "A public display like this means everyone's going to expect more." He touched her cheek. "A lot more, like say …"

"A wedding?" She leaned back and smiled. "How about we start with your father's and see where things go?"

"You mean it? Because I have witnesses."

"Oh, I mean it, Sheriff Charming." She kissed him again. "Witnesses or not, you got your wish. Like it or not, you are one hundred percent stuck with me."

"Oh, I like it." He smiled into her twinkling eyes. "I like it just fine."

Seth reached for her apron and tugged her into a deeper, more gossip-column-level kiss that had Serena's knees go weak and both of their kids groaning and exclaiming simultaneously, "Ew, Mom!" "Dad!"

Where the Heart Is

by Kayla Perrin

1

*J*ared Hollister pulled his black Lincoln Navigator into the parking lot of The Dive Bar, the aptly named hole in the wall on the edge of Sea Glass Bay. He was back in town and, before he saw any members of his family, he needed a drink.

Jared entered the dimly lit establishment and was immediately pulled back to nine years earlier when he'd taken up residence in this bar—with the help of a fake ID. Until his dad, Clay Hollister—the then-Sheriff of the town—had caught on to his antics, entered the bar, and sternly *guided* him out.

Surprisingly, a smile tugged at Jared's lips with the memory, even though being back in town had him on edge. Nine years ago, he'd been eighteen going on thirty-five—or so he'd believed. He had come to this bar to have a beer and contemplate his future with the weight of the world bearing down on his shoulders.

The place looked exactly the same. The barstool seats were still cracked. The sign advertising FREE BEER TOMORROW still had the lights missing over the "e" and "r" so it read, FREE BE TOMORROW. All kinds of alcohol lined the back of the bar, some top shelf, but mostly off label. People didn't come here for an elevated drinking experience. They came here to drown their sorrows.

At least, he had. Back then he'd had an agonizing choice. Take the scholarship to Kent State and play football or choose love and follow Dominique to UCLA and hope he still worked out his football dream.

He chose Kent State, and Dominique never spoke to him again. He heard just last year she'd married some tech millionaire.

Jared shoved his hands into his jean's pockets. There was a handful of people here, mostly seated alone, though there were at least a few two-seater tables occupied with smiling people. A couple of televisions mounted on the walls were airing sports, golf and baseball. Thankfully it wasn't football season. He wasn't sure he could come here if it were.

A beefy bartender was wiping down the counter, and Jared approached, sitting at a barstool on the far-left side of the bar. As the bartender made his way over, Jared recognized the man's face.

"Doug?" Jared said tentatively. This guy wasn't the lanky kid he'd played football with who couldn't put on weight no matter how many Twinkies he ate.

"Jared Hollister!" A smile erupted on Doug's face. "You're back in town, man."

"Yeah, my dad's getting married."

"I heard. That's great."

Jared shrugged. Was it? His mother, Leda Hollister, had been gone only two years, and his father was already moving on? If it were up to him, he wouldn't have shown his face for this event. But Seth had been on him to come back for the wedding. Said he owed it to Clay Hollister—the man who'd adopted him, Seth, and Van, and fostered Axel—to be there for him on his special day.

The way Jared saw it, Gail was taking the place of his adopted mother, and Jared had loved Leda Hollister as much as any person could love someone. It was her patience and kindness that had helped him stay on the right path after the tragedy that had thrown his world into a tailspin and landed him in foster care. Leda had been the glue that held his world, and the family, together. The idea that Gail was taking her place didn't sit well with him.

"What can I get you?" Doug asked.

"Beer. Whatever's on tap."

Doug scooped up a beer glass, filled it, then passed it to Jared. "There you go. On the house."

"Thanks," Jared said.

"So how's it out in Buffalo?" Doug asked. "Other than a lot colder than here?"

Jared drank a mouthful of the beer. The one topic he didn't want to talk about, though he knew he'd never be able to avoid it. He'd left this town seeking a bigger life … and for a moment, he'd had it. Then everything had gone to hell.

"Definitely colder," Jared said, "but I like it. It's a nice community. Great fans who support their sports teams, come hell or high water. As soon as I get my shoulder operated on, I'll be good as new and on the starting lineup again."

Doug's eyes expressed surprise. "Really? Well, that's great. That last hit you took … I thought your career was over."

"Hey, bartender, can I get another beer?" a bearded man in the middle of the bar demanded. The slur to his voice said he'd had a few already.

Doug wandered over to the guy, and Jared was glad that he'd been saved from having to continue to flub the truth regarding his failed football career. He wasn't sure if he was going to be on the starting lineup for the Bills once his shoulder was as good as new. They were contemplating dropping him.

He sipped more beer. It wasn't over for him yet, though. If Buffalo did let him go, his agent was trying to work a deal for him elsewhere.

"Come on, Dave, that's enough."

The female voice behind him was loud, with a defiant edge to it.

"Why not?" came a man's voice. "You're always turning me down. You ain't got no man."

Jared turned then. He saw the woman get up from a table by the window, and the man who'd been talking to her grabbed her arm. Instinctively, Jared slipped off his barstool and started toward them. The one thing he hated was men who felt it was their right to pressure a woman after she'd said no.

"Let go of my arm, Dave."

"You heard the lady," Jared said. As the woman turned toward him, her blunt bob no longer obstructed the view of her face, and recognition hit him like a kick to the gut. All the air whooshed out of his lungs.

Recognition flashed in her eyes as well, and her face lit up, but then Dave was back at it, reaching for her arm again. "Every woman needs a man. Let me be yours."

Jared stepped toward them, closing the distance with two large steps. "Didn't you hear the lady?" he asked, standing in front of Dave. "She said no."

Dave, who looked to be about forty, with an unkempt red beard and hair past his shoulders, looked at Jared in confusion. His eyes were slightly glossed.

"Who the heck are you?" he asked.

"Jared?" came the soft question from Nina's lips.

Oh, how he'd always enjoyed hearing her voice—the softness, the tenderness. So many times she had grounded him when he'd been stressed out. He didn't realize until right now how much he'd missed her over the years. Nina Thomas, his best friend in high school.

"Yeah." Jared turned to face her with a grin on his face.

"Well, Jared, or whoever you are," Dave said to Jared's back, "why don't you leave me and Nina alone. She likes me. She just needs a bit more time to realize it."

"I figured you might be coming back to town," Nina said, "but I wasn't sure. Since your dad is getting married."

"That's why I'm here," Jared said.

"Hey." Dave, who apparently didn't like being ignored, moved to stand between Jared and Nina. "You might be a big dude, but—"

"Dave, stop it." Nina rolled her eyes. "You really want to fight someone twice your size?"

Dave swallowed, his eyes seeming to register that fighting Jared would not be a good idea. "Whatever," he said. He dug money out of his jeans' pocket and tossed it onto the table next to Nina. "Call me when you're ready for me to rock your world."

"I won't be calling since my boyfriend's back in town." Nina sidled up to Jared and slipped an arm around his waist.

Dave's eyes nearly bulged out of their sockets.

"Jared Hollister," Nina went on. "Plays for the Buffalo Bills."

"Wait—*you're* Jared Hollister?" Dave thrust a hand forward, amused, Jared shook it. "It's an honor."

"Don't be bothering my girl anymore," Jared said.

Dave saluted him. "Scout's honor."

The guy was three sheets to the wind, that was for sure. Suppressing a giggle, Nina tugged on Jared's hand, and together they started for the bar's exit.

"I didn't know it was you, man," Dave continued as Nina and Jared slipped through the door. "I'm sorry!"

Once they were outside, Nina threw her arms around Jared and squealed. Jared held onto her, remembering how good it had always felt to hold her, especially when he'd been going through something rough. She'd been his rock, and he'd been hers … more than once they had saved each other from a troublesome situation by pretending to be part of a couple.

"Jared Hollister, it's really you!" Nina said as she eased out of the hug. She ran her palms down his arms, then took his hands in hers. "I never thought you'd ever come back to Sea Glass Bay."

"Well, I'm here." Jared extended their arms wide and took a moment to check her out beneath the soft lighting at the bar's entrance. He hadn't immediately recognized her because her hair was no longer in long braids, but in a straight bob cut that angled longer at the front of her face. Her body had filled out, her shapely hips and full chest made her look more like a woman than the teen he remembered. Her arms were well toned, which didn't surprise him. She'd been on the cheerleading squad, cheering him and the Sea Glass Bay Tigers on during their football games. He imagined she still had the strong thighs she'd developed doing gymnastics, something he couldn't quite tell beneath the flowing black skirt she wore.

Jared quickly averted his eyes and released her hands. Good grief, he was checking her out.

"You know," Nina began, "I wasn't sure if you'd come. Since you missed your mother's funeral. Not that you'd ever tell me."

She sounded a little irritated. And should he be surprised? Nina had been his best friend in high school, but he'd left her and everyone else in this town behind when he'd headed off to start his life as a football player.

What she didn't know, not even his own father knew, was that he *had* come back for his mother's funeral. He'd come quietly, paid his respects to Leda on his own terms, then left.

Jared just couldn't deal with the whole funeral thing—everybody coming over to the house and sharing wonderful stories about someone he hadn't been prepared to lose. The tears, the absolute goodbyes. The finality of it all.

So he'd come in without anyone knowing, went to the funeral home to see Leda and confirm for himself that she was gone. He'd said his goodbye privately and even went to the graveside after all the mourners had left to leave her flowers.

"Seth was gonna throw me in jail if I didn't show my face," Jared said, adding a rueful laugh. That had been the truth. Seth had threatened to hunt him down and throw him in jail if he didn't return for his father's wedding to Gail. "So here I am."

"Here you are. The star who has returned to grace us all with his presence."

Jared frowned. "Hey, don't say that."

Nina's lips morphed into a pout. "I'm sorry," she said. "I've had a bad day. That's why I'm here, after all. It's where we all go when we need to sit and mope."

"You were never the moping type," Jared said. Whenever she'd needed to reflect, the Nina he knew wouldn't come to a place like this. He could often find her on the beach instead, digging her toes in the sand as she dealt with whatever was on her mind. "And not at a place like The Dive Bar."

Nina hugged her torso. "Today I am."

"What's going on?" Jared asked. The door opened, and a lone patron walked between them down the steps. "How about we talk in my car?"

"Sure."

Jared led the way to his SUV, which was only a few steps away from the bar's entrance. "This is my vehicle," he said, walking to the passenger side.

"Nice ride."

"I like it." Jared opened the door for her, and she climbed inside. Then he rounded the Navigator and got in beside her. "So what's going on with you?" he asked.

"I feel kind of stupid," she said. "It's no big deal, honestly."

"It is a big deal if you're upset," Jared said.

"It's just … God. This is going to sound stupid. I found out that my ex and his new girlfriend are having a baby. Remember Olivia Newhart?"

"Yeah. You and Olivia were best gal friends. Always hanging out together, on the cheer squad together, playing soccer together …"

"And apparently sharing the same men. Not that I knew it at the time. I'm not even upset about it," she rambled on, "despite how it might seem right now. It's just unexpected, you know? I guess it's just one of those things that makes me realize that I failed. Marriage is supposed to last forever."

"Whoa, back up a moment. You're saying Olivia cheated with your *husband*, and now she's having his baby?"

"After he told me he didn't want kids. Was adamant about it, actually." Nina forced a smile. "I don't know why I'm upset. He's not worth it on any level. Not to mention we've been divorced for six months."

"You married Juan, right?"

"How did you know?"

"Axel told me. I wasn't surprised when I heard. You dated him on and off throughout high school. I always figured you two would end up married." Though he didn't know what she'd ever seen in him. Juan Suarez had always been arrogant and inattentive … things Nina had complained about often.

"For what it's worth," Jared said, "it's his loss."

"Oh, I know. We were never a good fit. It was just one of those dumb relationships that evolved from high school and …" Her voice trailed off.

Jared could have told her that, not that she would have listened. She had cried on his shoulder so many times over Juan, and so many times he'd wanted to tell her she would be better off leaving the guy. But that hadn't been his place.

"Anyway, I haven't talked to you in nine years about any of this stuff so I'm sure you don't want to hear about it now." Nina reached for the door handle. "Thanks for listening. It was good to see you again, Mr. NFL Star."

She was probably just teasing him, but the comment stung a little. It implied he thought he was too good for her—and that was why he hadn't been in touch.

But that hadn't been it.

"You don't have to run off so soon," Jared told her.

"I've got a twenty-minute walk home."

"Walk? No, let me drive you."

"I like walking. It's great exercise."

"It's dark," Jared said around a yawn that he couldn't keep suppressed. "I'll give you a ride."

"You're tired," Nina said. Her eyebrows shot up. "Did you drive here from Buffalo?"

"I stopped along the way. I'm heading to Seth's place, where I plan to climb right into bed. But I'll give you a ride home first."

"You don't have—"

"I want to. You can tell me more about Juan." He grinned widely. "It'll be just like old times."

Nina angled her head as she stared at him, her hair swaying as she did. "Are you saying I talked too much about Juan back then?"

"You're the first person from my past I've seen since getting back to town. Talking to you and hearing about Juan ... in a way, it's like I never left."

Something flashed in Nina's eyes, but Jared couldn't quite read her thoughts, and she didn't say.

Still, he could imagine what she was thinking. He'd walked away from Sea Glass Bay and let their friendship slowly die. And there was no good reason for that.

He felt like a fool. He'd walked away from Nina, his family, and everyone here looking for a different life. A life that wouldn't have a foundation of pain, like it had here in Sea Glass Bay.

He knew that to everybody it looked as though he'd simply walked away from *them*.

He started the car then faced Nina. "What's your address?"

2

*J*ared dropped Nina home, then headed to Seth's place. He gave his brother a heads up, sending a text to let him know that he was on his way.

When he arrived at Seth's, he parked in front of the house since the driveway was occupied. Pulling the key from the ignition, he sat for a moment and stared out the window at the cottage. It had been a long time since he'd seen his brother—seen any of his family. Seth and Axel had stayed in Sea Glass Bay, while he and Van had left. Van had joined the military, which took him all over the world on various missions, and Jared had left to pursue football. Over the years, he had only returned to Sea Glass Bay a few times, for short visits.

Jared exited the vehicle and got his suitcase from the back. Then he headed up the steps to the front door, but before he could knock, it opened. Seth's face erupted in a grin.

"Jared," Seth boomed, then opened his arms wide. "It is so good to see you."

Jared stepped into his brother's embrace, both of them holding each other and patting the other's back. It felt good, being back, seeing his brother. He'd missed him, and that fact was all the more clear right now.

"You didn't give me much choice, did you?" Jared said as he stepped backward. But he was smiling.

"You know you need to be here for Dad. Besides, it's been a long time since you were in Sea Glass Bay. Everyone misses you."

Jared nodded solemnly. "How's Dad doing?"

"Good," Seth answered. "Excited about the wedding. He'll be happy to know that you're in town."

"Thanks for keeping it a surprise." Jared had figured that was best, just in case he didn't make it. But he also wanted to see the look on his father's face when he showed up at the door.

"No problem," Seth said. He stepped back and pulled the door open wide. "Come in. How was your drive?"

"Long."

"You hungry?"

"I stopped to get food along the way. Mostly I'm just tired."

Footsteps thundered down the stairs, sounding like a freight train. As Jared looked to his right, he saw Matty bounding toward him.

"Uncle Jared!"

"Matty, haven't we talked about this?" Seth asked. *Walk.*

"Wow," Jared said, checking out the tall kid who was no longer a boy. "You have grown."

Matty beamed. "My dad says it must be something in the water."

Jared hugged the nephew he hadn't seen in years. And he felt that warmth that only being home can bring you. "Good to see you."

"I've got to head back upstairs to my game," Matty said hurriedly. "Talk to you later, Uncle Jared!"

Seth shook his head as his son took the stairs two at a time, instead of walking.

"I can't believe how big he is," Jared said. "I know I haven't been here for a minute, but still. He's almost a man."

"Yeah, time flies." Seth's gaze lingered in the direction of the stairs until he heard a door close, then he faced Jared again. "You sure you don't want a drink, or some toast?"

"Naw, I'm good."

"The bed's all set for you upstairs," Seth said. "Let me show you your room."

Jared followed Seth up the stairs, checking out the photos on the wall as he did. Photos of their parents, photos of him and his brothers, photos of them all together. Seth had remained firmly connected to their adopted family. But maybe it had been easier for him. When Clay and Leda had adopted him, he had already been in the foster care system since he was a baby. Essentially, Clay and Leda were the only parents he'd truly known.

Seth pushed open a door, revealing a minimally decorated room. There was a double bed with a basic blue comforter, a white dresser, and a white wooden chair in the corner. "Here you go."

"Thanks," Jared said. He placed his suitcase on the floor. "How's Gail?"

Gail, their father's fiancé, had been Leda's best friend, which was why the upcoming wedding didn't sit well with Jared for so many reasons. It was almost like the story Nina had just told him. You were friends with someone for years, then get involved with their man? It didn't seem right to him.

"Gail is good," Seth said. "Great. Dad is doing a lot better than before. I know you're not in agreement with the wedding, but Gail has really changed things for the better. Brought back the spark to his life. And for that, I'm truly happy."

Jared simply nodded, because he didn't want to get into his feelings on the matter. The way he saw it, no one could ever take Leda's place. He understood that his dad had to move on, but why with Gail? Why not someone else who hadn't been so close to Leda?

"You *are* staying here after the bachelor party, right?" Seth asked. "I don't see any point in you going back to Buffalo, then coming back for the wedding."

In other words, Seth didn't trust that Jared would return for the wedding if he left during the two weeks after the bachelor party and before the wedding date.

"I wasn't sure what I was going to do, but it's a fair drive to head back to New York State so yeah, I'll be sticking around." Unless something came up, like a meeting between his agent and another potential football team that might want to sign him. But he could always fly out to wherever was necessary and then return to Sea Glass Bay.

"Good, good," Seth said, sounding happy. "Now I'm heading out for a little bit. I have someone I need to see."

"Oh?" Jared's eyebrows rose. He could see by the glint in his brother's eye that the person he needed to see was a woman. "You're dating."

71

"Yeah, I've got someone special. But we'll talk about that later. I don't have much in the fridge, but if you're hungry help yourself to whatever's in there."

"Or I can go out and get a pizza. Lollapa-Pizza is still around, isn't it?" He could always pop by there and get a slice of their pizza, which was the best in the world in his opinion. Though the bed was calling to him after his long drive, even though it wasn't quite 9:30 p.m. yet. He figured he might be out for the night.

"Oh, you bet. That establishment isn't going nowhere," Seth told him.

"All right, bro. I'll see you in the morning."

As Jared settled into the spare bedroom, the heaviness that had clouded his heart before he'd left this town began to lift a little. Sea Glass Bay had been a place of so many memories, both bad and good. The bad—he'd lost his family. The good—he'd gained one when Clay and Leda Hollister had adopted him.

But during his senior year at high school, he had been thinking a lot about the loss of his biological family, and the sense of guilt that came from wondering why he hadn't been with them that day. He'd been at football practice while his family had been on the road heading to San Francisco—and when they'd been hit head on by an eighteen-wheeler.

It had always irked him when people said he'd been spared because he had a greater purpose. Hadn't his parents had a great purpose in life? What about his little sister?

Dominique hadn't understood his grief. She had told him that he needed to move on, that his parents would want him to. She talked about the great life they would have if he followed her to UCLA. And when she realized he was considering taking the football scholarship, she'd given him an ultimatum—football or her. Did he want to lose someone else who was important to him? She had stressed that, something that had truly bothered him. In a way, it had seemed like she'd been playing on the tragedy that had so deeply affected his life in order to get her way.

But it was Nina who told him to go after what he really was passionate about, and that had been football. Maybe he *had* been influenced by those who said he had a greater purpose after losing his family, because he believed his greater purpose was football. It was a sport both his parents had loved, and he would become an amazing success in their honor.

Jared stretched out on the bed, looking up at the ceiling. He had pursued football in his parents' honor, and ultimately, he had failed. The last thing he'd wanted to do was return to Sea Glass Bay as a failure. So he'd stayed away.

He just hoped no one talked to him about his career, because the sting of that failure was fresh. Too fresh to discuss.

Jared thought he would sleep in the next morning, given that he hadn't gotten much sleep in the days leading up to his trip to Sea Glass Bay, but with the time zone difference, he was up bright and early. He could hear Seth moving around in the bathroom as he got ready to head to work. Jared climbed out of bed and met him in the hallway on the second floor.

"Morning, Seth," Jared said.

Seth was dressed in his police-issued tan khakis and shirt. He pushed back his dark brown hair back, then fixed the sheriff's ball cap on his head. "Morning. How did you sleep?"

"I didn't expect to be up at six. I could use a bit more rest. Or a coffee. You have some here?"

"No, sorry. But there's a café not far from here, Wide Awake Café. They make the best coffee in the area. Stop in there and pick something up. Get a pastry, too. The owner, Serena, makes the best pastries. Tell her I sent you."

There was something about the way his brother said the woman's name that made Jared perk up. "Serena ... is she ...?"

A smile touched his brother's lips. "We'll talk about it later. I've got to get to work."

Seth left, and although Jared wanted to get more sleep, he decided he would follow his brother's advice and head to the Wide Awake Café. At this point, that's what he needed—to be wide awake.

He looked up the café on his phone, saw that it wasn't too far. Not that anything was far in Sea Glass Bay.

When he went into his vehicle a short time later, his eye caught something on the passenger side floor. He reached down to scoop it up. A wallet.

Nina's.

She would no doubt be looking for this. She would need it.

He was about to head straight to her house when he thought better of that. Why not get a coffee for Nina, too? He would knock lightly on the door, and if she was awake, she would answer. If she didn't, he'd leave her a note for her to contact him and save the coffee for later.

The Wide Awake Café was busy, and—surprise surprise—he found Seth there, a coffee in hand as he leaned over the counter talking to a beautiful blonde whose hair was pulled back in a long braid. Jared walked toward him and, seeing him, Seth quickly stood up tall, straightening the duty belt around his waist.

The blonde shot him a gaze, then looked at Seth.

"You must be Serena," Jared said, a hint of amusement in his voice. "I'm Jared."

"My brother," Seth explained.

"The one who arrived last night." Serena smiled and extended her hand. "Nice to meet you."

"Very nice to meet you." Jared shot Seth a knowing glance. "I hear great things about your coffee."

"We have a wide selection, as you can see on the board. And there's a special if you get a coffee and pastry."

"I suggest the apple fritter," Seth said. "You've outdone yourself, Serena."

She blushed. "Thanks, Seth."

Seth's walkie-talkie crackled. "Serena, I'll talk to you later. Jared—see you at eleven?"

"I'll be there."

At eleven, they had an appointment at the tuxedo shop for a fitting. Seth was pressing them all to be groomsmen for their father, and while Jared hadn't committed to that, he'd agreed to at least get sized for a tuxedo—just in case.

Serena was busy behind the counter, adding coffee to one of the carafes labeled "French Vanilla." A teenager, who looked like the spitting image of her, was placing muffins into a small cardboard box.

Jared waited his turn, then ordered a French Vanilla coffee for Nina and a house brew for himself. Like Seth, he also ordered an apple fritter. He ordered both coffees with cream and sugar, hoping Nina liked hers that way.

A short while later, he was back at her house. He knocked the door lightly; in case she wasn't yet awake.

It didn't take more than fifteen seconds for the door to open. Nina, dressed in a black nightshirt that read *Diva at Rest*, looked up at him in relief. "Did you find my wallet?"

Jared nodded toward the wallet, which he'd placed between the cups on the coffee tray. "I did."

"Oh, thank God." She reached for it. "I was so worried that I'd lost it."

"Thankfully it was in my vehicle. I figured you'd want it as soon as possible."

"Thank you so much." She pressed the wallet against her chest. "You want to come in? I don't have much time, but—"

"No, I'm heading to my dad's place. But I brought you a coffee. French Vanilla with cream and sugar. Hopefully you like your coffee that way."

"That's perfect, thank you."

She looked as beautiful dressed in a nightshirt with her hair pulled back under a headband as she did with a stylish dress and makeup. He sensed she was in brighter spirits than she had been last night but asked anyway. "How are you feeling this morning?"

She waved off his concern. "So much better. I was just … having a moment."

"I'm glad to hear you're feeling better." He passed her the coffee. "All right, enjoy your drink. We'll talk later."

Jared turned and started down the steps.

"Jared," Nina called.

He paused to look over his shoulder at her. "Yeah?"

"Don't you want my number?" she asked. "It'll be easier to stay in touch that way, don't you think?"

Chuckling, Jared shook his head. Where was his brain this morning?

"Of course," he said. Then he made his way back to the door.

*J*ared almost didn't recognize the house he had called home for nearly a decade. No longer a pale gray, the saltbox house was painted a bright yellow with white trim. But one thing was the same. The porch planks squeaked as they always had, causing Jared to reflexively perch himself on one leg, then do a quick sideways then forward move toward the door.

The move hadn't worked when he was a teen to keep from alerting Clay Hollister that he was sneaking in late, and it didn't work now. By the time Jared was raising his hand to knock, his father was opening the door.

His father looked down at him, his eyes registering surprise and then delight. "Jared?"

Jared smiled up at his father, who was still an imposing figure at six-foot-six compared to Jared's six-foot-one height. "Surprise."

Clay pulled him into a hug and held on as though his life depended on it. "You trying to kill your old man? I've already got enough gray."

Jared looked at his father's temples, which were graying a little, but his dark blond hair remained mostly unchanged from years before. "It's good to see you, Dad."

"Come in, come in. Did you drive from Buffalo? I see New York plates on that Lincoln Navigator."

Jared shouldn't have been surprised. As the former sheriff, his father had always been very observant. He spotted details in an instant. "I did," Jared told him. "Got in last night. Stayed with Seth so I could surprise you this morning."

"You're just in time for breakfast."

The smell of bacon and eggs had his stomach grumbling, making him realize that he needed more to eat than the apple fritter from the café—which had been just as delicious as Seth had promised.

"Clay, who is it?" came the female voice from inside the house.

Clay slung an arm around Jared's shoulder and guided him into the kitchen. "Gail, look who's come home."

Gail's lips formed a perfect "O" and her eyes widened. Then she rushed forward and threw her arms around Jared's waist. He hugged her back, surprised at her outburst of excitement.

"I'm sorry," she said as she broke the hug and looked up at him. She tucked her shoulder-length dark hair behind her ears. "I'm just so glad you're here." Her voice was ripe with emotion. "We didn't know if you'd be coming back."

Jared felt a modicum of guilt. He liked Gail, always had. She was a sweet woman whose friendship with his mother had been real. She was happy that he was here for the wedding but didn't know that he'd come back more out of a sense of obligation than excitement over his father's nuptials.

"I knew he'd come," Clay said, and while his father sounded certain, Jared knew he couldn't have felt as confident as he portrayed. Heck, Jared hadn't even known if he would be coming for the big event.

"Are you hungry?" Gail asked. "Of course you must be. We were just about to sit down to eat. I always make extra—Seth and Axel have a habit of dropping by, and those two have the appetite of growing boys, let me tell you." She wiped her hands on the blue and white checkered apron she was wearing. "Listen to me, rambling on. Would you like coffee or tea?"

"I'd love tea, actually," Jared said.

"I can brew you up some fresh mint from your mother's garden," Gail said.

77

"There's still mint out back?" Jared asked. Mint tea had been one of his mother's favorites, that and the iced tea she brewed in a pitcher set by the window.

"Growing like weeds," Clay said. "But Gail has a green thumb like your mother, and she knows just how to keep them under control."

"I'll have mint tea," Jared told Gail.

Clay put another place setting at the table, complete with a glass of water. Then he said, "Sit, Jared. Tell me everything that's going on in your life. How's your shoulder?"

Jared rotated his right shoulder, testing out how it felt. "I've injured my rotator cuff too many times," he admitted. "But it feels good now. I'll be back playing this season," he said, then looked away, not wanting his dad to see that he was telling a lie.

It wasn't exactly a lie, but Jared knew that nothing was confirmed yet. However, he was hopeful. And one had to remain positive, right?

"Don't overdo it," Clay said. "You don't want to push it too far and find that you've ruined your shoulder once and for all. It might be best to take a longer break."

The comment irritated him. His dad had always seemed to try to push him away from football, even now that he'd actually made it professionally.

"I've been seeing the best doctors, the best physical therapists, chiropractors. I'm in good shape."

"I understand that, but in case the worst happens, which I'm not saying it will"—Clay held up a hand when Jared made a face—"I'm only wondering if you've given thought to doing something else. Not that I don't believe in you, Son. But when it comes to careers like this that can be interrupted based on an injury, I think it just makes good sense to have a backup plan. Maybe coaching or—"

"I'm going to be fine," Jared said, unable to hide the irritation in his voice.

It was a good thing that Gail returned at that moment, holding a basket of freshly baked biscuits. The butter was already on the table. "You two help yourself to a biscuit, I'll get the eggs and bacon plated."

"Let me help you," Clay said. He got to his feet.

Jared didn't know if his father had gotten up to help Gail in an effort to step away from their conversation, but he was glad, nonetheless. He looked around the dining room, saw that Leda's touches were still everywhere. The sculpture of two pigeons on the bottom level of the dining room cabinet. The crocheted placemat on which the sculpture sat. Jared had always thought the sculpture was tacky, but man was he happy to see it now. He was even happier to see that the picture of Clay and Leda on their wedding day was still on the top level of the cabinet.

It made him feel a lot better to know that Leda's personal touches hadn't been erased from this house because his father was moving on. Leda Hollister would always be a part of the fabric of this house, no matter what. Her touch was everywhere. Even the sheer white curtains with embroidered blue butterflies had been Leda's touch. Jared hoped this place never changed.

Clay and Gail returned to the table, Gail holding two plates while Clay had one. She placed a plate of scrambled eggs with a heaping load of bacon and hash browns in front of Jared.

"Now this is what I call a breakfast," Jared said.

Clay patted his middle. "I have to keep making sure I work out so I stay in shape. Gail's feeding me as if she wants to fatten me up; make me unattractive to any other woman."

"Oh, stop it," Gail said. "You know you're gorgeous. You'll always be gorgeous in my eyes, even if you gained two-hundred pounds." She leaned down and gave Clay a kiss on the lips then slid into the chair beside him.

Jared looked at his father and Gail as they regarded each other. He thought about Seth's words: that the spark had come back into their father's eyes because of Gail.

He could see that spark in Clay's eyes right now, a spark that had once been there because of Leda.

And Jared wasn't sure that he liked it.

4

"Listen, Seth, I'm not sure I'm even going to be here for the wedding, much less that I want to be *in* it," Jared said into the phone as he sat in his car after breakfast at his father's. The homemade hash browns, crispy bacon, and those fluffy biscuits had been delicious, and Gail as accommodating as she could be, but Jared kept thinking about Leda and how no one could take her place.

"We talked about this," Seth said on the other end of the line. "You're not going to disappoint Dad."

"I may have to get back to Buffalo. I already told you that. I'm waiting for a call from my agent any time."

"You came back here in time to make this fitting," Seth said. "So you're going to be at the fitting."

"But—"

"Just in case," Seth stressed. "And Axel will be there, too. You haven't seen him yet, have you?"

"No." Jared hadn't yet seen his other brother, and he wanted to. He missed them all, even if he wasn't in touch as much as he should be. "All right, I'll go. I'm just saying I don't know if I'm going to be around for the wedding or not. So I shouldn't be part of any definite plans."

"Gail's a good woman," Seth said. "You know she is."

Jared's shoulders rose and fell with a heavy breath. His brother knew him too well. It wasn't that he thought Gail was a bad woman. She had always been a nice person, and he had enjoyed spending time with her when he'd been a kid. It was the fact that she was going to be taking his mother's place that he couldn't accept. How had his father moved on so quickly? He'd always said that Leda was the love of his life.

"Just be there for eleven," Seth said. "Are you at my place? I can swing by and pick you up."

"I'll meet you there," Jared said.

At eleven on the dot, Jared entered Lou's Clothing For Men, the most popular shop in Sea Glass Bay for men getting married, graduating, or needing a suit for business. A variety of smart-looking suits and tuxedos were displayed on male mannequins in the windows, as well as on racks around the store. There was a narrow hallway at the end of the shop with a floor-length mirror and a number of doors, obviously the change room area.

Seth, who'd been looking through one of the racks of suits, approached Jared immediately. He glanced at his watch. "Eleven o'clock, right on the dot."

"I thought Axel was coming."

"He is. But you know Axel, he's always a little bit late."

Ten minutes later, the door chimes sang. Jared quickly looked over his shoulder. When he saw his other brother, his black hair slicked back, his arms boasting tattoos, he smiled. Axel had the same face boyish Jared remembered from so long ago. And the same edge.

Axel's face broke out in a grin. The two brothers embraced each other.

"It's so good to see you, Axel."

"Good to see you too, bro." As Axel pulled back, Jared took note of the rest of him. He was wearing a white T-shirt which had some grease stains. Axel worked on cars, so that made sense. His hands were callused—occupational hazard—and his fingernails were darkened. His well-worn jeans looked as though he'd smeared his dirty hands over them, leaving grease marks.

"I did say eleven," Seth said.

"I was finishing up a car," Axel explained. "I left as soon as it was done."

"The problem is I don't have much time," Seth said. "I'm on my lunch break."

"I know, you've got an important job and I don't," Axel quipped. "Maybe I should just leave."

There was that edge Jared remembered. The Martinez fire, Jared had jokingly called it. Axel had always had a bit of a temper, but hadn't they all at times? They hadn't been the easiest boys for Clay and Leda Hollister, God bless them. Jared'd had his issues, being adopted after tragically losing his family. And Axel .... Well, it was hard when everyone in town knew that your mom was an addict and that's why you had to go into the foster care system.

"That's not what I said." Seth exhaled sharply. "At least you're here now."

"Then why get on my case?" Axel balled his hands into fists at his side.

Seth said nothing, and Jared quickly interjected to lighten the tension. "We need to have a beer and catch up, Axel. I'm sure there's lots to tell me."

"Yeah, for sure," Axel said.

Seth glanced at his watch, then smiled at the well-dressed attendant who walked over to them after finishing up with another customer. "The gang's all here, Steven. We can get started."

As the attendant helped them pick out a number of different styled suits from classic to modern, to single- and double-breasted tuxedos, the mood eased. "I like this one," Axel said, holding up a flashy burgundy jacket that there was no chance any of them would be wearing. "We can go for an 80's disco theme."

Jared laughed. "Dad will never go for that!"

"I'd almost pay to see him in that jacket though," Seth said, getting in on the fun.

"So where are you working now, Axel?" Jared asked. It was shameful, he should already know this.

"I'm working at Seaside Transmission."

"You always did like tinkering with cars." Jared smiled. "I still remember that time you hotwired Mrs. Harrison's car and ended up in a jail cell."

"She was over eighty, hadn't driven that car in years," Axel said. "I was just checking to see if it still worked."

"Ha!" Seth chimed in. "That's a new defense."

"Yeah, I was a little hellion," Axel said, lifting a pale gray suit from the rack. "I was lucky I didn't get a worse punishment. I guess it helped that our dad was the sheriff. And old lady Harrison was glad to have me cutting her lawn every week for a year. It was a fair punishment."

Clay had always been a fair man who had led with love, despite his sternness. It helped all of them grow into decent men.

"Any word on Van?" Jared asked. "Is he coming back for the wedding?"

"I'm waiting to hear from him," Seth said. "I'll just have to get his sizes."

Jared, Seth, and Axel tried on classic fit suits, modern fit, and also a of couple tuxedo options. Jared liked the modern black suit, as well as the black two-button tuxedo. Either would work for Clay. He was a classic man who didn't like anything over the top or exceptionally unique.

"I still think we should pick the red," Axel joked. "Watch Dad lose it."

"More like watch him have a heart attack on his wedding day." Seth smiled. In that moment, it was like old times. Though Seth had been older, and had become a father at a young age, he'd still been around to be a good influence to Jared. Just like Clay.

The three of them stood in the black tuxes, checking out their reflection in the mirror. Seth tall with dark brown locks, Axel his black hair and lightly tanned skin from his Mexican heritage, and Jared, biracial, the product of a black mother and white father. All three looked different, and no one would ever peg them for brothers, yet they were. They were brothers because of the love of Leda and Clay, who'd brought them together. And they'd formed their own special bond.

"Hey, let me take a selfie," Axel said. He retrieved his phone from his jean's pocket and held it up to take a mirror selfie that would capture all three of them.

Steven quickly made his way over. "Let me take it for you. You three look great in these tuxes. Is this the one you've decided on?"

They looked at each other, unsure, then Seth spoke. "This feels like the right one for Dad. But the modern suit is good, too .... Can we let you know?"

"Absolutely," Steven said.

As they began to remove the tuxedo jackets, Seth said, "I'm gonna have to run. My lunch break is almost over. But I'll see you two at home for dinner, right?"

By home, Seth meant the home they'd grown up in. "Yes," Jared said. "Dad invited me for dinner when I was there this morning. He said I needed to wear something nice, that we're taking family photos."

"I don't know if I can make it," Axel said. "Me leaving the shop has caused a backlog as it is."

"Try," Seth said. "If you can."

They all disappeared into a changeroom to finish undressing and redressing.

"So what's new with you?" Jared asked Axel when they were back in their regular clothes. "Dating?"

"No. There's no one tying me down." Axel snorted a laugh. "But you hear our brother's sweet on someone. Serena, who owns the coffee shop."

"Oh, yes. I've met her," Jared said. "Wide Awake Café. Seems as though she wakes Seth up every morning with her special brew and treats."

Seth shot a playful glare at Jared as he adjusted his duty belt. "Hey, I've already heard enough from the people in this town. I don't need to hear it from you two." But he was smiling, and Jared was happy to see it. He was glad his brother had found someone special.

Then Jared was thinking of Nina, whom we hadn't quite been able to stop thinking about since he'd gotten back to town. He didn't know why she was occupying so much of his thoughts. Hadn't he pushed thoughts of Nina, and pretty much everyone else in this town, out of his mind as time had gone on? But being here, he could feel his roots to the past growing again. Something he hadn't expected.

5

Though Gail's breakfast had left Jared full for most of the day, by the time he smelled the aromatic flavors coming from the kitchen, his stomach grumbled as though he hadn't eaten in days.

Gail greeted him with a sweet smile as he followed Clay into the house, and Jared felt a sense of guilt that he wasn't thrilled about her marrying his dad. Gail was a good woman. Honest, genuine. Patient. Clearly loving. He heard that she had been a godsend to his mother when she'd been ill. She had been by Leda's side through the horrible days as the cancer had ravaged her body. Jared had seen his mother only once during that awful time, and he'd hardly been able to stand it.

"Sit, put your feet up," Gail said, guiding Jared to the living room. He sank his body into the recliner. "Let me get you a glass of sweet tea. I make it the same way your mother did."

She headed off to the kitchen, and in no time returned with a tall glass of iced tea. She passed it to him, but before she could turn away, Jared took her by the hand. "Thank you, Gail." He paused, held her gaze. "For everything. For being there for my mother. And … for being here for my dad."

He hadn't expected to say that, but it felt right. No matter how he felt about the wedding, he couldn't deny that Gail had brought normalcy to his father's life.

Jared sipped the tea; it was sweet and refreshing, exactly as he remembered Leda used to make it. He got up and wandered to the dining room. "Anything I can help with?" he asked his dad.

"No, you just relax."

Clay was setting the dining room table, and Jared noticed there were seven place settings. "Who else is coming? Seth, Matty, maybe Axel. Me."

"The photographer," Clay said.

"Oh." That was odd, but this was a small town. The photographer was probably someone they knew well.

Gail whizzed in from the kitchen, untying her apron at the neck. "I believe in having a plate for anyone who comes to visit. She might not want to eat, but I'm going to offer her a meal anyway."

Yes, Jared realized, that was the small-town way.

Gail scooped her apron over her neck, beneath it she was wearing a pretty pink blouse and white pants. Her makeup was done nicely, and her hair was softly curled.

"We're going to do the pictures first, then eat," she said.

There was a knock at the door, then it opened. Seth and Matty sauntered into the house. "We're here!" Seth announced. "Man, does it ever smell good. Is that a pot roast?"

Gail nodded. "I know how much you love it, and how much Clay does, too."

"Hey, Uncle Jared," Matty said, then hurried over to hug him.

"Would you like some sweet tea?" Gail asked them.

"Absolutely," Seth replied.

Seth wandered into the kitchen, and Matty settled onto the sofa, then promptly pulled out his phone.

The doorbell rang. With everyone but Matty in the kitchen, Jared said, "I'll get the door."

When he opened it, his bottom jaw hit the floor. "Nina?"

She smiled up at him. "Hello."

"What are you doing here?" Jared asked. He noticed the Canon camera she was holding, a 6D. It was definitely a professional camera. She had a bag slung over her shoulder which he imagined held extra lenses and other camera supplies.

"I guess your dad didn't tell you. I'm doing the photography for their wedding."

Jared's eyes grew wide. "You're what?"

"I'm the photographer." Nina held up the camera.

Jared remembered that in addition to her sports, she had always been taking pictures in high school and had even been part of the photography club.

"You always said you planned to open a dance studio," Jared said. "Or be a personal trainer."

"I was a personal trainer for a bit," she said. "But you know me, I always loved photography. I'd go to soccer games, football games, and always bring my camera. Some friends would ask me to take photos of their children, some wanted videos of the games, so I'd do that. Then more people asked. Next thing I knew, I turned a hobby into a business."

"That's amazing," Jared said. "A woman of many talents, for sure."

"I love it. Every day is different, so I never get bored."

Jared remembered. She would always joke about being a Gemini, how that fact alone had her spreading herself in all different directions. She was on the cheer squad, the debate team, the soccer team, and of course, the photography club.

"Oh, hello," Gail said, coming into the foyer. Her smile was warm as her eyes landed on Nina.

"Hello, Gail. I was just telling Jared that I'm doing the photos for your wedding."

"Yes, and we love the photos you've taken so far. Our engagement photo on the beach was so beautiful."

Nina walked into the living room, greeting Clay, Seth, and Matty. "It's a lovely day," Nina said. "I think we should do all the photos in the backyard."

"Yes," Gail agreed. "In front of Leda's beautiful flower bushes. It'll be like she's with us in a tangible way."

Clay slipped an arm around Gail's waist and pulled her close. Leaning down, he kissed her temple.

"Mom was always proud of her flower bushes," Seth said. "Especially the climbing roses on the lattice."

"We want to find a way to include her in this." Gail's eyes veered toward Jared. "We're together because of her. And she's part of us, always will be."

Jared's lips pulled in a small smile. "I couldn't agree more."

Two times in two days Nina had seen Jared, when she hadn't seen him once in the nine years since he'd left, and he was interacting with her as if no time had passed at all.

As if he hadn't abandoned her.

Oh, they'd stayed in touch in the beginning. Then his responses had been less and less, until eventually there'd been no contact at all.

She wanted to be angry with him, but she still had a soft spot for him in her heart. She knew why he'd stayed away, that it was about his pain. Even looking at him now, she could see the hint of sadness in his eyes as he and the rest of the family gathered in front of the climbing rose bushes.

He'd always turned to her when he was sad or angry or even happy in the past. But that had been in high school. Perhaps it was silly for her to have expected them to stay up on the phone talking for hours about their grievances once he'd moved away.

"The party can start because I'm here now!"

At the sound of Axel's voice, everyone turned to him and erupted in cheers. Axel jogged over to everyone, smiling like a goofball.

"Perfect," Nina said. "You're just in time for the group photos in front of the rose bushes." She'd already taken some of each of them alone, and some of Clay and Gail together. Now it was time for Clay and Gail with their sons and grandson.

The Hollisters shuffled over to the rose bushes, which were in full bloom. The red looked incredible.

Nina's eyes lingered on Jared. He looked good in black slacks and a pale blue dress shirt. Better than good. He had a closely shaved beard and mustache that framed his full lips, and his black hair was closely cropped at the sides but about an inch in length on the top. Gone was the long hair that he'd often worn wild and free. She'd always joked that his natural loose curls were better suited on a girl.

That had been a lie, of course. The curls were uniquely his, and more than once she'd wanted to run her fingers through them. Pull his head to hers and compel him to kiss her.

She never would have done that, however. He was her best friend, and she'd never wanted to do anything to ruin their friendship—something she had made clear to Jared. Still, there were times she'd hoped that something would spark between them. Those times when she knew he was the perfect listener, and perfect in so many other ways.

But Juan had always been there, ready to swoop back in after every breakup and sweet talk her back into his world. Yet Nina had found herself hoping and wishing that Jared would make a move. That after she'd spilled her heart and guts out because of Juan, he would gather her in his arms and kiss her.

And yet, the one time he'd tried to do exactly that …

"Is this good?"

Nina's thoughts snapped back to the present at the sound of Gail's voice.

She quickly raised the camera and looked through the viewfinder. "Axel, how about you stand on Gail's left. Then Jared, then Matty and Seth. Great," she said when they'd rearranged themselves. "Perfect. Now everyone smile. Yes, that's beautiful."

And it was. While they all wished the fourth brother Van was there, to complete the family unit, Nina smiled as she snapped off several photographs of the Hollisters, who became more comfortable with each click of the lens. They exuded happiness and love. They weren't a family born of obligation, but one based on choice.

Nina sometimes wondered if Jared knew how lucky he was. There was no doubt that life had dealt him a horrible hand. He'd lost his mother, father, and sister in one horrible accident. But he'd been given a second chance. Because another set of parents who couldn't have their own children had wanted to provide love to children who needed it.

And Jared had needed it.

"Now let me get the three brothers together," Nina said. She repositioned them so that they were standing with the large oak behind them. "Look at each other, not me."

89

Nina snapped more photos, amazed at how gorgeous they were. The love between these three men was evident in the pictures.

"Jared, can I get you over here?" Nina guided him to a spot near the fence. "Now look at the camera and smile."

Nina placed her eye to the viewfinder. For a moment, the sight of Jared's charming smile made her heart skip a beat. It was just the kind of smile Nina loved on a man, one that was bright and earnest and sweet.

She drew in a deep breath, then began clicking off photo after photo. The camera really loved Jared. He had that special star quality.

But that was something she had already known, hadn't she? She'd seen photos of him during some of his football games, and he absolutely looked like a star. But the star quality wasn't something that came from the exterior with him. It came from the inside out.

She took more photos of Jared then of Seth then the rest of the family. Pictures in front of the fence, and pictures by the tree.

After a solid forty minutes, Nina was satisfied. "I think I have enough of what I need. This is great."

"It's a pity Van couldn't be here," Gail said.

"I know. But send me some family photos that include him." With the right photo, she might be able to digitally add him to one or more of the pictures she'd taken today and have it look natural." Or if he comes back to town with enough time, I can come back to get some pictures with him."

"Gotta run." Axel kissed Gail's cheek, then hugged Clay. "I'll see you later, Jared."

"Later," Jared said. Then he sidled up to Nina as she returned her various lenses to her camera bag. "Is this all going to go in the album? You won't just use the photos from the wedding day?"

"I was told you all might not be here on the wedding day," Nina said, and watched as Jared stuffed his fingers into the pockets on his pants. "So these will be helpful if you're not. And some of this I'll use for the video."

"You're doing the video, too?" Jared asked.

Nina nodded. "Gail was very generous to offer me the job of filming the wedding as well. I do have an assistant, but otherwise I'm pretty much a one-person operation. I'll do my best to make a stunning video of the day's event, and I'll pepper in pictures of family and the couple and all the people who mean something to them throughout." She shrugged. "You'll see. Hopefully you'll like it."

"I know I'm going to love it," Gail said, her eyes lighting up. "I saw what you did for Jazzy and Jeremiah's wedding, the way you incorporated their baby, Caleb, and the pictures of all their friends and family …. It added so much richness and meaning."

Nina's chest swelled with pride. "Thank you," she said. "I try."

"You do more than try. It's obvious you love what you do. That's what makes your work incredible. You have that special touch that makes your work unique. I think it's pictures just like these. Not of the wedding day alone, but of a family being a family."

Nina slung the camera bag over her shoulder. "I appreciate that." Gail's words were further affirmation that Nina was achieving what she hoped with her photos and videos. "All that's left now is the big day."

"You will stay for dinner, won't you?" Gail asked.

"Actually, I can't."

Clay came to stand beside Gail. "Gail's made her famous pot roast."

Jared's eyes volleyed between Nina, Seth, and Gail. "How do you all know each other?"

"We met at a yoga class," Clay explained.

"Yoga?" Jared laughed as if he couldn't imagine Clay sitting on a mat doing stretches.

"Yes, yoga," Clay said. "We do it on the beach. It's a beautiful setting, very calming. You should try it."

"It's a great class," Nina said. "Maybe you'll try it before you head back to Buffalo." She imagined it would be helpful for him.

"We'll see," Jared said noncommittally.

Nina patted her camera bag. "I'd better go. I wish I could stay for dinner, but I have to see my mother."

"Oh, yes. I need to talk to her as well," Gail said. "Ask her when I can go see her."

Jared shot Nina a concerned look. "Something going on?"

"Possibly a pending disaster in the kitchen."

Jared made a face. "What?"

"My mother's taken up baking," Nina explained and watched Jared's concern morph into an amused expression. "She's very

91

serious about it. My stepdad keeps complaining that his midsection is growing every day because of her." Nina chuckled. "And Gail isn't helping matters. She actually hired my mother to make one of the cakes for the wedding reception."

Jared shot a look at Gail. "Seriously?"

"She offered me an incredible deal, next to nothing really, as she's trying to get her name out there and establish her new business."

"But don't you want a professional wedding cake?" Jared asked.

"You haven't seen my mother's cakes," Nina interjected, squaring her jaw slightly. "She has become quite the master. She watched one YouTube video which led to probably ten thousand YouTube videos and then she decided that she had missed out on baking her entire life. She's been at it now for several months. Honestly, it's one of the reasons I keep working out as often as I do."

"You have an incredible body," Jared said. "I don't think you have anything to worry about."

Nina blushed. "Anyway, she wants me to do some testing of the cake recipe she's working on for Gail."

"Wow," Jared said. "I should stop by. Say hi to your mom while I'm in town."

"You just want to eat cake," Nina joked.

"Can I help you take anything to your car?" Jared asked.

"No," Nina told him. She exhaled softly. "I guess I'll see you around."

Before he could say anything else, she was off. The sooner she got away from Jared, the better. Being around him was making her think of old times with him.

And she didn't want to think of old times.

Because she knew that, sooner rather than later, Jared would be leaving. And once again, he would no longer be a part of her life.

6

The next morning, Jared went to the Wide Awake Café to start his day. Serena greeted him with a bright smile and a hello, reminding him he was in a small town, where people remembered you and greeted you earnestly.

He got himself a cappuccino this time, along with a blueberry muffin. He gave Serena a wave as he was leaving because she was dealing with another customer. He'd get to know her at a later time. With her being involved with Seth, he figured he would be seeing her at some point soon.

Jared stepped out of the café and onto the sidewalk, almost bumping into someone.

"Sorry about that," Jared quickly said.

"Jared? Jared Hollister!"

As Jared looked at the man, his face erupted in a grin. It was Coach Whalen. Grayer, his face visibly more wrinkled, but it was Coach. No doubt about it.

"Coach Whalen." Jared opened his arms and drew the older, shorter man into a hug. "It's so good to see you."

"As I live and breathe," Coach Whalen said, easing back to look at him. "Guess it took your dad getting married to bring you back to town."

Jared was going to hear this a lot, and it was true. "Yeah, it did. It's good to be back."

"You left to become a superstar and forgot all about us," Coach Whalen teased.

"Naw, that's not true. I could never forget about you guys. Especially not you, Coach Whalen."

"Please, call me Henry."

For a moment, Jared rolled the name around in his mind. He couldn't do it. "You're always going to be Coach Whalen to me."

The coach chuckled. "Okay." He paused. "How long are you in town for?"

How long indeed? Jared had planned to return to Buffalo after the bachelor party then come back here for the wedding. But did that make any sense? It's just that he was in a football frame of mind, wanting to get the contract situation resolved before he came back for the wedding.

"Probably until the wedding," Jared said. "So a couple of weeks."

"You going back to Buffalo?" The coach looked at him with a hopeful expression.

Jared knew what he was asking. If anyone knew what was going on with his career, it was probably Coach Whalen. Jared told him the truth. "I'm not sure. My shoulder hasn't quite healed properly and … it's causing some issues."

"But they could keep you on the roster still, they must know your potential."

Jared'd had the same arguments with his agent. The man was trying. But the discussions with Buffalo weren't going well, and Jared was all but certain that he would be cut. With no specific time frame as to when he could play in the future without further injuring his shoulder, he was dead weight.

Even if Buffalo didn't want him, another team might pick him up. But he knew that was unlikely with the current state of his rotator cuff.

"You know how sports are," Jared said, forcing a smile. "Everything's up in the air. You think you're down, then you get that call and find out you're back on top." He chuckled, hoping to convey a nonchalance he didn't feel. His career was on the line. He had left to pursue bigger and brighter things, always hoping that when he came back here, he'd be coming back as a guy who'd made it.

Not as a guy who'd tried and failed.

"I talk to my kids about you all the time," Coach Whalen said. "Tell them that I had one superstar who left and got drafted into the NFL. Hey"—his eyes lit up—"do you have time tomorrow? I'd love for you to talk to my guys. I can rally them all up, we can meet at the school football field, say for 3:00 p.m. You tell them your story. There are a couple of guys I think could really benefit from hearing how you picked yourself up after tragedy. One guy in particular, Daniel Aucoin. He's currently in foster care right now. I keep worrying that he's going to take the wrong road."

Though Jared had been momentarily wallowing in the sorrow of thinking of how his career had gone down the toilet, the mention of talking to kids made his spirits rise. It was something he loved to do. "Sure." It would be a good way to pass some of the time while in town. "I'd be happy to."

"Great," Coach Whalen said. "Why don't we exchange numbers, or would you prefer me to send you a message on social media?"

Jared took out his phone. "You're family to me. Here's my number."

Jared drove around Sea Glass Bay while drinking his coffee, reacquainting himself with the town he'd once called home. The post office, the library, the sports complex, the movie theater.

The cemetery.

A lump lodged in his throat as he drove by the burial ground. It was always odd to him that graveyards were such beautiful-looking places, with landscaped lawns and sprawling trees—as if they were happy spaces. He drove on by. He'd gone there twice—for his biological family and then for Leda—but he didn't like visiting them there.

He drove to the boardwalk, a place of happier memories, and parked his vehicle. It was early. He wondered if he'd find Clay and Gail on the beach doing yoga.

Jared strolled past the various shops and eateries, getting caught up in the sounds of happy people out enjoying the gorgeous morning. He walked in the middle of the roadway so that he wouldn't have to talk to anyone. He wanted to go to the beach.

The weather was warm and comfortable with a cool breeze coming off the water. His eyes trailed up and down the stretch of sand, but he didn't see a group of people doing yoga. Some people were jogging, some were doing stretches. A couple was walking hand-in-hand near the water's edge.

Jared went to the right, toward the stretch of rocks where he'd used to sit and reflect. Someone was sitting there, he noticed as he got closer.

Not just someone, he realized.

Nina.

A rolled-up yoga mat was resting on the rock beside where she sat. Either the exercise class had already finished, or it would be starting soon.

Jared picked up his pace as he headed toward her. Seeing her out here, on the very rock where they used to hang to talk about life, a feeling he couldn't quite describe began to stir in his chest.

She didn't even notice him as he approached. She was lost in her thoughts.

"Hey," Jared said softly.

Nina whipped her head toward his, her eyes widening as she saw him. "Jared, what are you doing here?"

Even if he didn't hear the quiver in her voice, he couldn't miss the moisture in her eyes. "Have you been crying?"

She glanced away, dipped her toe in the sand.

Jared perched his butt on the rock beside her. "So you still come to our spot when something's bothering you. Tell me what's wrong."

"I shouldn't be sitting here feeling sorry for myself," Nina said. "I have so much to do. Especially today."

"You know you can talk to me," Jared said. "I'm here for you."

Nina looked off into the distance, as though weighing whether or not she could trust his words.

"I know I haven't been around. But ..." Jared hesitated. He hadn't left her behind just because he'd wanted to, his ego had been hurt. He had hoped that after deciding that he wasn't going to follow

Dominique to UCLA—encouraged by Nina herself to follow his own dream—that maybe, *finally*, he could show her how he really felt. Sure, Dominique had been his girlfriend his senior year of high school, but he'd known deep down she wasn't the right one for him. And after yet another fight with Juan, Jared had hoped that Nina would realize he wasn't right for her either.

That was why he'd leaned in to kiss her that summer night, but she'd pulled back with a stunned expression on her face and asked him what he was doing.

She'd rejected him, which had stung—more than it should have. Her rejection was a big part of the reason he'd let their friendship fade into the past.

Something that he now realized was immature.

Nina exhaled harshly. "So I told you that Juan and I split. We've been officially divorced for several months, but we had a storage unit we were sharing after we sold the house. It wasn't a problem before, but now that Olivia is moving in with him, he needs the space to put some of her things, plus stuff that was occupying the extra bedroom, as that's going to be the baby's room."

"Okay."

"He told me that I have only three days to get my stuff out of the storage unit. The problem is I don't have anywhere to go. He's given me almost no notice."

"He's got to understand that. He needs to give you time."

"I told him that, and he pretty much told me too bad. He's the one who's been paying for it. And …" Nina's shoulders drooped.

"Hey," Jared said. He placed his finger beneath her chin and turned her face toward him. "We'll find something."

"With such short notice?"

"There are a lot of people in this town who have space. Maybe even my dad. Maybe he can fit some things in his garage."

"I don't want to be a burden to people."

"Friends help friends. It's not a burden."

"Friends also don't disappear from each other's lives," she said, flashing him a knowing expression.

"You know I hated losing people," Jared said.

97

"Yet you were okay losing me."

Why didn't he just tell her that he'd been hurt? And when he'd seen her go back to Juan yet another time, he couldn't do it. Couldn't stay in touch with her while her relationship with Juan grew deeper.

Because he was going to lose her, too. Lose her once and for all to Juan through marriage, and that's exactly what had happened.

Jared looked out at the shimmering water of the bay. Why didn't he just admit the truth to her? How he felt about the rejection, about Juan …

But he said nothing about that. Instead, he said, "Let me talk to Seth. He knows a lot of people, maybe he'll know someone who's got some space to lease immediately."

"You don't have to. This is my problem, not yours."

Jared took her hand and gave it a reassuring squeeze. "Whatever your problem, I'm here for you. I may have failed you these past years, but I'm here now. Again."

"But for how long?" she asked.

Jared didn't know what to say, so he told her the truth. "No matter how long I'm here for, I'm not going to disappear from your life again. I know that was wrong and that it hurt you." It had hurt him, too. "So just know that I'm here for you, and I'll be coming back to town regularly even when I do leave."

Nina's lips slowly lifted in a grin. In her eyes, he saw a spark of trust. "You promise?" she asked.

"I promise."

7

$\mathcal{L}$ater that day, Jared was thrilled when Seth got back to him, letting him know that he had found someone who was willing to forgo rent and loan Nina the space she needed for as long as necessary. "It's a woman named Cecily Perkins. She's got a shed at the back of her house that's unoccupied. Used to be filled with her son's stuff, but he moved to Texas so now it's empty. I recently helped her out with a cat issue, so she's happy to let Nina use it for free."

"Cat issue?" Jared asked.

"Don't ask," Seth said. "She said Nina can bring her things by as soon as she needs to."

"Thanks, Seth," Jared said, beaming from ear to ear. He was thrilled and knew that Nina would be relieved.

He hung up from Seth then called Nina and told her the good news.

"Yes, I know Mrs. Perkins," she said. "Lovely lady. Probably a little lonely now that her son has moved away. I don't know how to thank you, Jared."

"No need. Seth said he'd helped her out with a cat issue, whatever that means, so she's just returning the favor." In that moment, Jared realized that this was another one of the benefits of a small town. You couldn't necessarily just call up someone in a bigger city and get something like this for free. But Mrs. Perkins was refusing any sort of payment.

"But the favor should be for Seth," Nina said.

"He's happy to help, Nina. Please don't worry about it."

She nodded. "You're right. I need this. Oh Jared, thank you so much."

"You're welcome." Jared knew that she probably would have found something on her own, but it helped having a brother as the town's sheriff, who had been able to get results sooner. Besides, she didn't have the luxury of time.

"You said you have stuff to move," Jared said, "and you don't have much time."

"That's right."

"How about I help you now? Between the two of us, we can get a good start even if we don't move everything today."

"That would be great," Nina said. "Can you come at one?"

"I'll be there."

Several hours later, Jared and Nina had moved most of her big items from Juan's storage unit into Cecily Perkins's shed. It was getting later into the evening, and Nina didn't want to move every last item of hers and impose on Cecily, as the woman was spending much of her time fussing over them, offering them food and drink at regular intervals.

"You've been so wonderful to allow me this space, Mrs. Perkins," Nina said, passing the empty drinking glass to the older woman. "And that lemonade, it hit the spot."

"If you'd like to join me for dinner, you're more than welcome."

"Maybe tomorrow for lunch," Nina said. "But I'll bring the food. It's the least I can do."

They all said their goodbyes, and minutes later Nina and Jared were back in his vehicle. "We got a good amount accomplished today," Nina said, smiling with satisfaction. "I can't believe it."

"There's nothing we can't do when we set our minds to it," Jared said, facing her as he started his vehicle. "Isn't that what we always said?"

"I remember *you* saying that when you asked me to help you cheat on those algebra tests you didn't study for."

Jared laughed. "Yeah, algebra was always too tough for me."

"Are you hungry?"

"You just told Mrs. Perkins that you didn't want dinner."

"That's because I was hoping you and I could have dinner," Nina said. "Just the two of us. Let me take you out." When Jared's eyes widened slightly, she clarified. "Dinner as a way to pay you back for helping me."

"I don't need any payback." His expression softened. "Think of it as me making amends for not being here for you all these years."

"Fine, that debt is paid. But after all that time slugging boxes for me, I would love for us to just do something fun. Pizza and roller-skating at Lollapa-Pizza?"

"Lollapa-Pizza?" Jared's eyes lit up. "I've been dying to get back there to have a slice. I can't refuse that offer."

"Even better, tonight is old school night. We can get ready, head there in a couple of hours."

"Old school night? You know I'm a sucker for old school."

"Great," Nina said. "Then it's a date."

Nina hadn't meant to say *date*, but she hoped that Jared didn't read into her words. Still, she felt light, happy. She wanted to do something that was easygoing and fun. She'd spent too many days with the truth about Olivia and Juan weighing her down. She felt stupid even being upset about it, but it did hurt. Then Juan's ultimatum that she get her stuff out of his place within a few days had added to her stress.

Finally, she could breathe, and she had Jared to thank for that.

As Nina stood in front of her bathroom mirror, making sure her hair looked just right, she wondered why she was taking the extra time beautifying herself if this wasn't a date?

Because she wanted to look good, to represent exactly how she was feeling. There was nothing wrong with that.

The place was just how Jared remembered it, as if he had stepped through a door that led to nine years in the past. The old-school arcade with its dinging, ringing machines, and flashing lights, the family tables where people sat, gorging on pizza, and the indoor roller rink with its multicolored lights and mirrored disco ball spinning above the middle of the rink.

"I haven't been on roller skates in years," Jared said. "Not since I left Sea Glass Bay."

"You want to eat first or hit the rink?" Nina asked.

"I'm starving."

"So am I."

They secured a table, and as they looked at the menu, Nina said, "Pepperoni, ham, pineapple. What do you think?"

Jared looked at Nina as though she had sprouted a second head. "*Pineapple?*"

"Yeah. Life is short. Live a little."

Jared was suddenly remembering the Hollister family tradition—the test. Anyone who liked pineapple on a pizza was essentially not to be trusted. Nina had never liked pineapple on pizza before.

His stomach sank. "Wow, a lot has changed over the years."

Nina started to laugh. "Honestly, if you could see the look on your face. You look absolutely horrified! I just figured I would tease you about your obsession because you used to make such a big deal about it back in the day."

"I did?"

"Oh yeah. Pretty much every time we came here to have pizza." Nina's lips flattened. "You don't remember?"

Now Jared cracked a smile. "Now I'm teasing *you*. Of course I remember."

It was still a big deal for him, but as he thought about it, he realized it wasn't really about the pizza. It was about his connection to the Hollisters. It was the shared family joke that meant something to him.

"So what *do* you want to have on the pizza?" Jared asked.

"I feel like having a pepperoni pizza oozing with extra cheese."

"That sounds perfect."

No sooner had Nina lowered her menu, the playful expression on her face morphed into horror. "Oh my God, don't look," she said.

Jared threw a quick gaze over his shoulder. Across from him, Nina squealed. "I told you not to look!"

Jared wanted to look again, but given Nina's distress, he didn't. Then he saw what had gotten her attention. Juan. With Olivia. Walking hand-in-hand toward the skate rental counter.

"Is she actually going to get on roller skates while she's pregnant?" Nina asked.

Her mood had gone from happy to sour in an instant. "You want us to leave?" Jared asked.

"No. It doesn't matter."

"But it looks like it does."

"Oh my God, they're coming over here."

Moments later, Juan was at the table, grinning at them as though they were all on good terms. "Nina, hi. Jared—I heard you were back in town." Juan extended a hand. "How's it going, man?"

"I'm good," Jared responded. His gaze went to Olivia. "I hear you and Olivia are together. Congratulations."

Olivia sidled up to Juan, gripping his arm as though she expected Nina to physically come between them. "Hello, Nina," Olivia said. Her voice was tentative. "I've called you."

"I've been busy," Nina said, her tone clipped.

"It's great to see you," Juan gushed. "I've watched so many of your games. You know we're big fans in this town."

"Thank you," Jared said.

Olivia's eyes darted between Nina and Jared, as if something just clicked. "Is there something going on here? Are you two together?"

Nina's eyes widened, but she said nothing.

"I'm just in town for my dad's wedding," Jared said.

"But Nina, you always had a thing for Jared," Olivia went on. "As much as you dated Juan, Jared was always there for you. I always thought … maybe …"

"If that's what makes you feel better about going after my man." Nina waved a dismissive hand. "You know what, I don't care. I wish you both well." Then she beckoned the waitress. "I'm ready to order, Jared. I'm famished."

Juan got the hint and took Olivia by the hand. "Enjoy your pizza," he said. "Good to see you."

"Thanks, good to see you, too," Jared replied. Then the moment Juan and Olivia were out of earshot, he said to Nina, "You okay?"

Her smile returned. "I am now."

8

*J*ared was starting to get into a routine. Coffee and a pastry at Wide Awake Café to start his day, something he was starting to wonder how he'd survive without when he left. Yes, the coffee was that good.

For yet another morning he joined his father and Gail for breakfast, where she'd made so much food, he wondered how she expected it to be eaten by three people. But she explained, "Seth is going to drop by when he gets a chance, and I'm going to bring a plate to Axel at the shop."

"Maybe I can bring a plate for Nina," Jared suggested. "I'm going to help her move the rest of her stuff to Mrs. Perkins's place when I leave here."

"Absolutely," she said.

"Don't forget Matty," Clay said. "He's coming by to help me with my computer. He can always be bribed with food."

As Jared watched Gail head into the kitchen to prepare plates of food just as his mother would have, he could feel the love in this house. Seeing Clay happy and content, the corner of Jared's heart that had been shaded by darkness began to fill with light.

Still, he felt the need to talk to his dad. So as Gail busied herself in the kitchen, and Clay wandered to the back patio window to stare outside, Jared saw his chance.

"Dad," Jared said softly, standing to his right.

Clay faced him. "Yes, Son?"

"Gail is a lovely lady," Jared found himself saying. "But you always said that Mom was the only one for you. That the first time you saw her, you knew she would be your forever. So I don't understand how barely two years after she's gone, you're moving on ... with her friend."

There. He'd said it.

Clay opened the back door, and Jared followed him outside. "I loved your mother as much as any man could ever love a woman," he said when the door was firmly closed behind them. "She *was* my forever. But she was taken away from me, something I prayed would never happen. Except it did, and I was lost. I didn't think I would ever be with anyone else, then Gail was there. She saw me through my grief. And then .... Something sparked. Something I never expected. Something real and wonderful. Almost as if your mother was pulling the strings from above."

Jared's lips twisted with doubt. To him, it still felt wrong that he was with Gail, although maybe that was childish of him.

"But her friend?" Jared asked. "It makes me wonder, was she ever interested in you before? Were you ever interested in her?"

"No. Absolutely not," Clay said adamantly. "We never saw each other as anything other than friends. That's what I'm saying, Son. It's like your mother was working on this from above. She knew I was lost and needed someone. Who else would she choose but Gail, someone she trusted implicitly."

Jared's gaze wandered to his mother's rose bushes. He supposed in a way, his father had a point. Who would Leda have chosen? Someone she could trust to take care of Clay. And there was no doubt that Gail was taking care of him.

Clay placed a hand on his shoulder. "This doesn't take away from the love I have for your mother. What it's shown me is that, unexpectedly, you can be blessed with love a second time. That's what I have been. I've been blessed a lot, Son. With you and Seth and Van and Axel. And now, with a second chance at love."

Even when Jared left a short while later to meet up with Nina, Clay's words about love and second chances stayed with him.

Jared looked up at the sign for the high school, and smiled as he remembered his days here. Home of the Tigers. Jared had played a number of sports before concentrating on football in his last two years. He and the quarterback had worked effortlessly together, Jared so often able to wiggle his way out of the other team's defensemen to make himself available to catch the ball. He had wowed the crowds here and at away games.

The image of the orange and black tiger graced the school sign. His years playing football had been the glory days for the school. Getting a scholarship to Kent State had been a big deal, something Dominique hadn't understood. Her ultimatum had hurt him. The one person he wanted to talk to about it was Nina. Nina had encouraged him to choose his passion—if Dominique was right for him, she'd be there when he graduated from college.

Jared parked, got out of the vehicle, and made his way around to the back of the school to the football field. Coach Whalen saw him and raised his hand in an immediate wave. Jared waved back, and his way over to the bleachers, where a number of teenagers were sitting. Mostly boys, but a few girls, too. Probably the girlfriends of some of the players.

"Jared!" The coach's face lit up. "Everyone, Jared Hollister. In the flesh. You've heard me talk about him so much."

There were excited murmurs in the crowd. Jared smiled at the kids, and they smiled back, some looking shy, even a little intimidated amid their excitement.

Nina was there, too, he noticed. Holding her camera.

"I brought you all here today so you could hear Jared's story. Which is why I didn't want your parents here. I want Jared to be able to focus on you without any distractions." The coach looked over the crowd, and his gaze landed to the right on a tall boy with messy brown hair sitting near the back of the bleachers. Then he continued. "It wasn't always easy for Jared. But he concentrated on football, and as you know he not only left here with a scholarship to Kent State, he went on to be drafted by the Buffalo Bills."

The kids clapped, some hooted. Jared's chest swelled with pride.

106

"Thank you," Jared said, facing the crowd at large. "What I want to stress to you is that I'm just a kid from Sea Glass Bay who worked hard and made something happen. I'm not special, I'm not lucky. But I was determined, I busted my butt. There's no reason that you guys can't do the same." He paused. "How many of you want to play professional football?"

A few hands flew up. Some of the guys shrugged. "If you want to get a football scholarship, or even end up playing in the NFL, you have to show up and do the work. I know, sometimes Coach Whalen can be tough, he can be demanding, but he knows what he's doing, so listen to him."

"But now he's retiring," one of the boys said. "So what's gonna happen now?"

Jared shot a look at the coach. "You're retiring?"

He shrugged. "I promised my wife Nancy that I wouldn't keep coaching until I dropped. I'm old now."

Jared couldn't imagine Coach ever retiring. He was an icon, a legend.

"Whoever takes over for me will be great," Coach Whalen said. There were a few *boos*. "I'll still be around a lot. You know me. I won't be able to stay away." He faced Jared. "Continue, Jared."

Jared told the kids about his love of the game, and some of the highlights while playing for the Sea Glass Bay Tigers. He told them about both his excitement and his fear after getting a football scholarship at Kent State in Ohio, a Division One school, and how important it was to keep up his grades in order to play. "Don't think you'll get a free pass just because you can throw a ball or rush it into the endzone. Your grades matter. Even if you do end up playing professionally, you never know how long your career will be. You need to be prepared for another career."

The words tasted sour on Jared's tongue. He was in that same predicament, yet the idea of walking away from the game he loved was not sitting well with him. He was definitely *not* prepared.

He was certain that his agent, Arnold Bancroft, could get him a new deal. He'd been doing everything possible to make sure his shoulder was in tip top shape.

"My dad said you might not be playing football again because of your shoulder," one of the kids said.

Jared opened his mouth to speak but didn't know what to say. He opted for the truth as he knew it. "I'm waiting to hear back from my agent as we speak."

The boys had other questions, and Jared answered them. Mostly they wanted to hear about his technique when he worked with the quarterback, how they had become the "Dream Team" as they'd been known, and about the one play that had garnered Jared attention and fame in this region of California. "Is it true that you fell on the field, got up, broke through a tackle attempt, and basically were falling into the end zone after being fouled, but *still* somehow managed to turn and catch the ball?"

"It's true. I think my dad might even have some video footage of that somewhere," Jared went on. Though, knowing his father, who had always stressed that he should make sure he studied something tangible that could land him a career outside of football, if need be, he might have thrown the tape away.

After a good forty minutes, Coach Whalen said, "I want to thank Jared for coming out today. For agreeing to spend some time with you. We are all hoping he gets another contract. He's a stellar player, and a great guy."

Some of the kids came up for autographs, and Jared obliged. Nina stood back, taking pictures unobtrusively. Jared noticed the boy Coach Whalen had looked toward in the beginning was standing to the side with an intense expression on his face. The coach went over to him and after the rest of the group dispersed, he brought the kid toward Jared. "This is Daniel Aucoin. Would you mind spending a few minutes with him? He's going through a bit of a rough time— he's in foster care like you were. He was raised by a single mother and …" Coach Whalen shrugged. "He can tell you."

Jared looked at the kid with compassion. He now understood that the expression on his face mirrored some of the mixed emotions Jared had felt when he'd been his age. The desire to belong, the guilt of moving on when your family had been taken from you. It was a mixed bag of emotions and you didn't always know the right way to feel.

"You're in foster care," Jared said. "Are you with a good family?"

Daniel nodded.

Jared noticed Nina getting closer. She snapped a photo of the two of them. She looked especially lovely in a pair of white jeans, a white T-shirt fitted at the waist, and white sandals. Lowering the camera, she raised a hand in a goodbye to Jared. He waved back, then turned his attention fully to Daniel.

"What's your story?" Jared asked. "Mine—I lost my whole family in a tragic car accident when I was nine. I bounced around in foster care for a couple of years before ending up with a truly amazing family, and they adopted me. If you're like me, maybe you feel some guilt that you're moving on from your past. But we have to move on. We have no choice."

"I'm still mad at my mom. She shouldn't have been drinking. It was just me and her. If she cared about me, how could she get drunk and get in her car?" Daniel's voice grew thick with emotion. He looked at the ground. "It was a stupid thing to do. Now I'm alone."

"I understand," Jared said. Though he hadn't been angry with his family for heading to San Francisco that day, he *had* felt bad that he hadn't been with them. But he knew what it was to feel alone.

"But you said something I'm sure you're wrong about," Jared continued. You said, 'If she cared about me.' I don't know much about your mother, but I'm sure she loved you. I know there's no way she would've ever wanted to leave you. You gotta forgive the mistake that she paid the price for. I know, you're paying a price too, but put your anger and sadness into something positive that will motivate you to move forward. Did she like to watch you play football?"

Daniel raised his head, his eyes perking up. "She was my biggest fan."

"What do you play?"

"Quarterback."

"Why don't I give you my number, and before I leave town we can get together and practice some plays. If you want. Wide receiver and quarterback—that's the best combo in my opinion."

Daniel's face lit up with excitement. "For real?"

Jared placed a gentle hand on the kid's shoulder, emotion swirling inside him at Daniel's happy reaction. There was hope for this kid, just as there had been hope for him. "It would be my pleasure."

On Friday night, Jared walked into Hanks for the bachelor party, holding his breath as he did. He was late, conflicted over even coming here. Not because he didn't want to support his father. He knew that nothing was going to change the fact that he and Gail were getting married. His stress tonight came from knowing that he was going to see so many people in Sea Glass Bay, people who had known him, had no doubt cheered him on, and might all be disappointed that he had fallen short of his goals.

Today of all days, he had gotten the final word.

Cut.

No one else wants you.

His future in the NFL was …. Well, it was no longer uncertain. It was over.

Jared tried not to think about the bad news. Later, he would let it really sink in.

As he entered fully into the bar, he saw a couple of eyes widen. As his eyes landed on his old high school buddy, Kevin Macklin, he heard the claps begin. Slowly, but steadily, until it was a thunderous applause. Jared looked behind him, not certain if this reaction was for him or if his dad had just walked in.

Kevin Macklin approached him immediately. "Jared! Long time, buddy. I always knew you'd make pro."

Jared looked around at the warm faces. The eyes filled with wonder. He was used to people looking at him as a celebrity because he played sports and people knew his name. But he didn't expect this reaction here, in his hometown, where he'd grown up with many of these people who had simply known him as Jared.

Coach Whalen walked toward him and hugged him. "Everyone's so happy you're here. Look at them all."

This was overwhelming. And undeserved. Jared made a gesture as if patting the air, indicating that everyone could stop the applause now. This night wasn't about him, it was about his father.

Axel came over to him, pulled him into a hard hug, and held on for a long moment.

"How's the rotator cuff?" Kevin Macklin asked when he and Axel separated.

Jared shrugged. "Working on it."

"Dad's over there," Axel said.

Jared made his way through the crowd with his brother, seeing more familiar faces. Almost everyone extended a hand, wanting to say hi to him. It was a welcome Jared hadn't expected.

Seth was standing beside their dad, both had beers in their hands.

A smile broke out on Clay's face. "Thought you weren't going to make it, Son."

"I'm here. I'll always be here for you, Dad."

"Let me get you a beer," Seth said.

After about an hour and a half of eating, reconnecting, and drinking, Jared spotted Nina in the crowd. She was taking pictures.

His chest tightened as he looked at her. So beautiful. Inside and out. He hoped she was doing better now that the situation with Juan had been dealt with.

Her face brightened when she saw him. She wound her way through the crowd toward him. "Smile," she said. He quickly obeyed, and she snapped off a photo.

"You look good," she said to him, and again Jared felt that stirring in his gut. He wanted to kiss her.

"Why are you here?" he asked.

111

"I'm working. Taking photos to capture the event."

"That's great. You seem to have really found your groove and something that you like. I'm happy for you."

Nina shrugged. "Thanks."

The music lowered and then Clay's voice boomed through the microphone. "Hello?" He waited until he had everyone's attention. "Thank you all so much for coming here today. I really feel special and honored that you are part of this. Honestly, from the bottom of my heart, it means so much." His eyes floated over the crowd. "All of you know that I was married before, to the love of my life, Leda. And I never thought there'd be another woman for me. But I've been blessed to have found a rare and special love a second time. For that, I'm eternally grateful."

There were cheers in the crowd. Someone whistled. There were murmurs of "Good for you" and "You deserve it, Sheriff."

"Now most of you know that Leda and I weren't blessed enough to have our own children biologically, but we did have children. Four great boys. Most of you know Seth because he's the current sheriff. Hopefully you haven't gotten on his bad side and spent a night in the jail." Everyone laughed.

"Axel has worked on many of your cars," Clay went on. "My other son, Van, is in the military. He isn't here right now, but I hope he will be for the big day."

Clay turned toward Jared. "And Jared, whom you all know, has really done well for himself. He probably hasn't heard me say this enough, but I'm proud of him. He was talented from a young age, he knew that. Football this, football that. Poor Leda, she never understood the game. But she understood the basics. We were all proud of Jared. Even when he got drafted to play with Buffalo instead of San Francisco."

There was more chuckling, and when it subsided, Clay continued in a more serious tone. "I just want to say that I'm happy to have three of my four sons here. As for Jared .... Well, Hank, will you play that tape?"

People angled themselves toward one of the two big screen televisions in the room, and Jared did the same. Moments later, the NFL theme song began to play. For a moment Jared was confused, his heart started racing as he wondered what was going on.

Then a video began to play. A picture of him as a teenage boy in his football uniform came onto the screen, his curly hair wild and free, Jared holding his helmet under his arm. There were a few chuckles, but they were laughs of joy and admiration.

The music changed from the NFL theme to something upbeat. Then came some clips of Jared on the high school football field, including his most memorable play. That clip morphed into one where he was catching the ball in the end zone as he played against the Miami Dolphins. Then catching another ball and running with it. Then another touchdown. Then a one-armed catch at the two-yard line and a jump into the end zone that had the crowd going crazy. Jared remembered that game well. That touchdown had won them the game.

There were more highlights of his career. Incredible catches, some of him dancing in the end zone, shaking that wild, curly hair. As the video came to an end, words flashed on the now black screen: *We are all so proud of you, Jared.*

Tears were filling Jared's eyes.

"Come over here, Son," Clay said through the applause now filling the bar.

Jared began to walk, he caught Nina's gaze. She was holding the camera but not taking any pictures. He was happy for that. What must he look like with his moist eyes and stunned expression?

As Jared joined his father, Clay said, "I'm proud of you, Son. I know you've had some setbacks, and sometimes that's what life does. Gives you setbacks that you think you can't get beyond. But you can. Even if getting beyond it is a life you didn't expect. But I just wanted you to know that I am proud of what you've done and the man you've become."

As friends and family began to clap again, Jared pinched the bridge of his nose. He didn't want the tears to fall. He wasn't prepared for this. His father, a man of so few words when it came to expressing how he was feeling, had just told him and the world how much he was proud of him.

How much he loved him.

"I can't believe ...." Jared cleared his throat because it was clogged with emotion. "I can't believe you did all this for me. I didn't even know you'd seen all those games."

"Not only seen them, but taped them," Seth told him.

Jared couldn't speak. He was stunned.

"I love you, Son," Clay said. He wrapped his arms around him. People whistled and cheered, ecstatic to see this touching moment between father and son.

As Jared held onto Clay, feeling closer to the past than he had in so long, he thought about his father's words. He'd lost his family, but he'd been given a second chance to have a family who loved and cared for him. A family who had given him everything his own parents would have wanted for him. If his mother and father could have chosen anyone to raise him, they would have chosen Clay and Leda. Jared had no doubt about that.

"Dad, can I talk to you outside for a minute?"

"Sure, Son," Clay said, looking at him with concern.

Jared led the way to the patio doors, and they stepped outside. He moved to the far corner of the outdoor eating area so that no one would be able to listen in on their conversation.

"What is it?" Clay asked. "Are you upset about the video?"

"No, I'm not upset about that. I'm overwhelmed. Surprised. But that whole tribute feels undeserved. Especially today."

"Why?"

"Because I heard from my agent this morning. I'm done with Buffalo. They cut me. I'm probably done with football altogether."

"Oh, Jared." Clay clamped a hand down on his shoulder. "I'm so sorry."

"So this, today of all days ..."

"You think that tribute is contingent on whether or not you continue on in the NFL? Did you see all the love everyone here has for you? I'm proud of you, and so is everyone else in this town."

Jared let the words settle over him. "It's crazy, because I feel like I failed. I only had three good seasons."

"Something happened out of your control. And you still made the best of it when you were playing and in pain. We're here for you if you need us. That's what family does. This whole town is practically your family."

Clay was right. Jared knew that.

"I don't know exactly what you were going through when you left, but I know you were in pain. Leda and I tried to fill the void after you'd lost your family. Maybe we didn't do the best job—"

"Of course you did," Jared said, interjecting. "You and Mom weren't the problem."

"You've dealt with your pain alone these past years. You've stayed away. Even when your mother died. I'm not gonna lie to you, Son. It hurt me that you didn't come back home for her funeral." Clay looked away before continuing. "I needed you then. And you needed us."

Jared knew this was the time to reveal the secret he'd kept. "I did come back, Dad."

Clay's eyes widened as he looked at him. "But you didn't."

"I did. I just ... I couldn't deal with the whole funeral thing. It was too much. I came, saw Mom privately at the funeral home. Said my goodbyes to her there. Then, after the service I went to the graveside and left flowers."

"I never knew," Clay said, looking confused.

"That was the point. I never told anyone."

Jared looked to his right as the patio door opened and Seth emerged. "Everything okay?" he asked as he approached them.

"Yeah," Jared said. "Just talking to Dad. I told him something. I know you all think I abandoned you and never came back for Mom's funeral. But I did. I saw her at the funeral home and left flowers at the graveside."

"I know," Seth said softly.

Jared's eyebrows shot up. "You do?"

"Yeah. I saw you at the graveside."

"But I never saw you," Jared said.

"I stayed back," Seth explained. "I left you alone because I realized that you didn't want us to know you were in town. You wanted your space to deal with the loss your way."

"I did," Jared admitted softly. "I didn't think I could handle my grief and everyone else's as well. But now I realize ... I realize that family is what helps you get through it. When my mom, dad, and sister died, I didn't have that family to lean on. I didn't have anyone to turn to, to help me deal with the loss."

"Thanks for telling me," Clay said. He hugged Jared. "It really does mean a lot to know that you did come. I know I don't open up and share my feelings all that well. Maybe that's why you felt you couldn't turn to me. But know that from the depths of my heart, I love you."

Jared's eyes misted again. That had always been what Leda had said. "I miss her, dad."

"I know," Clay said. "I do, too."

Jared smiled at his father. "I love you, Dad. You and Leda chose me, and for that I'm forever grateful."

"It was fate," Seth said, his voice sounding gruff. "We were all meant to be family." Then he pulled them all into a group hug. "Now before anyone else comes out here and sees the Hollister men weeping at a bachelor party, let's get back inside."

10

*H*ours later, as the bachelor party was winding down, Jared saw Nina packing up her camera bag. She was getting ready to leave.

Today had been a whirlwind of emotions, with him laying his feelings on the line in ways he hadn't expected. Now, he had to do it one more time.

He approached her as she was slinging the camera bag over her shoulder. "Let me help you to your car," he offered.

"Okay," Nina said.

They went outside into the cool night air. Jared tipped his head backward, glancing up at the moon. The moon had always looked more spectacular in Sea Glass Bay, from the way it hung in the sky to the way it reflected on the water.

"You totally surprised me with the video," Jared said, facing her. "I'm very impressed with your skills."

"It was all your father's idea. He gave me the tapes, told me he wanted to celebrate you in a big way."

"I never realized he was so proud of me," Jared said.

"Come on," Nina said softly. "You had to know."

"Maybe I should have, but he never explicitly said the things I wanted him to say. I don't know …. Sometimes when you're left to fill in the blanks you come to the wrong conclusion."

They reached Nina's vehicle, and she pulled her key out of her crossbody bag. The car beeped, lights flashing as she unlocked the door remotely. "You're right about that," she said softly.

Jared stepped toward her, he gently touched her face. Her eyes widened in surprise. Before he lost his nerve, he continued. "Remember that night after graduation? When I tried to kiss you and you pulled away?"

She nodded. "Yes. I've thought about that so many times and I regret it. I just … I was surprised. And there was Juan."

"I think you knew what we had back then. A solid foundation for a great relationship. But we had other people in our lives, probably a great buffer to keep from exploring what we could have had. Maybe we were both afraid. Or maybe just I was. But when I tried to kiss you, and you rejected me …. That's one of the reasons I left and didn't look back. I couldn't stand the idea of watching you go down the wrong path with Juan, a guy who'd hurt you so many times and didn't deserve you."

Her eyes narrowed in surprise. "That's why you stayed away?"

"Part of it. But I'm here now. And … unless I'm crazy, I think there's still something between us. Something that we can both explore now that we're older, more mature, with no one standing in our way."

Nina's lips parted, but she didn't say a word. She didn't have to. Jared could see it in her eyes, and the soft invitation of her parted lips.

So he accepted that invitation, lowered his head, and softly kissed her. She didn't pull away. Instead, after a moment, she gripped his collar and pulled him closer.

He eased back, smiling. Yes. There was something between them. Something real. There always had been.

The light in her eyes fizzled after a moment. "But you're going to leave again."

"I'm not."

She angled her head, looking at him as though she hadn't heard him correctly.

So he repeated himself. "I'm not leaving. I'm not running."

"But your career?"

"With Buffalo … is over. In fact, I don't think I'll ever play again. That's another reason I hesitated to come back here. I felt like a failure. But my dad said something to me I can't stop thinking about. That sometimes life doesn't give you the path you want, but it gives you another path that's just as rewarding."

"What do you mean by that? Because I don't want to get my hopes up—"

"Sea Glass Bay is my home, and I have felt a huge weight off my shoulders just being back here. You know what they say about how when a door closes, a window opens? Well, that window opened for me tonight. Coach Whalen is retiring. He just said to me that if I want, I can be the new football coach at the school. That no one in their right mind would refuse me."

A tentative smile spread on Nina's face. "Oh, Jared. That would be wonderful."

"I've always loved talking to kids. And when I went there to talk to the kids, I realized I could make a difference. I had no clue that coaching could be a possibility, but I know the sport; I played it professionally. This is something I can do. And it will keep me in town." He paused. "But mostly I want to stay for my family—and for you."

Their eyes locked and held. Nina seemed to be trying to assess whether or not she could trust him completely. Trust him to not abandon her again.

"I'm not going anywhere," he said. "I'm gonna stay with Seth or my dad until I can get myself a place. Then I'm going to prove to you that I'll always be there for you, Nina. I never want you out of my life again."

"I want the same thing." She slipped her arms around his waist and tipped up on her toes. "Maybe it's good that we didn't try before, because you would've left, I would've been hurt, and we would've had a burned bridge between us. But now …"

Now there was nothing standing in their way.

"Now, I want to kiss those lips again, because they are so tempting," Jared said, his voice husky.

Nina leaned in even closer and looked him dead in the eye. "So what's stopping you?"

"Nothing," Jared said. "Absolutely nothing."

Then he kissed her again, right there beneath the spectacular moon in Sea Glass Bay. And he knew absolutely, not only physically but in his heart, that he had come back home.

A Place to Belong

by Melinda Curtis

From the moment the auto repair shop door swung closed behind him, Axel Martinez knew he'd made a mistake coming back to Sea Glass Bay Automotive. Not one to back down from the hard stuff, he planted his steel-toed work boots on the concrete floor of the closed shop and looked around.

Standing toolboxes and electronic diagnostic equipment lined the side and back walls. An old Ford sedan occupied a far bay, hood up. Car lifts sat empty in two of the three other bays. To his right, a small waiting room and office had been made with plate glass running waist high to the ceiling.

Sea Glass Bay Automotive was a mechanic's dream. Well-cared for and large enough to make a good living. Axel wanted to buy it. He'd scheduled a meeting here with the owner, Dennis Hammond, and his real estate agent, Sam Bell.

But he'd been stood up.

Axel stuffed his hands in his grease-stained coverall pockets. "I was supposed to meet Mr. Bell and Mr. Hammond?" He hadn't meant that to come out as a question. There was no question about whether he had an appointment. The question was why hadn't the men honored it.

Axel glanced toward the exits. First, the small door behind him and then the rear exit behind Penny Bell Carlson, his high school crush and Mr. Bell's daughter.

"Dad had something come up. He sent me instead." Penny's cheeks flamed red.

If history was any indicator, her blush was deeper when she lied than when she was embarrassed, which meant—

History?

Axel hated the past. He tried to find something positive here, in the present. All he found was Penny.

She looked better than what he remembered from a decade ago. She still had her All-American, girl next-door looks; blonde, blue-eyed, trim body, classy clothes. He hadn't taken in more than a glimpse of her in what seemed like forever. Penny stayed in her circle of friends and family in Sea Glass Bay, and he stayed in his.

Axel kept his oil-stained hands in his coverall pockets, glancing over his shoulder at the exit once more. Girls like Penny weren't supposed to give guys from the wrong side of the tracks a second look.

Except she had. That one time.

The fallout hadn't been pretty. Axel worked his jaw at the memory.

Forget the past!

A sound from the auto shop's office door drew Axel's attention.

A little blond boy of about three pressed his body against the glass door, flattening his palms near his face, smushing his nose and open mouth against the glass in what seemed like a silent plea for help. A large blue sippy cup hung neglected from his hand, then dropped to roll around at his feet.

"Oh, no," Penny said in a panicked voice. She ran between the service bays to the office, her black high heels tapping on the concrete with the same urgency Axel's blood was tapping at his temples. "Trey woke up. I'm coming, sweetie."

"Trey?" Axel glanced around the shop, imprinting the image of the place he'd once worked into his memory, storing it along with the other things he'd been unable to have in his lifetime because of what his mother was, and the chip he'd carried on his shoulder as a result of it. "What kind of name is Trey?"

124

"We're judging names now?" Penny opened the door for the boy and swung him into her arms. "That's rich coming from you, *Alexander*." She smoothed the boy's haystack hair away from his face with all the love Axel had longed for as a child. "His name is Brett John Carlson the Third. *Trey*."

"Named him after Brett, did you?" Her ex-husband. Axel generally kept to himself, but even he'd heard about Penny's messy divorce brought upon by Brett's two-timing. Just the thought of the high school golden boy and bully gave rise to angry bitterness. "Let's hope this little guy makes a better go of things than his father."

Shut up–shut up–shut up!

Penny frowned at him.

"Sorry." Axel removed his hands from his pockets, curled his fingers, crossed his arms, and tucked his fists into his armpits, trying to lock himself and his emotions up tight. Penny was the last person in the world he wanted to pick a fight with. She'd been nice to him in school—not that he'd always deserved it. And she'd been nice to him today by showing up and telling him in person that Sea Glass Bay Automotive was out of his reach, like that Ferrari he dreamed of owning someday. She hadn't said as much, but Axel could read the writing on the wall.

Penny was still frowning at him, Trey's head tucked under her chin. The toddler stared at Axel, too, but without the frown.

Axel tried to charm the little guy with a smile, all without loosening the arms over his chest. "I'm generally a background player, kid. I don't speak until I'm spoken to."

"That's new," Penny murmured.

Axel supposed he was different than when they'd been in school. Back then, he'd popped off on the regular. Arms still tightly crossed, Axel bent at the knees to look Trey in his big blue eyes. "Sometimes the pendulum swings, kiddo. Smart-mouthed teens can learn to think before getting into trouble."

"Smart-mouthed teens aren't always looking for trouble, but they always seem to find it." Penny's frown seemed to be giving way at the corners.

"I've stayed out of trouble since graduation." Alex straightened, giving the kid another smile. "Hard lessons learned. I'm a good guy now. No trouble at all." He straightened, glanced around the shop, and sighed. "Not that everyone seems to believe it."

"This has nothing to do with who you are, Axel," Penny said gently. But her cheeks were pinkening again.

"I won't kid myself. I'm not stupid."

"I know that." Penny's voice was still soft. She was being nice to him again.

He had a weak spot for people who were nice to him.

"I just thought ..." Axel's arms loosened. His fists unfurled. His hands dropped to his sides. "I thought that the past was in the past. I thought people had forgotten that I'm the son of the town drug addict. Or that I was the motorhead delinquent who liked taking fast cars for joy rides." He made a silent apology to Dennis Hammond and Sam Bell, both of whom had great taste in cars. No wonder they didn't want to take his interest in buying the place seriously.

Penny's little boy stared at Axel with big, blue, puppy-dog eyes.

"Axel ..." Penny's gaze softened to something resembling pity.

Geez-o-Pete. I have to get out of here.

But the lock was off his emotions, and they tumbled out, falling between them with a thud. "I'm not the guy who lets anger run his mouth anymore. I'm not the guy who lets frustration guide his fists anymore. I'm not even the guy who kisses the first girl to be nice to him. But what Sea Glass Bay sees ..." He sighed. "What this town sees is apparently something different than who I am today. That's why you're here, isn't it?"

"Hang on." Penny scoffed, cheeks a soft pink. "I wasn't the first girl to be nice to you. Or the first girl you kissed, if memory serves."

"But you were the only one ..." *Who meant something to me.* Axel glanced at the exit once more. "I didn't come here to skip down memory lane. I've been saving ... and I was hoping ..." He shook his head.

"You want to start your own auto repair shop," she finished for him, closing the distance between them with slow steps, hips swaying because of those almost-hypnotic heels ...

Those heels should be outlawed for use by single mothers.

"My own shop. Yes." Axel forced his gaze to the ceiling, hating that he felt vulnerable baring his fragile dream to her. "That's why

I'm here, right? But if your dad and Dennis didn't show up, I don't know that any offer I make would be accepted anyway and ..."

Don't you dare talk down to yourself!

His foster mother's voice rang between his ears as if Leda Hollister had hold of his shoulders and was trying to shake some sense into that thick head of his. She'd been dead and buried for two years and yet he could swear she was the angel who rode shotgun on his shoulder.

"Axel ..." Penny began in that gentle way of hers. "If you were a serious player for this business, you'd have to qualify for a million-dollar loan. That's how much the property and business itself are listed for." Her gaze roamed Axel's face as if there was a riddle to be solved somewhere between his lips and his eyebrows. "Did you get pre-qualified?"

Go to a bank?

Axel gave a quick shake of his head.

"Have you ever bought real estate before?"

Axel shook his head again, focusing on the cute boy in Penny's arms so that she wouldn't see how unfit he was for this thing called adulting. "I'm a newbie when it comes to things like bank loans." And relationships with girls from the right side of town. "Never had one. I've paid for all my vehicles in cash." He tickled the little nugget's feet. "Don't you think that's smart, buddy?"

Stricken by shyness, the little dude tucked his feet up, folded in on himself, and hid his face against Penny's chest.

"Yeah, I'm shy around strangers, too," Axel admitted, simultaneously coming to terms with the fact that his dream would remain just that—a dream.

It was time to go.

He gave the shop one last, longing look, taking in Penny's shapely legs out of the corner of his eye because he was a man, after all, and she was his kind of woman. Which meant like everything else, she was out of reach.

"Are you serious about this?" Penny asked suddenly, so close now that if she turned her shoulder it would bump into his.

"I am, but guys like me ..."

"Guys like you should get pre-approved for financing," Penny said firmly. Her unwavering tone matched the determined look in her eye, although why she was determined was beyond Axel. "I can refer you to Cindy at Bayside Mortgage Company. She doesn't intimidate first-time property buyers."

He didn't admit he had no idea what a mortgage company was. "Don't I need to talk to a bank?"

"No. Cindy works with lots of different banks. She finds financing so you don't have to waste time sitting in a string of banks and filling out paperwork to apply for loans." Penny explained it all so simply and without talking down to him.

"That's helpful." Axel glanced around, hopes rising. "So I might be able to buy this place after all?" Own his own shop. Set his own rules. Be his own boss.

"No," Penny said gently. "I say that not only because you'd need to put twenty percent of the purchase price down in cash—"

Two-hundred-thousand dollars?

Axel closed his fingers, crossed his arms, and tucked his fists into his armpits again. He'd saved a lot, just not enough apparently.

"—but there's also the fact that you stole Dennis Hammond's Corvette back in the day." Despite balancing a rug rat on her hip and shouldering a tote that was big enough to hold a small television, Penny placed a hand on Axel's wrist and gently loosened his grip on himself. "Dennis is old school. He's never going to sell his life's work to you. And if he did, he'd charge such a premium that it wouldn't make financial sense."

"Hey, I was in middle school when the incident in question happened." A hot-wiring prodigy of his mother's car-thieving drug dealer. "Technically I didn't steal his Corvette because I brought it back." In fact, that was where his foster father Clay Hollister—who'd been the town sheriff at the time—had caught him. "It's called joyriding, which is a right-of-passage. Innocent fun. And besides, Dennis doesn't hold a grudge. He hired me to work here after graduation. He knows what I'm capable of." Those last words felt negative.

Don't you dare talk down to yourself, Alexander! I mean it.

Axel lightly tickled Trey's ribs. The kid gave him a tentative smile.

"We both know Sheriff Hollister twisted Mr. Hammond's arm to hire you." Penny fiddled with Trey's hair again. "Your parents are saints."

"*Foster* parents," Axel murmured. He didn't call Leda and Carl Hollister Mom and Dad. He'd never been given that right. "And yeah, Leda *was* a saint." His chest felt tight just thinking about her being gone. Hot on the heels of that feeling came the mixed emotions he had with Clay selling the house where he'd almost felt like part of the Hollister family. Axel rubbed at the sudden tightness in his chest. He was the only foster kid Clay and Leda hadn't adopted, and that still had the power to sting. "Some dreams aren't meant to be."

"Just because this opportunity is out of reach, doesn't mean they all are." Penny looked equal parts sympathetic and optimistic.

It was the optimistic part that Axel found hard to believe. "I appreciate the offer, Penny, but it's obvious I'm never going to succeed here." And by *here*, he meant in Sea Glass Bay. He mustered a smile for Trey. "Nice meeting you, kid." He tickled the boy's foot lightly again. "See you later."

"Bye-bye," Trey said, as he squirmed and giggled. "Be good." Then he continued to repeat, "Bye-bye," as if he enjoyed hearing the sound of his own voice.

Axel headed for the exit, striding out with his shoulders back and unapologetic steps that would have made Leda proud.

"Trey!" Penny lifted the suddenly silent three-year-old in front of her. "Say that again," she commanded because her son had stopped talking the moment the door shut behind Axel. "*Bye-bye. Be good.*"

Trey nestled his head beneath her chin, mute.

Penny's heart scaled up her throat.

Every child is different.

How many times had Dr. Inman told her that? Not that Brett had listened once. He was more likely to say there was something wrong with Trey, words dripping with disappointment.

Penny's jaw thrust out. Trey was three. The average three-year-old had a vocabulary of about two hundred words and spoke in three- to four-word sentences. But not Trey. He rarely spoke one word, let alone four in a string. At least, not until today. Not until he'd met Axel.

Her son had spoken. And he'd spoken to the one man from Penny's past that she had regrets about.

Axel still had the power to draw her near. He was just so … so … inexplicably appealing.

That lean frame that looked like it could withstand the strongest storm, and probably had. Those dark as midnight eyes that had seen, and still saw, too much. Black hair with a rebellious glint of red in it. Everything about Axel Martinez was magnetic to her. In elementary school he'd been scrawny, squirrely, and smart-mouthed, which often made him a target of the bigger boys, as did the way he missed a lot of school, which prevented him from forming strong friendships. Those absences were because of his mother.

Or at least, that's what Penny's mother told her the day she'd asked about Axel when he'd missed the class Valentine's Day party in the fifth grade. During that conversation, Penny's father had told her to stay away from kids like Axel. Kids with addicts for parents, he meant, as if it was a foregone conclusion that they'd become addicted, too.

Then the Hollisters took Axel in and made him go to middle school on the regular. That was back when Sheriff Hollister had talked Axel's mother into entering rehab in Humboldt. No one had seen her in Sea Glass Bay since. Not that folks had forgotten.

Axel used to thumb his nose at anyone who held the specter of his mother against him. In school, he'd been determined to do things his way, speaking out when he wasn't supposed to, standing up to bullies without being asked to. Penny had admired his courage because she didn't have the same *chutzpah*. She'd followed the rules even if they didn't make sense, which meant she'd also gone along with the crowd, even if deep down she hadn't wanted to.

And then there'd been that kiss during the high school graduation dance. That one fabulous kiss before Brett had pulled them apart and punched Axel in the face, knocking him to the ground and demanding he keep his grubby hands off Brett's girl. At the time, she hadn't been Brett's girlfriend, although things had been moving in that direction.

Penny drew Trey closer, seeking comfort.

Everything had changed that night. And not for the better, not in the long run, unless she counted Trey.

But what if this was her do-over? Penny could help Axel find a location to open his own auto repair shop, one he could afford. That's what good realtors did. They found properties to fulfill people's dreams, whether it was for a home or a business. They didn't sit in the office and process paperwork for other realtors.

Penny didn't move other than to draw in a deep breath. Axel didn't want her help. Just like Brett no longer wanted her.

When something's defective, you send it back, Brett had told her.

Penny held on tighter to her beautiful baby boy. He wasn't defective.

Trey reached a hand toward the door and made a grabbing motion. "Want him."

Those few precious words ...

Tears filled Penny's eyes. "You want Axel?"

"Want Acks," Trey wailed.

Gathering her courage, Penny scurried toward the door, flinging it open. For her son, she would do anything. "Axel! Axel, wait!" She ran into the parking lot. "Wait!"

"I'm still here." Axel was sitting on the tailgate of his white truck, peeling his coveralls from his legs. His work boots lay on the asphalt, along with balled-up black socks. Beneath his work clothes, he'd worn a blue T-shirt and black basketball shorts. He reached for a pair of black flip-flops. "Do you need help locking up? The office door is tricky. You have to lift the handle before turning the mechanism."

"No, I ..." Penny glanced down at Trey, who was grinning at Axel. "Can you tickle Trey again?"

Axel shot her a cautious look. "Why?"

"Because ..." Penny hesitated, protective of her secrets. But honestly, what did she have to lose? "Trey talked to you. He ... he rarely says more than one word at a time."

"Speech delay?" Axel hopped down from the tailgate and gathered his work clothes and boots into a bundle that he tucked in the corner of the truck bed behind the cab.

"How do you know about speech delays?" Penny's ex-husband hadn't known.

"My mother was … unreliable." Alex framed his mother's situation so matter-of-factly, as if it was no big deal to be raised by a drug addict. "I spent a lot of time in and out of foster homes with a variety of kids. Special needs. Speech delays. English as a second language. Kids with emotional setbacks. You name it. I've seen it." Axel grabbed a metal water bottle and took a long drink, during which time Penny's mind continued to be blown. He was so nonchalant about the whole thing. "Have you taught him to sign?"

"Yes." Penny drew a calming breath and stared into Trey's bright blue eyes, so full of intelligence and warmth, her heart aching with love and swelled with hope. *Hope?* She'd tried to believe Dr. Inman, but she hadn't had much in the way of hope materialize. Until today. Until Axel. Penny drew a calming breath. "Please. Talk to him again." Penny settled Trey more securely on her hip. "You want to talk to Axel, don't you, sweetie?"

Trey hid his head under her chin and held out his hand, three middle fingers curled toward his palm. He shook it from side-to-side.

"Yes," Penny translated, staring up at Axel with tear-filled eyes. "Yes, he wants to talk to you."

"That's because I'm easy to talk to." Axel chucked Trey beneath his chin. "Not that anybody outside of my foster family knows it—not even your mom, little man."

Trey giggled but said nothing.

"Don't you want to say bye-bye to Axel?" Penny jiggled Trey a little, feeling a bit desperate for a repeat performance from her son.

"Geez-o-Pete, you're tense, Penny. Of course, he's not going to perform on command." Axel's phone buzzed in the truck. "Hey, look. I've got family dinner in a few. Why don't you go inside and lock up? Me and Trey need to have a meeting of the minds." Axel held out his faintly grease-stained hands and Trey fell right into his arms.

Penny's jaw dropped again. Not because Axel's hands weren't pristine—they were a working man's hands—but because her son didn't go easily to strangers.

"Penny? Pen?" Axel reached over and nudged her chin upward with a gentle touch, closing her open mouth. "I've got places to be and I'm sure your little man needs dinner."

"Right." She nodded. "I'll go lock up."

"Don't forget the sippy cup. And to lift the office door handle." Axel turned away, pointing out things to her son. His tire. His truck. The seagull flying overhead.

"Bird fly," Trey said with certainty, earning Axel's praise.

Penny's breath caught.

Everything had changed for Penny the night Axel had kissed her. And not for the better.

Maybe this was a sign. Maybe she could get her life back on track. She and Trey and …

She didn't dare include Axel in that thought. But the idea hovered there like a single, sherbet-tinged cloud on the horizon of a brand-new day.

2

"Yes on casserole, salad, and vegetables. No on breadsticks." Axel practically tumbled into his seat at the dining room table of his last and longest foster home just as food was being dished up.

The old saltbox hadn't changed in years. The creaky floors, the meant-to-be lived on furniture, the family photos. It was the closest thing Axel had to call home. The dining room table was where weighty things were discussed and celebrations shared with his foster family.

Seth, the oldest of the foster boys, always sat to Clay's right, as he did now. Axel, among the youngest, had always sat to Leda's right, across from Jared, who nodded to Axel now. The Hollister's fourth foster son was Van, who sat between Axel and Clay when he was home. His chair was empty.

So much was the same, and yet, things had changed. Seth's teenage son Matty often took Van's seat, although he was out with friends tonight. And Leda's chair was now Gail's. She and Clay were getting married in two weeks, selling their respective houses, and moving into something that would never be Axel's home. Although, legally, this wasn't his home either.

"Did you wash your hands?" With a plate of food in front of him, Clay sat back in his chair, waiting for everyone to be seated to begin eating. He'd been a tall, imposing figure when he'd taken Axel in. Not much had changed since then, except the graying of his blond hair.

Gail stood at the opposite end of the table, dishing out Axel's plate the way Leda used to. Her dark hair brushed her shoulders, the same shoulders that had carried Axel and the Hollister men through the grief over losing Leda. She'd been their rock. "Axel's a grown man, Clay. I'm sure he washed up."

"Yes, I did. I used the hall bathroom." Axel held out his hands, flipping them over and back the way he used to as a kid. "I shaved today, too, in case that matters—which it shouldn't, by the way."

"Long day at work?" Seth's dark brown hair was crisply cut, his posture square and businesslike. "I hear Old Man Abernathe brought his 1957 Chevy to Seaside Transmission for a rebuild. Is that why you're late?"

"Technically, five minutes isn't late, not even when you punch a timecard." Axel accepted his plate from Gail. "I had some errands to run. And traffic was bad. Terrible, even. The summer tourists have arrived early this year. Don't you hate the tourists? I hate the tourists. Except the ones whose cars break down." He was babbling. He hadn't told his foster family about his dream of owning his own garage. They'd pepper him with questions and counsel. He wanted to do this on his own. To stop himself from saying more, Axel drank deeply from his water glass.

Seth and Clay exchanged glances. Jared's eyebrows were raised.

Axel swallowed a groan.

"Maybe we should hear more about those errands," Clay said slowly. "You seem ... tightly wound."

Axel set his glass down. "Tightly wound is Seth's department." As boisterous was for Jared and strategic thinking was for Van. "I just keep to myself, remember?"

"Normally, yes. But you're very chatty today." Seth gave him the kind of look a police officer gave a potential perp, which was fitting considering he'd become sheriff when Clay retired.

Axel hunched his shoulders and shoveled food in his mouth.

"Leda used to tease you boys about being chatty." Gail slid into her seat and laid a paper napkin across her lap. "She said boys only become chatty when they're chasing girls."

Jared snorted. Seth let out a bark of laughter. Axel choked on a bite of chicken and broccoli casserole.

"I'm sorry," Gail said immediately, placing a hand on Axel's shoulder. "I was joking but—"

"But you hit pay dirt!" Seth crowed, setting Axel's teeth on edge.

"Tone it down, Seth," Jared cautioned. He and Axel were similar in age and watched out for each other.

"Tone it down?" Seth was on a roll and not to be stopped. "Don't you see what's happening here? Axel is running at the mouth?"

"I'll bet he's found a date for the wedding." Nodding, Jared gave Axel an approving smile.

"Maybe." Leaning back, Clay studied Axel, who tried to ignore him. "There was that time before he graduated that he was chatty."

"Because of a *girl*." Seth puffed out his chest.

Axel sighed.

"Back then, Axel was so chatty that Leda and I thought he'd turned a corner," Clay said slowly, his gaze on his food. "But then Axel came home with a black eye and became tight-lipped again."

"Not only that, but he was also extra quiet for weeks after that." Seth sat back in his chair, so like Clay in his body language they could have been blood family. "Who was that girl he had the fight over?"

Penny.

"I don't recall." Jared covered for Axel. He'd been there that night and knew everything. "But he was fighting with Brett Carlson. I hear he's still a jerk."

"Fighting …" Clay shook his head.

"Hang on. I wasn't fighting. I did what you told me and *didn't* hit him back!" Although Axel had wanted to. If truth be told, he still wanted to give Brett some payback, especially after meeting little Trey today and hearing about his delayed development.

Penny had looked desperately hopeful when she'd told Axel about the boy's journey. In Axel's experience, the reason to look desperately hopeful came from being let down too many times by someone you were supposed to depend upon. In Axel's case, that had been his mother. And in Penny's case, he assumed it had been Brett. The jerk had stolen the innocent joy from her pretty blue eyes.

One thing Brett had been unable to take from Penny was her beauty. Seeing her holding another man's child should have been a turnoff. Likewise, having her deliver the news that Dennis Hammond wouldn't seriously consider Axel's offer for the garage should have been a lust killer. But all seeing her had done was reawaken the attraction he'd felt toward Penny ten years ago.

"I was proud of you that day, Axel," Clay said in a gruff voice. "Leda was, too."

That's my boy, Leda seemed to whisper in Axel's head.

Jared nodded toward Axel. "He should have decked Brett. I would have."

Immediately, Clay and Seth argued against violence.

"What's done is done," Gail said, signaling for calm. "Leda told me that was the day she knew you were going to be all right, Axel. And look at you. You should be proud of yourself."

Caught off guard for her praise, Axel couldn't think of a thing to say. All he'd done in the past ten years was put in an honest day's work at various places around town where he could learn everything there was to know about repairing cars.

Seth scoffed. "Axel was fine the day he walked through our front door. *I* made sure of that."

That elicited chuckles and eye rolls from everyone at the table.

"But that still doesn't answer the question about who made our little Axel such a Chatty Cathy today." Seth speared a big piece of broccoli. "We're still waiting for your answer."

"*You're* still waiting, you mean," Gail teased. "Some people like to keep their private lives private."

"This is a judgment-free zone." Clay regarded his fiancée fondly.

While the assembled enjoyed a friendly round of bickering, Axel managed to clean his plate. "Thank you for the food. Family dinners are the best." He escaped to the kitchen and rinsed his plate.

And then because he felt guilty for rushing off, he put the rest of the casserole away and set the empty dish in the sink to soak.

He was just about to escape out the back when Gail entered the kitchen. She set her plate on the counter, took one look at Axel, then crossed the kitchen, opened the back door, and gestured for him to follow her.

That was unusual.

Axel walked out and joined Gail on the rear porch swing, his arms crossed over his chest and his hands tucked in his armpits. "The food was delicious. Thank you."

"Like you tasted any of it." Gail tried to laugh, failed, and took Axel's hand, tugging his arms loose. "Is it me? Is that why you're bolting out of here? I know not all you boys are supportive of our marriage. I don't intend to take Leda's place in your heart or your father's."

It was the kind of gesture a mother made to a son; the kind of gesture Leda had made to Axel too many times to count. The kind of gesture he couldn't recall his mother ever making. His mother …. A woman who'd refused to relinquish her legal claim on Axel but had then dropped out of sight upon being released from rehab.

Axel swallowed thickly. "It's not you."

Gail withdrew her hand, clasping both of hers in her lap. "Before your father and I began dating, you, Matty, and Seth would show up for family dinners and stay for an hour, sometimes longer. And now …"

Much as Axel didn't want his foster family butting into his business, he knew what it felt like to be an outsider. He didn't want that for Gail. "I have a second job. I wasn't going to tell anyone because … I didn't think I'd be working there long." Only long enough to build some extra money into his bank account to buy Sea Glass Bay Automotive.

"A second job? Why?" She leaned in closer, sending the swing a bit cockeyed. "Are you overextended? I have some money stashed away. I could—"

"It's not like that," he reassured her.

She patiently waited to hear him tell her more. That was the thing about Gail. She had enough patience to outlast Axel's silences.

When he wasn't chatty from seeing Penny, that is.

"I've been saving to buy my own garage." The admission slipped out of Axel in a whisper, the way secrets someone wanted to keep private sometimes did.

Gail squeezed his hand again. "That's wonderful. I'm so proud of you. Your mother would be proud of you, too." She gathered him into her arms for a quick hug, just as Leda would have done.

Axel's throat constricted as if he was still that little boy taking care of an unreliable parent, trying so hard to hold their life together while guiltily dreaming about having a perfect mother and a life that was normal, safe, and respectable.

He sat back, staring at the nearby blooming bougainvillea and Leda's red roses, needing space.

Gail set her feet on the porch, halting the swing. "You don't want to tell Clay or your brothers about starting your own business. Why not?"

"I'm trying to do this on my own." Without Hollister endorsements or assistance.

Gail nodded slowly. "Can I tell you a story?"

Something inside Axel melted.

This. This was why Leda and Gail had been friends. They were a lot alike—nurturing, steady, kind. And yet, they were different, too. There was the feeling that Gail was neutral, like Switzerland, rather than part of Clay's team, as Leda had been.

"When your mother first became ill," Gail began in a low voice. "Leda didn't want to ask anyone for help. She didn't want to receive special treatment or be a burden to anyone."

Axel nodded, remembering.

"But we all ignored her wishes and gave her our support, both emotionally and physically. That's what family does. They chip in. They lend a hand without being asked or despite being told to stay away." Gail drew a deep breath. "You should tell them. They'd be happy for you."

"All due respect, Gail ... Clay would want to weigh in on my decisions. And he wouldn't just want me to listen. He'd want me to take his advice. Same with Seth." It wouldn't matter that they'd never run their own businesses, unless he counted the sheriff's office.

"They'd want you to do it their way." Gail nodded, proving again that she understood. "I'm beginning to see your point." The way she empathized ..... The tone and heavy cadence ...

Axel noted every worry line on her face. "Clay does it to you, too."

"He doesn't. I love him and we get along fine." Gail tried to deny it, but there was no conviction in her words.

And suddenly, Axel remembered something she'd mentioned months ago at the dinner table. "You wanted a bridal shower, a rehearsal dinner, and a special honeymoon." All the trappings given to a bride.

"Oh, that." Gail looked away, glancing toward the garden with a slight frown. "I'm too old for those things. Plus we've both been married before, even if the last time I got hitched was a courthouse elopement." This last was said with ill-disguised remorse before she plowed on with forced cheer. "Anyway .... Why do I need a bridal shower?" A popular bar and grill in town. "And Seth hired an event planner." Who was only planning the ceremony and reception, not anything leading up to the big event.

"I hear Clay's practical voice in your words." Axel stood, staring at the caring woman who'd won his foster father's heart. "My best advice to you since you're marrying Clay is to be true to yourself. I know he's a good partner to you—that you have a great relationship. But your needs should be met, too. You're not just mending his broken heart with your love, but he should be instinctively fulfilling your heart's desires, too."

Gail stayed quiet for a long moment, and he made a move to return to the house.

"Hang on." She caught his hand. "I've always meant to ask. Why do you call your father Clay?"

Hurt balled in his gut as Axel headed toward the side yard. "Because he didn't fight for me."

Trey's giggles filled Penny's small apartment while she made dinner and checked real estate listings on her phone.

Penny had been unable to shake Axel's disappointment about the auto shop being out of reach. She was determined to help him find a good property to open his business, whether his pride wouldn't let him admit he wanted her help or not.

"Things are going to be different from now on," she murmured, stirring the boiling noodles. She was going to be more proactive about her real estate career, rather than being the backup for her father and other agents. Helping Axel was a great way to start. It had nothing to do with how he inspired Trey to be more verbal or how he lit a fire deep inside of Penny that had gone out after her divorce—or if she was to be honest with herself, long before her divorce.

In the living room, Maple, their Dachshund, let out a playful sound, half-whine, half-growl.

"Trey, are you and Maple playing nice?" Her son sometimes hugged the dog too tight.

"Yes," came Trey's verbal reply. The word in itself was new and made Penny's heart soar with happiness.

A small ball bounced into the kitchen. Maple charged in after it, wagging her tail happily as she picked it up and trotted back to the living room.

Penny's phone buzzed with a message. It was from Brett.

Hanson has the sniffles. You should keep Trey this weekend.

Hanson was Brett's other biological son and almost the same age as Trey.

Penny released a long breath. She'd gladly keep Trey and shower him with all the love his father didn't give him. She opened her calendar app and made note that Brett had once more given up his visitation rights. That was six times this year. Once a month, almost like clockwork.

It wasn't that Penny was going to challenge Brett for sole custody. But she had ammunition in case Brett decided he and his new bride wanted Trey on a more permanent basis. He was that kind of entitled man. If she'd chosen Axel ten years ago and their marriage had fallen apart, she'd have more trust in Axel than she did in Brett.

And wasn't that telling?

She sent back a brief affirmative reply to her ex and then drained the noodles, realizing that Trey and Maple were too quiet. She hurried to the living room where she found Trey climbing the bookshelf like a jungle gym. Maple sat watching him. Thankfully, the shelf was attached firmly to the wall. Also, thankfully, Trey was skilled at scaling the bookshelf, not that she in any way approved of the exercise.

"Hey, my little monkey. No climbing in the house, remember?" She plucked him into the safety of her arms.

"No, Mama." Another two-word sentence that thrilled her. "Top-top-top."

Regardless of her happiness in the words tumbling from her son's lips, there was safety to be considered and a schedule to keep. "It's time for dinner." And then bath time, bedtime, and a few cherished moments of quiet for Penny.

"No." Trey also made the sign, tapping his index and middle finger against his thumb.

"Yes." Penny wasn't about to get upset at his rebellious attitude if he was talking. "You need to feed Maple. Look at her. She's so hungry she might just eat her ball if you don't feed her." She carried Trey into the kitchen, followed by a prancing Maple.

The little dog ran right to her bowl, wriggling with excitement at the prospect of dinner.

"No," Trey said again, crossing his arms over his chest much the same way Axel had at the garage today. "I go top."

A distraction was called for. "If you feed Maple and eat your dinner, we can get ice cream." Penny said the words, simultaneously signing them.

Trey slumped in defeat, dropping his hands and lowering his shoulders. He gave Maple a scoop of dog food and then climbed into his seat at the small kitchen table, sitting on the booster in his chair.

A short time later, Penny was driving them to the Deep Sea Diner. It'd be a quick trip, one that would delay Trey's bedtime by an hour. But today was a celebration, after all. Trey was talking and Penny was taking her career seriously. The road ahead was flat and clear.

And then the car sputtered and chugged as if overtaken by a coughing fit. And then the coughing fit overcame the engine and it died.

Thankfully, the car had enough momentum for Penny to pull onto a less busy side street and park.

"Shoot." Penny tried several times to restart the car, but to no avail. She glanced in the rearview mirror. Trey's eyes were closed, his sweet face tilted to one side in slumber.

She called her insurance's tow truck service, relieved when the dispatcher said someone would be there right away.

If she'd taken her job more seriously, she could afford a new car, or at least, a reliable car.

While she waited for the tow truck, Penny searched more real estate listings in Sea Glass Bay, looking for something that would fit Axel's needs and budget, an amount she'd arbitrarily set for him.

A tow truck pulled up in front of her.

"That was fast." Penny got out to meet the driver, whose smile was heart-poundingly familiar. "Axel? I thought you had a family dinner."

"I did. And then a shift for the tow company." He glanced at her car with an assessing look in his eye. "What seems to be the problem?"

She related the car's symptoms as she handed over the keys. "Trey's asleep in the back. We were going to get ice cream."

"Let's see if I can fix it before he wakes up and wonders where his dessert is." Axel got behind the wheel but couldn't get the car to start either. He popped the hood and came around to the front to look at the engine. "Why don't you sit in the front seat and turn it over when I'm ready?"

"Sure." He was so calm about her breakdown, not blaming her as Brett would have done, even though it wasn't her fault. Her ex found fault in everything about Penny.

Axel got some tools from the tow truck and began taking things apart. His hands and arms were strong, dexterous, and—*dare she think it*—sexy. Ten years ago, he'd placed those hands on her shoulders, looking deep into her eyes before sliding his hands around her back, drawing her close, and kissing her tenderly.

Penny sighed. Axel knew his way around a woman, an engine, and who knew what else.

Axel leaned around the hood to look at her. "Turn it over. I bet this engine hums now."

Forget the engine. She was humming. Penny fumbled with the keys, embarrassed by her train of thought.

The engine caught immediately without a cough or a gasp.

Axel lowered the hood and came to stand outside her car door, leaning down to smile at her. "Your air filter was caked with dirt and filled with leaves. It looks like it hasn't been changed in ten years. Do you park under a tree?"

"Every day at the office." Her car was ten years old, and Brett had been in charge of servicing it, so this little hiccup came as no surprise. "Thank you so much." She extended her credit card toward him.

His smile disappeared. "No charge. And if you buy a new air filter, I'll change it. Also no charge."

A part of her rebelled at his charity. "Let me buy you an ice cream, then. Trey would love to see you."

Axel hesitated.

"Come on. You must have a break or something coming up. And I owe you." For more than help with her car. She owed him for what happened ten years ago. "I insist."

"Are you going to the Deep Sea Diner?" There was uncertainty in his eyes.

She didn't want him to look uncertain when he looked at her. But she knew that to get to that point, they needed to talk about what had happened a decade ago. And that wasn't a conversation for the very public Deep Sea Diner.

3

"This is not a date," Axel muttered to himself as he parked at the far end of the Deep Sea Diner's parking lot. He'd called dispatch and told them he was taking an early dinner break. "Penny just wants to thank me, not date me."

All the same, his heart beat a little faster.

Axel hopped down and walked over to Penny's car. She was getting Trey out of his safety seat. The Deep Sea Diner was busy. He saw Seth's teenage son, Matty, in a window booth with his friends, including his girlfriend Kimberly. They all seemed to look his way.

"This is a bad idea," Axel said, imagining Seth teasing him at their next family dinner.

"Ice cream is never a bad idea." Penny lifted Trey to her hip and shut the rear car door.

"The whole town will be talking about us by morning." *Including Brett.* Axel backed up. "I don't want to cause you any trouble."

Penny frowned. "You aren't any trouble. You've never been any trouble." She rolled her shoulders back. "If anything, I caused you grief and—"

"Water under the bridge." Axel didn't want to talk about the past. "Fudge and nuts."

"Excuse me?"

145

"That's what I like on my ice cream." Where was his cool? He reached for Trey as if he had every right to carry her kid around.

She didn't hand him over. "If you walk in the Deep Sea Diner carrying Trey, people *will* talk."

He grimaced but was already accepting the inevitable. "I can handle gossip." He'd learned early to let most of it slide off his back. It was the hurts caused by exclusion that he carried around. "Look, I'm either going to carry Trey or pay for ice cream. Your choice."

"You're not paying. I invited you." Penny handed over the slumbering toddler. "Why don't you get us a table outside on the ocean-side patio? I'll go in and pay."

He nodded, carrying the boy to a table on the west side of the restaurant.

The sun was going down and the breeze coming off the ocean was kicking up. Axel turned his back on the horizon to shelter Trey from the wind.

If things had gone differently ten years ago, this kid would have been mine.

Well, not this kid.

Trey stirred, blinking at his surroundings, aiming sleepy eyes up at Axel. "Acks."

"That's right. We're having ice cream. Your mom should be back any minute."

"Acks." Trey came more fully awake. He placed his two palms on Axel's cheeks, excitement in his wide eyes. "Truck. Truck. Truck."

"You like trucks, do you?" Axel smiled. "I'm driving another truck tonight. A bigger truck." The kid would get a kick out of sitting in the cab of the tow truck.

Penny sat across from them, placing a tray with their orders on the table. "Why are you driving a tow truck? I thought you worked at Seaside Transmission?"

"I'm saving for …" Axel shrugged, setting Trey on the bench next to him and handing the toddler a plastic bowl shaped like a seashell with a scoop of vanilla ice cream inside. He claimed his sundae with fudge sauce and nuts, and some of the napkins, which he anchored on the table with his truck keys. "You know why I'm saving." A rainy day, apparently, since his money didn't seem to be any good in Sea Glass Bay.

She scooped the cherry from the swirl of whipped cream on top of her strawberry milkshake almost without taking her eyes off Axel. "I want to talk to you about that."

Axel perked up. "Did Mr. Hammond change his mind?"

"No. But I'd like to help you look for a place to open your own shop." The wind blew her blonde hair away from her face. "I'd hate to see you give up on your dream."

Axel shook his head. "Everybody takes their broken cars to Hammond's. If I open a shop, they won't come."

"That's not …. You've got a drip on your chin, baby." Penny reached across the table, plucked a napkin from beneath Axel's keys, and waved it toward her son, who took the napkin but did nothing with it. "That's not true, Axel."

"It is and you know it," Axel said evenly. "If I want my own shop, I need to move. Maybe somewhere like Humboldt where no one knows me." Not that he wanted to leave. Not that much of anything was keeping him here except his foster family.

His gaze traced the curve of Penny's lips. Longing seemed to trace a path around his foolish heart.

"Wow." Penny put a straw between those lips he couldn't stop looking at and drank her milkshake. "The Axel I grew up with would be determined to prove everyone wrong."

"I told you." Axel wiped the ice cream dripping down Trey's chin before it fell on his shirt, earning a glowing smile from Penny. "I've changed. I'm more of a realist now." A man who knew his place, which was nowhere near the woman sitting across from him.

Don't you dare talk down to yourself, Alexander!

Penny scoffed. "Realists take facts into account. They crunch numbers. I'm going to prove you can open a business here." Penny glanced at the other patrons on the seaside patio. "Michael." Penny waved at Michael Britain, who'd graduated with them and sat at the next table with his wife and kids. "What do you think of Axel opening his own auto repair shop? Would you take your car to him?"

"Heck, yeah." Michael flashed Axel a quick smile. "He helped my wife change her flat tire at the beach one afternoon. You think Old Man Hammond would do that?"

"No way," Michael's wife answered for them.

147

Penny turned the other way, spotting another of their former classmates, this one sitting by himself. "And how about you, Daniel? Would you take your car to Axel if he opened a repair shop?"

Mouth full of onion rings, Daniel nodded, swallowed, and explained himself, "I'd go to the guy who helped me start my junker in the high school parking lot after a football game before anyone else."

"Glad to help, man." Axel caught another drip from Trey's chin.

"See?" Penny said triumphantly. "Get over the past, Axel."

His cell phone buzzed with a call from dispatch. "Break's over. Thanks for the ice cream." He took a last bite, savoring the sundae's sweetness and the determined glint in Penny's blue eyes.

"We're not done with our discussion." Penny pounded her plastic milkshake cup on the table a few times, like a judge pounding a gavel to get their way.

"If I can't buy the best repair shop in town, I think we are." Axel chucked Trey beneath the chin. "Be good, little man."

"Yes." Trey nodded. "I'm good."

"You're good, too, Axel," Penny told him. "I wish you could see it."

Her words stuck with Axel throughout his shift.

The next day, the wind coming off the ocean was cool and determined to drive Axel away from the beach. He was having none of it.

"Why does everything have to be an uphill battle?" Axel pushed on, marching to a picnic bench tucked away on the stretch of Sea Glass Beach where he liked to eat his lunch. He turned off the music playing in his ear, content to listen to the ocean.

Kids laughed and shouted as they splashed in the waves. Somewhere, music played, tune indistinct above the crashing waves and the *whoosh* of the wind. Seagulls swooped and squawked. Beach noise was a welcome change from the roar of engines and whine of machinery at Seaside Transmission.

Axel sat down on the picnic bench and unlaced his work boots, thinking one of the voices from the beach sounded like his name had been called. He disregarded that thought. No one ever called to him down here. He swung his feet around, dug his toes in the sand, and opened his lunch bag.

"*Alexander!*" Penny appeared at the paved sidewalk a few feet away, out of breath. She wore a fancy blue dress and those same black high heels she'd had on yesterday. "I chased you all the way from Seaside Transmission. Didn't you hear me?"

Axel pointed to his earbuds. "I was listening to music."

"While you power walked down here." Penny slipped off her shoes and approached, every step a tantalizing sway of hips. She brushed sand off the picnic bench on her side and sat daintily across from him. "Thanks for the workout."

"You're welcome." Axel set out his lunch. A double-decker turkey and cheese sandwich, potato salad, and two pears. "Why are you stalking me?"

Her mouth hung open a moment. "This has nothing to do with …"

He raised an eyebrow, biting back a smile when her cheeks bloomed a soft, attractive pink.

Penny leaned her forearms on the picnic table. "I told you. I want to be your realtor."

Axel wanted to replace realtor with another noun, like girlfriend or lover. But he knew better than to wish for things he couldn't have. "I don't want to waste your time."

"I have time to spare." She rolled those baby blues like they were still in high school. "Currently, my dad has me working as his assistant, even though I have my license. Frankly, since the divorce, I was happy with the role. But now …" She paused, shifting on the bench, lowering her voice as if they weren't alone and she didn't want anyone to hear her confession. "I want to step it up. It's just that …. No one who comes to Bell Realty wants to hire me as their agent. You'd be doing me a favor by letting me help you."

Axel chewed on his sandwich and on her words while the sounds of the beach filled the silence between them. "You need me," he said finally.

"We need each other." She rolled her eyes again, looking adorable. "Axel, you have big dreams. But to get there, you need to start out small. I can help you."

Axel took his time replying. "I'm listening."

"There are several other properties for sale locally that might work for you."

"Ones with three service bays?" That was his dream, after all.

"No."

"Ones with lifts?"

"No."

Axel sighed. He wasn't fond of working underneath a vehicle lying on his back. "Not interested."

Penny tossed her hands. "Can you at least look?"

"Now? This is my lunch break." And what she'd found didn't sound like they fit his dream at all.

"After work?"

"I've got a tow truck shift again tonight." Axel finished his sandwich and offered her a pear.

Penny accepted his gift, but not his brush-off. "You're going to get your own shop, Axel. I'm going to make sure of it. Are you working tomorrow night?"

He shook his head.

"Then it's settled. I'll set everything up for the property viewings and text you the schedule." She handed him her business card. "All I need is your phone number."

He chewed slowly, looking at her as if he had all the time in the world to just look …

And remember that kiss a decade ago …

And the bloody aftermath …

Because it was important to remember that he was Axel Martinez, and that she was Penny Bell Carlson from the other side of town. The only way they had a future together was if he moved to her side of town. And to do that, he'd need an engine repair shop with three service bays.

Perhaps aware of the divide between them, her gaze swept the table, avoiding him. "Are you going to the high school reunion dinner and dance on Friday?"

"No." Axel recoiled so hard he nearly fell backward off the picnic bench. "Why would I?"

Penny's gaze found his. There was a plea in those blue eyes. "To reconnect with old friends."

He frowned slightly. He avoided socializing with his former classmates.

"Some of the teachers and administration are coming back, too."

His frown hardened. He'd frequently spent time in the principal's office and even more time in detention, sent there by teachers. "Where are you going with this?"

Penny looked like she was having a hard time holding onto her smile. It fell twice before she said, "We should go together."

"No." Axel checked the time on his phone, making sure he wouldn't be late returning. "Why would I want to reacquaint myself with high school bullies, the royal court, and staff who didn't like me?"

"Because …" Penny hesitated; lips parted slightly in that way of hers he was coming to recognize as shock. "Because I need someone to have my back. It's not going to be easy for me either."

"Because Brett is going with his new wife?" Axel guessed. "Don't go, Penny. From where I'm sitting, anything would be better than attending the reunion, even hosting a bridal shower for Gail." His words drifted off into the wind, like his dreams and Gail's. "Somebody should give her a bridal shower," he added as an afterthought. "She deserves one."

"I could do it." Penny pounced on the idea. "I could throw Gail a shower if you look at the properties I have in mind and go to the reunion with me."

Axel nearly fell off the bench again. "You can't throw Gail a shower. It should be given by one of her girlfriends."

"Or her soon-to-be stepson," Penny said with a bright smile.

He didn't understand her optimism. It threw a curve ball that made him ignore the stepson label. "It's too late. There are less than two weeks until the wedding."

"It's not too late. I can make it happen." She seemed so certain, just as certain as when she talked about him opening his own business. "How does Saturday sound?"

Axel rubbed at the furrows in his brow. "This is a lot to throw at a man on his lunch hour."

"Life comes at you fast, Axel. If you don't keep up, you'll be left behind." She stood, smoothing her dress and giving him a smile the likes of which a young Penny Bell had never given him before— confident … triumphant … *sexy*. "We'll start looking at properties tomorrow night. You'll need to pick me up at five for the reunion Friday. Wear a tie. I'll make all the arrangements for Gail's shower this weekend. You just need to send me a guest list and get her there."

"But ..." Axel couldn't think of a single argument he hadn't already tried.

Penny walked barefoot to the sidewalk, then balanced on one foot as she put on first one high heel and then another.

Hoo-boy. Axel swallowed longing. He swallowed hope. But he didn't swallow either hard enough.

Penny walked away without looking back, as if she was certain Axel would do everything she asked.

Funny thing was ...

He wanted to.

4

"What are you doing here?" Axel eyed Penny suspiciously when she was waiting for him outside the transmission shop at noon the next day. He looked ruggedly handsome in his stained work coveralls with the sleeves rolled up to his elbows.

Penny stuffed her attraction back in its hiding place. She'd had the best success with Axel yesterday when she was commanding. Falling to his charm would get her nowhere. "You didn't send me a guest list for the shower." She fell into step next to him as he headed for the beach, presumably to his shaded picnic table. "I need you to make some decisions about cake, decorations, adult beverages, games, and—"

"Before this gets out of hand, I have to talk to Gail." He walked faster, lengthening his strides, as if he could outwalk Penny and her demands.

It was a good thing Penny had worn red ballet flats with her long blue dress today. It gave her a better chance of keeping up. "Okay. You can call Gail while you eat lunch."

"This isn't the kind of conversation you have over the phone when it's out-of-the-blue." Axel sounded prickly.

"Are you chickening out?" Penny grabbed onto his shoulder, a little breathless from his power walk. She stared into those dark chocolate eyes, seeking the truth. "You are."

He heaved a sigh. "Penny …" There was so much emotion in his voice, just in those two syllables. And his eyes …

"You're afraid." *Of what?*

He began walking again.

She didn't let go of his arm, dragging behind him like a too-small anchor chained to a large, powerful yacht.

Axel glanced down at her hand.

Penny still didn't let go.

He heaved another sigh. "When I was a kid, every day was different. There was no routine." His tone was as taut as a stretched wire. "I never knew what to expect when I came home from school."

"That's why you didn't come to school some days."

He nodded, checking for traffic before crossing the road to the beach. "It was less stressful to me to be there through my mom's ups-and-downs in emotions, because I was used to that, but when I opened our apartment door never knowing if she was going to be there … or not …. That was harder."

Penny could only imagine what he meant by "or not." She squeezed his arm, wishing she could ease the pain of his past.

"And when I did go to school, I was never sure where I stood. The kids all had their friends and …"

"You didn't fit in." And worse, his clothes never seemed to be the right size. They certainly had never been a current style. "At least, not until you were taken in by the Hollisters."

"Yeah." Axel drew Penny down the path to the picnic table that was partially hidden beneath a cluster of pines. "Clay and Leda gave me a traditional home, one with rules and routines. I like knowing where I fit into things. And I like routine."

"And everything I proposed is anything but routine." Penny's spirits sank. She'd been banking on Axel to jumpstart her career and ease the awkwardness of the reunion.

"Yes. It's all very sudden—I'm not good with surprises or impulsive decisions." He sat down on the bench and removed his work boots. "I'm glad you understand."

Penny sat across from him. "I understand, but that doesn't mean you're off the hook on anything." She'd been looking forward to, hopefully, another kiss this weekend, never expecting him to back out of their deal.

Axel gave her a long-suffering look.

Penny was at a crossroad. She could either give in, like the good little girl she'd been all her life, following the path of least resistance. Or she could be bold, which was what she'd admired in Axel and Brett when she was a teenager.

Penny closed her eyes, thinking about the example she wanted to set for Trey, who was spending the day with her mother. She wanted to be bold and go after what she wanted, so that her child would do the same. There was just the trepidation inside her to be dealt with.

Be bold. Take charge.

Penny swallowed, opened her eyes and stood, walking around the table to sit next to Axel. From her seat, she could see the beach and the ocean. But no one was close. No one could hear what she had to say.

"You and me, Axel …. We always feel safer in the background. We're not like the carefree vacationers out there or the achievers whose touch turns everything into gold. You've had a less than normal childhood which made you more careful than most. And I've let others make decisions for me for so long that when Brett left me, I didn't know what to do." So she'd done practically nothing. "But that all changed the other day when I met you at the garage. You have a dream, and it reminded me that I should have dreams, too."

"I don't take any responsibility for that. You probably felt relieved that Trey started speaking."

"My impetus for change was a combination of seeing you again, hearing your dreams, and watching Trey blossom."

Be bold.

"Also …" Penny turned to Axel and kissed him.

He didn't lurch back in surprise or horror. His arm came around her tenderly until his hand rested on her hip. He kissed her long, slow, and deep, without any of the heat of their long-ago kiss or any of the passion she'd expected from this sexy, complicated man.

Penny drew back, caught up in the warmth in his eyes. "Hi."

"Hi." He gave her a wry smile. "Well, that is one way to convince me the unexpected can be good. I guess this means I'm looking for a place to open up shop, you have a date for the reunion, and Gail is going to have a bridal shower." Axel sighed, but this time it seemed more for dramatic effect than because he was unhappy. "Show me your ideas for the shower while I eat. I'll get you that list tonight."

Penny dug her phone from her purse. "You won't regret this."

"I already do."

"Who requested access to the Parnell property on Seventh?" Penny's father came out of his office after Penny had seen Axel. He scanned the two other agents present, skipping over Penny.

"Is there a problem?" Penny stood, knees suddenly weak.

"Other than the fact that I wasn't informed? No." Dad shook his head.

"I requested access codes to the Parnell lockbox." Penny squared her shoulders. "And two other properties."

Her father approached Penny's desk. "Which realtor asked you to arrange showings?" Dad glanced around the office.

Be bold.

"No one, Dad. I have a client of my own." A handsome client who kissed like a dream and made her heart pound.

"You?" Her father's brow clouded.

"Yes." Penny locked her knees and swiped at her suddenly hot cheeks. "I thought it was time I became more proactive."

Everyone in the office was silent, including her father.

And then he broke out in a grin. "Excellent. Who's the client?"

"Axel … *Alexander* Martinez."

Dad's grin faded. "He's not worth your time if he still goes by that hoodlum nickname. We don't take on clients who can't afford property."

Be bold.

"He's saved up to buy a business, Dad. That makes him legit." Penny scoffed to cover her nerves. "Besides, what's in a name? Don't you still call Dennis Hammond *The Hammer?*"

"That's different." Dad's arms were crossed, and his features closed off.

"It's not and you know it." Penny mirrored his body language, thinking of Axel, channeling his chip-on-my-shoulder attitude. "You always said you wanted me to take over Bell Realty when you retire. Everyone who walks through that door who asks for you can buy anything they want. If I want clients to ask for me, I need to start small. I know what I'm doing. You just have to trust me."

After a moment, her dad nodded.

It was a powerful moment for Penny. She had her father's support. And Axel's.

What could possibly go wrong?

5

unning late. I'll pick you up at seven.

Axel stared at Penny's text long enough that Gail noticed.

"Important message?" Gail served Axel a slice of chocolate Bundt cake at the dinner table. None of his foster brothers were around.

He'd come by the house after work to broach the subject of Gail's bridal shower. "A real estate agent wants to show me some options to open my own repair shop."

"That's a big step, Son." Clay lowered his fork. "Are you ready to manage something like that?"

"Of course, he is," Gail said staunchly.

Unbidden, old resentments rose to the surface. "I'm ready for a lot of things you wouldn't expect from me, *Clay*, like starting a business and dating someone with a kid. I'm even throwing Gail a bridal shower this weekend."

Gail and Clay glanced from Axel to each other and back again.

"How nice of you, Axel," Gail murmured, her eyes brimming with tears.

Now that everything was out on the table, Axel pushed onward, trying to lighten his tone. "I need a list of attendees from you, Gail. Everything is taken care of. All you have to do is show up and enjoy the experience of being a bride."

"Gail, I didn't realize this was so important to you." Clay faltered, swallowed, started again. "Tell me what you need, Axel. I'll help you pull this off."

"I didn't want to cause a fuss." Gail placed her palms on her cheeks. "I only mentioned it to Axel because …"

"Because she never got those things before." Even though Gail was tap dancing around the facts, Axel didn't plan to. "Gail deserves to feel special."

"She does," Clay agreed, voice thick with emotion. "I'm proud of you for taking that on. I'm proud of you in so many ways. I'm sure you've thought out everything you need to about this business idea, Son."

Son.

Axel wasn't Clay's son. He never would be.

"My name is *Axel*. You made it very clear that I wasn't your son when you wouldn't challenge Ava Martinez for the right to be my father." Suddenly out of breath, Axel couldn't stay in the house another minute.

He bolted for the door, running down the steps the way he had when he was a kid and things didn't go his way. Racing for the sidewalk the way he had the day Clay and Leda broke the news that they wouldn't be adopting him. He'd run into the street and been hit by a car. Luckily, Old Man Abernathe had been driving at a snail's pace. Still, Axel's leg had been broken and there was no more talk of adoption after that.

Penny pulled up to the curb just as Axel reached the sidewalk, windows down and engine running rough again. "Sorry I'm late."

"You're right on time." Axel climbed into the front seat.

"Acks!" Trey cried from his car seat in the back where he held a Spiderman action figure. "Look!"

"Hey, buddy. I like Spiderman, too." Axel pushed a smile past the guilt he felt over the words he'd thrown at Clay, glancing back toward the house where Clay and Gail stood in the doorway, holding hands.

We love you, Alexander.

Head muddled with emotion, Axel couldn't tell if that was Leda's voice in his head or Gail's.

He turned his back to the door. "I could use some really good news right now, Penny, like a property I can afford with three service bays and a lift." Something he'd be proud to show Clay or any of the doubters in town.

Penny caught Axel's hand and gave it a squeeze. "The good news is that Cindy pre-approved you for a loan. I have three options to show you today. All in your budget."

Axel felt Clay's gaze on his back, resisting the urge to return to the house and apologize. "And the bad news?" There was always bad news.

"There is no bad news." And Penny laughed when she said it, as if she believed it.

In his heart, Axel wanted to believe it, too.

"This is op-tion num-ber one." Penny parked in the driveway of Oceanside Beetles, a garage specializing in repairing Volkswagens. Excitement had her hands trembling nearly as much as her shaky words. She didn't want to let Axel down. "Harry Parnell wants to retire. He leases this property. He's selling the business and offering four weeks of help transitioning things to the new owner." She retrieved a sheet of paper with the business specifications on it and rattled off how much Harry had made annually in the past five years. "You'd have to pick up the lease and pay Harry for the business. But your loan will cover that, and it's worth it."

"Repairing Volkswagens." Axel sounded doubtful and looked forlorn. He'd been in a funk since she'd picked him up.

Penny pushed on. "His sales seem to indicate it's a lucrative business. The price includes all his tools and parts inventory, plus some old vans and bugs in the back."

Admittedly, the business wasn't as well-cared for as Mr. Hammond's. Weeds had claimed the fence border but did nothing to soften the abandoned look of the rusted vehicles on the other side of the chain link.

Axel stared at the shop, probably taking note of the office's cracked window and the faded sign. "It's only got one service bay and ... it's Volkswagens."

Find the bright side, Penny.

"You say Volkswagen as if it's a bad thing. Bug owners are loyal to the brand. You have a built-in clientele. Did you hear the numbers he's making? That's a decent living for a one-man show."

Axel crossed his arms over his chest, tucking his hands away. "But it's got a ceiling in terms of business size. There's only one service bay. And it's *Volkswagens*."

Penny's spirits sank. "I get it. You're doubtful you can expand beyond his current clientele." Penny hadn't thought of that. She checked her listing sheet. "I thought it said something about two bays though ….And yes. It does say two." She got out of the car and went to peek in the window. "It's a double. One behind the other." Two bays had to mean something. She hurried back to the car.

"The bay setup is inconvenient." Axel still sat in his closed position. "What if I can't get the car blocking the door to start? The car in back would be trapped. Customers would be angry."

"I hadn't thought about that." Penny knew she was supposed to be upbeat, learning more about what Axel wanted in a property with every showing, but she was taking his rejection personally. "Why don't you think about this one while we head over to the next option?"

Axel grunted.

"Acks needs ice cream." Trey grinned at Penny in the rearview mirror. He was becoming better at verbal communication every day, just as Dr. Inman had promised. "Ice cream is good."

"Mommy will need ice cream after this." Penny couldn't keep the sarcasm from her tone. "Honestly, Axel. I think you'd jump at the chance if the business was called Oceanside Corvettes."

"Why, Penny." Axel's arms loosened and he almost smiled. "I didn't think you knew me that well."

"I know you, all right." Heartened, Penny started the car. "I know you care too much about what people think nowadays. The Axel I—" *fell in love with* "—admired would judge people and things by their merits and expect the same of them."

That hint of a smile on his face became a real one. "If I would've known you spent so much time studying me, Penny, I would have tried stealing a kiss sooner than the graduation dance."

The thought thrilled her so much she pressed down too hard on the accelerator as she backed out of the driveway, making one wheel bounce over the curb. "Sorry."

"Wheee!" Trey giggled.

"I know owning a business is scary." She put the car in drive and headed toward the next property. "You can do this. I believe you can do hard things, like turn a lump of coal into a diamond."

"You're looking to make a sale," he grumped.

"You betcha." Penny chuckled. "And don't forget you owe me a date at the reunion, even if I don't find you a property you like today. I'm still coordinating the bridal shower." Which was turning out to be a lot of fun to plan.

"Funny you should say that." Axel flashed his phone at her. "Gail just sent me a guest list."

Thank heavens.

"Ice cream." Trey kicked his feet against the back of her seat. "Mama. Ice cream."

"Later, Trey," Penny promised.

"Now-now-now." Trey continued to kick.

"No ice cream if you can't sit still, Trey," Axel said, an oddly stern note to his voice.

Trey stilled. "Okay."

Axel clapped a hand over his eyes. "Geez-o-Pete, I sound like Clay. I apologize."

Axel looked so stricken that Penny laughed. "We all turn into our parents eventually. We take on too much responsibility and forget what it was like to be spontaneous or to dream big."

"Are you dreaming big, Penny?" Axel propped his elbow on her center console and put his chin in his hand as he stared at her.

She liked it when his attention was turned her way. "I haven't been spontaneous or allowed myself to dream big," she admitted. "Until now. Until this." She risked a glance at this enigmatic, enticing man. "Until you."

"Now you're going to make me blush." Not likely. His grin was too wicked, and those dark eyes sparkled.

It was time to say more about what happened ten years ago.

Penny pulled over. "Axel, the night you kissed me was the one real thing in my high school experience. And I walked away from it. From you. Everything would have been different after that if I'd stood up for myself or held onto you." Although holding onto him had seemed cowardly at the time. "I despised Brett for throwing that punch, but I went with him anyway because … because I was scared. I'm sorry about that. I should have stood by you." And been with him, the way she wanted to be now.

Giving in to impulse, she brushed the dark hair out of his eyes and pressed a quick kiss to his lips.

"That was nice," he murmured, staring at her mouth.

Penny suppressed a shiver and a smile. "The point I'm trying to make is that if you want to be happy, you have to choose a path that makes you happy. And sometimes, just making that choice makes you nervous or scared."

"You're saying that I need to swallow my fears about change and set my pride aside when it comes to going into business for myself." The warmth in his eyes stole her breath, so it was a good thing he kept on talking. "I've never thought bad of you for choosing Brett. And I don't mean to be difficult on this property search, but …"

"You're going to be," she finished for him.

He nodded. "And I may need time to think things through, weigh my options." He ran the back of his hand over her cheek in a touch that was feather-light. "My foster family would say I spend too much time alone in my head and not enough time doing things."

"I hope that's not true." Because she wanted him to take steps toward a bigger future, one that might include her and Trey.

"You want me to buy this? For six figures?" Axel stared at what looked like a two-story box. A two-story box that looked like a strong wind would blow it over. It looked like many of the apartments he'd shared with his mother. "This is what Clay would call a caution."

"I call it a project." Penny had on her optimistic cap. "It's a two-car garage that is extra deep with a two-bedroom apartment built over it. That'll save you rent. The neighborhood is zoned multi-use, commercial and residential. Two houses down is a law firm. Across the street is a doctor's office."

"The paint is peeling. The garage door needs replacing." Axel glanced around. "And there's a yard filled mostly with weeds."

"Sweat equity will get you far." Penny drew out her spec sheet and read him the particulars, square footage, and property taxes. "You'd have to equip the garage with all your own tools and spread the word that you were in business. But it's definitely cheaper than the first place we looked at." She nudged his shoulder. "You could service Corvettes here."

Axel continued to stare at the ramshackle building. It was a wreck, plain and simple. "I'm not sure I have enough imagination to picture how it could be."

"Let's explore what's inside." Penny turned off the engine. "You'll see."

He doubted it.

"Ice cream?" Trey asked hopefully.

"Trey's got the right idea." This wasn't so much a business opportunity as a multi-year project. "How am I supposed to fix the building while I'm fixing cars?"

"I'm sure you'll figure that out as you weigh your options." Penny got out and removed Trey from his car seat.

Reluctantly, Axel got out, too. He took Trey from her. The little dude nestled into his arms as if it were a safe and familiar resting place. Axel rubbed his back, taking some comfort in Trey's calm as he followed Penny to the main floor door. "It can't be as bad as it looks."

But it could.

The concrete floor was grease stained and cracked. It would need to be repoured. The walls weren't insulated, unless you counted thick cobwebs. "It smells like wood rot."

"It smells like a bargain. Don't you see? In its current condition, we can talk them down in price." Penny walked toward the rear of the garage. "There's an office back here and a stairwell to the apartment."

The "office" was the size of a closet. The stairs, steep and narrow. Upstairs, the kitchen cabinets were from the 1960s with scalloped trim. The wallpaper behind the stove featured copper teapots and orange flowers. The carpet was a dirty green shag. The bedrooms had brown wood paneling. The bathroom was pink and just as dated and worn as the rest of the place.

Despite that, Penny was walking around and talking with enthusiasm. "What a steal."

There was a robbery in the making here, all right. But it wasn't Axel who'd be doing the stealing. "This is the kind of place that Clay and Seth expect me to buy."

I'm proud of you, Son.

Clay wouldn't be if Axel bought this.

Penny frowned. "It's a fixer, which will save you thousands of dollars. You don't think your family will respect you for investing wisely?"

He shook his head.

"With the proper investment and care, your investment will increase twenty-five percent in value in five years."

"During which time, I'll be bankrupt."

Penny squared her shoulders. "I seem to recall you buying a wreck of a car when we were in high school. It didn't even run when you bought it."

Axel nodded. "I sold it for a pretty profit."

"You can do that here. Fix it. Establish a business. Sell and move to a better location." She said all the right things.

"There's just one problem." He met her gaze, not sure if he wanted to admit what was holding him back. At her nod, he pressed on. "If I buy this, no one in town will be surprised."

"You don't know that."

"I do," he insisted. "I would much rather buy the best." Like Sea Glass Bay Automotive.

Penny took Trey from him. "And if you can't afford the best?"

"Maybe I should keep working." He hoped that didn't mean their date was going to be canceled. "But that's a moot point. Didn't you say you had three properties to show me?"

"I have three options." Penny carried Trey downstairs and out to the car, buckling him into his safety seat before returning to the property to lock up. "None of the options is the diamond you're looking for, unless you consider these diamonds in the rough."

"Surprise me." Axel got into her car, aware of the chill in the air. And it wasn't coming from the sun moving lower on the horizon. Penny was disappointed in him.

She drove toward the highway, parking at the curb of Carlson Cars. "You want to dip your toe a little bit in the auto repair waters? This is it." She gestured toward the used car lot.

Axel's gaze caught on a red Corvette. "Where?"

Penny pointed toward the back of the lot. "You see that big van back there? You can equip it with tools and parts, and drive to your customers."

"It's a food truck." He couldn't take his eyes off the swirl of bright red colors on the vehicle, including a ten-foot hot dog painted on the side.

"Axel." Penny took his hand and gave it a squeeze. "We made a deal. I throw Gail a bridal shower, you'd be my date at the high school reunion, and …"

"And you'd be my realtor," he said absently, still staring at the van.

Penny released his hand and pulled away from the curb. "I can't be your realtor, Axel, not until you realize that dreams should be for your own satisfaction, not to impress someone else."

6

"*Y*ou look gorgeous." Axel handed Penny a blue orchid corsage on Friday night and tugged at his tie. He'd taken off work early to clean up. He'd ironed black slacks and a blue dress shirt. But his preparations were nothing compared to Penny's.

She wore a slinky black dress that hit her mid-thigh. Her blonde hair was in a sophisticated twist at the nape of her neck. Sparkly silver heels that made her nearly as tall as he was. And for one brief second, she smiled at him as if his reaction to her appearance was just what she'd been hoping for.

Axel wanted to kiss her, but since she'd shown him property two days ago, she'd limited their interactions to brief text messages asking him to approve details for Gail's bridal shower, which was going to be held at The Tipsy Table on Saturday afternoon. She wasn't the only one avoiding someone. Axel was avoiding Clay's requests to come over and talk.

"You clean up nice." Penny invited him inside her apartment, removed the wrist corsage from its package and slipped it on. "Who am I kidding? You look so handsome that someone's going to steal you away tonight." She laughed, but it was a hollow sound.

Axel wanted her optimism, her joy, or the intense look he saw in her eyes before she kissed him. But he'd disappointed her on the property search. She couldn't understand his need to be bullet-proof in the community or with family, and he couldn't give up the desire for the one business he truly wanted.

"No one's going to take me from your side," Axel said with conviction, tugging at his tie. He reached for Penny's hand, twining their fingers together. "This is our do-over, remember?" Ten years in the making. "Where's Trey?"

"With my parents." She didn't look at him as she unbound their fingers. "We should get going. Wouldn't want to miss dinner."

Axel wanted exactly that, but he escorted her to his truck anyway.

The drive to the high school gymnasium was quiet. A line had formed at the gym, a line with fancy-dressed couples, including Jared and his date, Nina.

Axel parked and hurried around to open Penny's door. He was late. She got out on her own. Apparently, the new Penny, the one he'd inspired to take charge of her life, didn't have room for an overly cautious, former foster kid who was afraid no one would like Alexander Martinez.

I'm proud of you, Son.

Axel needed to act like he deserved Clay's praise. He'd visit him tomorrow during the shower and apologize. He'd thank Clay for his support, patience, and kindness toward a messed-up kid, a boy who'd bluffed his way through life pretending to be tough.

Penny flashed him a cautious smile.

Penny likes the real me.

The man in the grease-stained coveralls who enjoyed putting his toes in the sand during his lunch hour. She'd kissed him at his picnic bench. Didn't that mean she could love him even if he didn't run the largest repair garage in Sea Glass Bay?

He wanted that desperately because …

I love Penny.

Axel drew a deep, slow breath.

He loved the way she empathized with his childhood. He loved the way she saw through his bluntness to his vulnerabilities. He loved that she tried to steer him toward success but could admit her own limits in helping him.

I can't be your realtor, Axel, not until you realize that dreams should be for your own satisfaction.

"Penny." He caught her hand once more, anxious because love had T-boned him, and he had no time to settle on words that could convey what he felt in a way that didn't sound desperate or vulnerable. "I'm sorry. I'm sorry I didn't like anything you showed me. That doesn't mean you can't show me other prospects. That doesn't mean we can't see each other while I wait for the right place to come on the market. In between looking, we could take Trey to the beach or go for ice cream, maybe have a nice dinner, just the two of us."

"Thank you but …" She lifted her palm to his cheek. "We tried looking and you rejected properties because you're not ready to make your dream a reality. I have to think of my future, Axel. Mine and Trey's. When I … fall in love again, it has to be with someone who's moving his life forward, not someone who …" Her hand fell away.

"Not someone who's scared of change," he finished for her, caught between the scars of the past and defense against scars in the future. But he loved her. He loved her and he had to explain. "I want to be that person, Penny. I wish I could have been that person the night I kissed you all those years ago. But I was afraid that if I made waves in town by punching Brett that Clay and Leda would give up on me."

"And I was afraid of doing something for myself."

"Admittedly, it takes me time to get used to the idea of something new," Axel allowed. "But I'm ready to embrace the idea of starting out small. At least, when it comes to opening an auto repair shop. As for other new things … I'm ready to embrace a different kind of life … with you and Trey."

"Oh, Axel. Even taking small steps of change is a big step in itself." Penny wrapped her arms around his neck. "I want that, too. I'm sorry if I've been pushing too much. I promise to go slow."

Harsh laughter filled the air.

"All is right with the world, Jules." Brett strutted forward with Julie Haney on his arm. Brett wasn't just wearing a tie. He was wearing an expensive-looking black suit. Even his shiny black shoes looked like he'd spent a fortune on them. Brett was everything Axel wasn't, had everything Axel didn't. Except for Penny. "I'm here with you, Jules, and Penny's with her class of guy. Low class, that is." Brett chuckled, coming to a halt in front of Penny and Axel, managing to smile down on the pair even though he wasn't as tall as Axel.

Instinctively, Axel tucked her behind him.

That seemed to goad Brett into attack-mode. "I should have picked better bloodlines to breed with. But this is too low, Penny. I don't approve of my son hanging out with garbage. At this rate, that kid will never talk."

Penny gasped.

Axel forced himself to laugh. "Listen to yourself, Brett. Talking about your son without love or pride." He glanced over his shoulder at Penny, noting the hurt in her blue eyes and wanting to protect her from ever being hurt again. "Let's head inside, Penny. There's too much stink in the air out here." He guided her toward the gymnasium sidewalk where he saw Jared and Nina had stepped out of line to move toward them.

"Hey!" Brett grabbed Axel's arm. "Nobody talks to me like that."

"Somebody should." Axel jerked free. "You're a bully and a cheat. You always have been. You paid Kevin Evans to do your homework in high school. You claimed Jared only got the starting spot on the football team ahead of you because of a mysterious trick knee. You sell used cars that break down the moment they leave the lot. You were two-timing your wife with Julie. And I wouldn't be surprised if you were still cheating at something …" Normally, Axel would have stopped there. But Brett's attack on Penny was too much. "You know, I saw your Mercedes parked out at Pinnacle Point the other night. Odd place for a married man to be, don't you—"

With a feral sound, Brett swung a fist toward Axel's face.

Axel blocked the blow with his forearm and countered with an uppercut that connected with his rival's chin.

Brett crumpled like a blade of fresh cut grass in a gust of unexpected wind. A cheer rose from those waiting to enter the gymnasium, which—when combined with Brett's collapse—would have been immensely satisfying if Penny hadn't rushed forward with Julie to attend to the jerk.

"He's breathing," Penny said.

Jared appeared at Axel's side. "Come on, man. Give Brett some breathing room."

"Why? I'm not going to hit him again." There was no need. Brett was passed out. Axel should have been crowing with satisfaction. Instead, he was staring at Penny getting to her feet. "I didn't mean to hit him so hard."

Before she could reply, Jared dragged Axel to the far side of the parking lot. "Do you know what Brett's going to do the moment he comes to? He's going to call the sheriff. We need to call Seth first."

"Brett Carlson wants to press charges." An hour later, Seth sat in a chair across from Axel in the sheriff office's conference room.

Clay sat next to Seth. Jared sat next to Axel. Not that it mattered. There weren't two sides here. All the Hollister men were frowning at Axel.

"At the risk of repeating myself," Axel said flatly. "Brett took the first swing."

"Which I saw," Jared added, although that didn't stop him from frowning.

"Violence never solved anything." But Clay's opinion lacked its usual finality.

"But in this case, it made me feel better." Axel thrust his chin in the air. "That blow was ten years coming. And before you start in on the lecture, Seth, I plan to apologize to the jerk." If for no other reason than because Penny might forgive him if he did. "And while I'm on the apology train, I want to say I'm sorry for the other night." Axel met Clay's gaze.

Seth pinched the bridge of his nose. "Axel, what have you done now?"

"Nothing." Clay pointed at Axel with one finger. "He just needs to hear that I'm his father and you're his brothers, no matter what the courts say. I don't need a paper signed by a judge to claim you as my son, Axel."

Axel's mouth dropped open. Seth lowered the hand from in front of his face.

But Clay wasn't finished. "It was obvious to us that you wanted our relationship to be legal. Heck, you ran out the door when we tried to have this conversation the first time and broke your leg."

"Mom made us swear not to bring up the topic of adoption again," Jared added, loosening his red suit tie. "She was afraid you'd do more than run out in the street. She was afraid you'd run away."

Clay nodded. "We tried convincing Ava a second time, but she was convinced that once she found a good place to live and a decent job, that you'd be better off with her." He cleared his throat. "I don't think she ever got her life together to a point she felt comfortable coming back for you. And that's a shame, because you've grown into a man she'd have been proud of."

The table fell silent.

"You're a Hollister, Axel," Seth said, voice just as thick with emotion as Clay's had been. "We all believe it."

"Through thick and thin," Jared chimed in.

"We love you." Clay put just the right accent on the conversation.

"Maybe I shouldn't have belted Brett and caused all this trouble," Axel admitted slowly, although then he might never have learned how they felt about him.

"What trouble?" Jared clapped a hand on Axel's shoulder. "We got out of dancing."

"*Ha!* Jared hates to dance." Seth reached across the table and poked Jared's shoulder. And then he sobered. "Why are you acting like you've murdered someone? I brought you down here to make a statement, not arrest you. Everyone saw Brett take the first swing."

"And everyone thought he got what he deserved." Jared stared at Seth as if thinking about what he deserved for poking his shoulder.

"If anyone says *he touched me first* I'm going to stop the proverbial car the same way our parents did when we were kids." Clay shook his finger at each of them in turn.

It was like they were all kids again and on a road trip. They grinned at each other.

"You're not in trouble, Son," Clay said, holding Axel's gaze. "We're all here to support you, not berate you."

"I haven't always been here for you lately." Jared picked up where their father had left off. "But what Dad says is right. We're family."

"I wouldn't tease you so much if you weren't my little brother," Seth said with a wry smile. "I didn't realize this has been an issue with you. We should have come clean about this years ago, I guess."

"Among other things." Clay—*Dad*—began to smile. "Apparently, Axel is the only one of you brave enough to tell me I'm too bossy—that I need to pay attention more to others' needs. Yours. My future wife's. Things in this family are going to change."

Family.

Misty-eyed, Axel got to his feet and hugged the only man who'd ever cared enough to be his father.

And then Jared wrapped his arms around them just moments before Seth did the same.

Family.

Axel hadn't thought he fully belonged to them or to Sea Glass Bay, not until that moment. He hadn't thought they'd loved him for who he was, not until that moment.

The conference room door swung open.

"I don't know what's going on here, but I want in." That was Gail. She inched her way into the family embrace, whispering, "Someone should have called me sooner. I should have been here for my boy at the first sign of trouble rather than hearing about it through the grapevine."

Son. My little brother. My boy. Family.

"I guess I'll have to start calling you two Mom and Dad."

"That's music to my ears," Clay said gruffly.

Axel was caught in the tangle of arms and in a circle of love.

But he wouldn't have it any other way with the Hollisters.

Now he had to make it right with Penny.

7

*P*enny stared at Axel's text message one more time.
Meet me at the two-story box after work.

Because exercise was on her list of things to get reacquainted with, she'd put Trey in his stroller after she left Bell Realty and pushed him toward the property listing. She waited at an intersection to cross the street, staring at her phone. Why did Axel want to meet at a property he'd rejected?

It had been two days since Axel had punched Brett's lights out. She'd been afraid Axel had hit him so hard that Brett's nose had been broken—that he'd killed him. Thank heavens, he hadn't.

But they hadn't talked since then. Axel had been whisked away by Sheriff Hollister and Brett had been taken to the hospital for concussion watch.

Penny tried not to take any pleasure in Brett's comeuppance. But wow, those assembled sure had.

She sighed and crossed the street. Axel probably blamed her for the ensuing trouble because that seemed the only reason he hadn't called her since.

Ahead, Axel pulled into the driveway of the listing. Tall, thick Cypress hedges hid him from sight.

"Acks!" Trey reached his hands forward. "I want Acks."

"Me, too, honey." Penny pushed the stroller at a faster clip until she reached the listing's driveway and came to an abrupt halt. "What are you doing?"

Axel was taping a big paper sign on the paint-flaking garage door with duct tape. "I'm staking a claim." He turned and strode toward her, allowing her to read his work.

"Future Home of Axel's Auto Repair." That had a nice ring to it, except … "You didn't make an offer through another realtor, did you?"

"No." He wrapped his arms around her and swung her through the air. "You're my real estate agent. I'm just making sure that the Penny I want to marry knows that I was serious the other day about taking steps to move forward." He set her down.

Penny was suddenly shy. "You don't blame me?"

"Not one bit."

"Acks! Acks! Pick me!" Trey twisted in his stroller, reaching for the man who'd stolen both their hearts.

"I pick you both, buddy." Axel released Penny, who landed on two feet, breathless. He turned to take Trey from the stroller. "I may still make mistakes. But I'll always choose the two of you." He settled Trey on his hip and faced Penny. "Right before I punched Brett—which was the wrong thing to do—I was thinking how much I loved you, Penny. I know I'll never quite shake the past and that feeling that I'm being judged, even when I shouldn't care. But I'm willing to step out of my comfort zone into something that isn't the exact replica of my dream."

"Back up a second." Penny found her footing. "You love me?" The question came out on a squeaky whisper.

"You and the nugget." Axel nodded. "I know you might not forgive me for decking Brett the other day, but that's the last time I step out of line." His smile wavered. "I mean, I'll try not to step out of line anymore. Because I love you, Penny. I love your optimism and your methodical way of approaching life. I love that you think about what you, me, and Trey need. I love that you think things through while I might overthink everything. I—"

"Stop talking," she commanded.

"Oh." Axel looked crestfallen.

"Stop talking so I can tell you I love you, too." She threw her arms around the two loves of her life. "I love you. I think I always have. And I want to make things better for you, now and always."

"I never knew family hugs were so wonderful," Axel murmured in her ear.

She drew back enough to glance up at him. "What does that mean?"

"File that under conversations for later." He kissed her. Briefly, because Trey was chanting, "Acks, Acks, Acks." He set her son down and turned to face the two-story property. "This is just the first step in our future." Then he stared down at her with so much warmth in those dark eyes of his that she wanted to cry.

Instead, she took his hand and Trey's. "Our future. I like the sound of that." She wasn't letting go of Axel again. "Mr. and Mrs. Alexander Martinez. And son."

"Yeah, about that …" Axel made the I-love-you gesture in sign language—first to Trey and then to Penny, which melted her heart. "Clay and Gail are making it official."

"Getting married?" Penny had no idea why Axel was telling her what she already knew.

"Yes, but that's not what I meant …" His smile was as broad as the ocean's horizon. "They're adopting me." He bussed her lips with an enthusiastic kiss. "I'm going to be a Hollister. I'm finally going to belong." He kissed her thoroughly.

And while their lips got reacquainted, Trey marched around them shouting, "I love Mommy! I love Acks! I love Maple! I love ice cream!"

Their kiss dissolved into chuckles. His arms loosened enough that she could gaze up into his deep, dark eyes while Trey continued to march and chant.

"You've always belonged, Axel." To the Hollisters. And in some way, to her. "And whether I'm called Mrs. Hollister or Mrs. Martinez … my last name doesn't matter as long as you love me."

"I do, baby. Now and forever."

Claiming the
Soldier's Heart

by Cari Lynn Webb

1

*H*e was early.

And everything was all wrong.

Van Hollister sat alone in his rental car outside his family's home in Sea Glass Bay and skipped his gaze over the slanted *For Sale* sign in the front yard then up on the empty front porch.

It was too early to knock on the front door and yell surprise. Dawn was still a good fifteen minutes away. And it was far too late to accept another assignment and disappear on his next mission overseas.

You'll come home when you're called. When it's right and it's time, you'll return.

Van's brother, Seth, had called when their father had gotten engaged over Christmas. Then Seth had informed Van that he had to be home for the June nuptials.

Now, it was June.

Their father's wedding was in one week.

Van was back. And nothing about any of it felt right.

He climbed out of the rental car, turned away from the two-story house and the only place he'd ever called home. He ached, deep down in his chest. In his core. But time was supposed to heal. And distance, too. He'd kept that for the past two years, ever since he'd said his final goodbye to his mom in the cancer ward of Sea Glass Bay's hospital.

Van picked up his pace, crossed the street and headed toward the beach. That grief only shadowed him like a sandstorm.

His feet barely sank into the cool sand when his name echoed across the shoreline. *Van!*

"Van! Over here!" The overly bright voice bounced around him again.

Van turned. Took in the more than a dozen early risers gathered less than one-hundred yards away. A tall man in a pale blue T-shirt and long board shorts held the hand of a dark-haired woman in yoga pants. The pair broke away from the group and headed toward Van. *Dad and Gail. The groom and bride-to-be.*

Van wanted to run. But the sand suddenly felt more like quicksand and anchored him firmly in place.

"Van." Gail stepped forward, lifted her arms as if to embrace Van then she reached for his hands instead. The warmth in her grip matched the warmth in her wide eyes. Her bright smile never wavered. "I told your father that was you. We're so glad you're here."

Van eased his hand free and rubbed the back of his neck. He wanted a hug from his mother. The kind that had always settled everything inside him. Even if only for a moment. He was home. Yet, his mom was gone. It had been two years. He shouldn't still hurt. Not this bad. He cleared his throat. "Flight came in earlier than expected."

"Welcome home, Son." His dad held out his hand as if he understood Van's reservations.

Sheriff Clay Hollister had offered the same handshake to a wary, scared fourteen-year-old Van the first time Van had walked into the Hollister house. Four years later, Van had left home to begin his military career and the handshakes had been traded for strong embraces full of love and emotion. The kind a father and son shared.

Van took his dad's hand and skimmed over the obligatory *it's good to be home.* "What are you guys doing out here?"

Gail wrapped her arm around his father's waist. "It's almost time for our Salute the Sun Yoga Flow class."

Van gaped at his dad. The former sheriff had always been fit thanks to daily sessions at the gym and long beach runs. "Dad, you're doing yoga now?"

"It took some convincing from Gail." Clay laughed. "But I'm here now and I like it."

Van had always considered himself an exercise traditionalist like his father. And like his dad, a woman had changed Van's mind, too.

"It took quite a lot of bargaining." Gail hugged Clay, easy and affectionate, then patted his dad's chest. "And some encouragement from Elise."

Elise. Van stilled and sank deeper into that quicksand. He scanned the group and watched an all-too-familiar woman separate from the others. The last time he'd seen Elise Harper had been on this very same beach. Except then it'd been only Van and Elise, the seagulls, and one unforgettable kiss.

"Hey Van." Elise slowed beside Gail. Her long auburn hair was secured in a ponytail, her smile was reserved, and her gaze guarded. "You're home."

From Elise, Van wanted to hear *it's good to see you*, because it was more than good to see her. He knew her auburn hair had natural streaks of red. Knew her eyes were the deepest shade of green he'd ever seen. Knew she'd left an imprint on his memories that even two years later had yet to fade. Yeah, it was really good to see her. He said, "Just got in."

"And Van is just in time for our sun salutations." Gail smiled.

"You're joining us?" Elise's eyebrows pulled together.

It wasn't all right. He could see it in her narrowed gaze. That night on the beach with Elise he'd claimed not to need holistic healing like yoga. He'd made other claims too, like their time together was nothing more than a passing moment. One he'd look back on with fondness. But seeing Elise now, his pulse picked up. Still, it was nothing he couldn't manage. After all, he was only home for now, not for good. "Yeah. Eight hours on a plane. My body could use the stretch."

"Come on then." Gail motioned toward the group. "Let's find our spot."

Van chose a spot off to the side with a straight-line view of Elise. He was grateful for the yoga session that allowed him to avoid talking. His dad was getting remarried to his late wife's best friend. And Van didn't like it. Not one bit. But he had to face it.

Van focused on Elise. On his breath. On moving from one pose to the next. And searched for his center. Nothing about being home again settled him.

Nothing, except one green-eyed woman who moved with the grace of a dancer and had a voice that curled through him and soothed every restless place inside him. She'd done the same that night on the beach, too. Two strangers had sought solace beside the ocean waves and found each other. He'd gone to the water to grieve his mom. Elise had been grieving the end of her marriage. They'd both recognized the timing was off and if they'd slept together, it would be for all the wrong reasons. So they'd simply taken comfort in each other's presence from sunset until sunrise, sharing more about themselves than they should have. Yet in the early morning hours, it wasn't regret Van had felt.

Thankfully, Van found comfort in Elise's presence now. And by the end of the class, he almost felt steady.

"Van, you looked like a professional out there." Clay ran his hands through his blond hair. The sides were only just starting to gray and only highlighted the deep wisdom inside his all-too perceptive gaze. "You could teach the class."

"How long have you been practicing?" Gail asked.

"Two years." Van looked at Elise.

Her surprised gaze searched Van's.

Yeah, Van had made a lot of claims that night with Elise and most of them had been plain wrong. He kept his gaze fixed on Elise and added, "Yoga has been something of a lifesaver."

Elise tightened her ponytail then ran her palms over her loose tank top as if putting herself back together.

"That settles it. I'm cooking a big welcome home breakfast," Gail announced and pulled out her cell phone. "I'll just text everyone. It's the perfect start to the week now that all the Hollister boys are home. Elise, you must join us, too."

"Gail's blueberry cream cheese French toast is legendary," his father said.

"I never could resist French toast." Elise's hands fluttered to her sides as if she couldn't find a ready excuse to decline. "I just need to drop the extra mats at my place and then I'll be over."

"I'll help Elise." Van gathered several blue yoga mats and waited for his dad and Gail to head back to the house.

"You don't need to carry those." Elise rolled another mat and secured the Velcro straps around it. "I can handle it."

But Van couldn't handle stepping inside his parent's house without his mom being there. Not quite yet. "You're doing me the favor."

Elise paused, then fell into step beside him. "Want to talk about it?"

She'd cut straight to the heart of things two years ago on this same stretch of beach. He'd hedged then, the same as he did now. "I don't know where to begin."

Last time she'd simply smiled and said: We have all night. How about I go first?

Elise bumped her shoulder against his, bringing Van back into the present. She chuckled. "How about you start with 'Elise, you look great. It's so good to see you again.'"

2

Van's laughter spilled around Elise like her favorite song.

He sobered and said, "Now you won't believe me if I told you that it *is* good to see you again."

Would you believe me if I told you I've thought about you every single day for the past two years? Elise blinked as if a warning light flashed, signaling a dangerous swell at the beach. Proceed with caution. She kept her focus on the sidewalk. "How have you been?"

"Good. Busy." He shifted beside her. His arm brushed against hers and her gaze slanted toward him. He ran a hand through his hair, shifting the wavy dark brown strands. "How about you?"

"Same." Except now her heart raced. And when she looked at Van, she wanted his arms around her. Wanted to feel again like she had that one night. With him. When she'd felt seen and heard and understood.

But she'd hurt the next day. And the day after and so many more. From missing him. Even though she'd had no right. They'd both known one night was all it'd ever be. They'd both known, but her heart, it seemed, hadn't listened. Van would leave again this time, too. After all, he was career military, and she knew from Gail and Clay that his work still kept him away. Good thing her heart was set on pause now.

He stopped on the sidewalk and faced her. His gaze trailed over her face, sharp and sincere. "Look, you know I can't talk about what I've been doing. I'm not being dismissive on purpose."

Elise nodded. He'd told her on the beach he was a former Green Beret and his work involved military intelligence and classified assignments. She tipped her head and eyed him. "I'm not asking what you've been doing, Van. Just how you've been since . . ."

"Since my mom passed," he finished for her. "Or since my father got engaged to Gail."

Or since our one, heart-stealing kiss. She started up the stairs to the small porch of her rental cottage before she fell into his deep brown gaze and tried to soothe the pain and hurt inside him. But he wasn't hers to soothe.

"I'm supposed to tell you that I'm good. It's great to be home." Van handed her the yoga mats. Distress wrapped around his voice and tightened his words. "And that I'm really happy for my dad and Gail. And I can't wait to celebrate their wedding this weekend."

Elise stacked the extra yoga mats behind the wicker rocker and faced him. "Are you all those things?"

He rubbed his palms together as if searching for warmth. "I want to be."

"Then what are you really feeling?" she asked. Besides lost. It was there in his gaze. In his face. And his lowered shoulders. And it called to her, urging her to reach for him. She kept her arms locked at her sides.

"Terrified," he admitted, his voice whisper soft. "Terrified to step into the house without my mom there. Terrified I'll never really be happy for Gail and my dad. Terrified I'm getting it all wrong, including right now."

She stilled. "Right now."

He nodded. "Tell me to keep my feelings to myself and deal with them on my own. That we aren't even friends. Not really. That I shouldn't burden you with my problems."

The seat of the rocker bumped against the back of her knees. Her heart bumped inside her chest.

"Tell me I'm inconsiderate. Disrespectful. That I should've texted or called you," he challenged. "Tell me that you forgot about me that very same day."

"Did you forget?" she countered.

"Not a minute. Not a second of that night." His words were a vow. A curse. A balm.

Her breath caught. She wasn't alone in her memories.

"Tell me you have a boyfriend." He moved toward her. His gaze intense, his voice urgent. "That you're head over heels in love. And that he loves you more than you ever imagined possible."

"And if I don't tell you any of that?" Elise stepped closer to him and set her palm over his heart. If she curled her fingers in his T-shirt, she could pull him to her. "Then what?"

"Then I might kiss you." He never moved. Only his gaze trailed over her face as if updating his memory. "Kiss you like I've wanted to since I walked away from you that morning two years ago. Ridiculous, isn't it?"

Not so very. Her voice sounded fragile even to her. "Why don't you?"

His eyes widened, heat flared like a bonfire then disappointment seeped in, dousing those flames. "I don't like to start things I can't finish. And you, Elise Harper, deserve to be loved for a lifetime, not a moment."

"But all we have is one week." All she really had was now. Her battle with breast cancer had taught her that lesson.

"One night wasn't enough two years ago." He brushed the backs of his knuckles across her cheek and captured a stray piece of her hair in his fingers. Regret shifted across his small smile into his words. "And I can guarantee it won't be enough now."

And she could guarantee she wouldn't get hurt this time. Her heart wasn't part of the conversation. It wasn't bruised and tender like last time. She was stronger. A cancer survivor, who lived in the present. Besides, it was a kiss, not a promise. She searched his face. But he deserved more, too. And promises from the heart she could never give him. She lowered her arm. "So what do we do?"

"We go to breakfast." He tucked her hair behind her ear and stepped back. "And we don't start things we can't finish."

"I don't want you to be right." She wanted to kiss him. Change both their minds. Prove one week was more than enough and all they'd need to finish whatever this was. Then they'd walk away in

186

seven days unscathed. But life wasn't fair and even best intentions weren't always enough. Best to leave the past in the past. She smiled at him. "Sounds like it's breakfast with an old friend then."

"Friends. I can work with that." He grinned and followed her down the porch steps. "I think we've talked enough about me. How have you been?"

Elise spread her arms wide and spun in a slow circle on the sidewalk rather than hug Van. "I'm five years cancer free."

"That's fantastic," Van said. "How did you celebrate?"

"I visited the medical team that got me through and spent time with current breast cancer patients." *Then I watched the sunset at our bench on the beach. Lifted a glass of wine to another day and to you—a good part of my past.*

"And have you set goals for the next five years?" he asked.

"Not yet," she hedged. The future wasn't something Elise ever considered. Thinking too far ahead wasn't a risk she could take. "I'm enjoying the present. And focusing on the here and the now."

"And now it looks like we're here." Van stopped on the sidewalk outside his family's home. "I'm not sure I can do this."

"I thought the same thing when I went for my first chemo treatment. Then a good friend arrived and told me: *I would take away your pain if I could. But if you need a shoulder to lean on or a hand to hold, I'll be right here beside you.*" Elise captured his hand in hers and linked their fingers together. "Now, I offer you the same."

Van studied their joined hands then his grip tightened around hers. He said, "Okay. Let's do this."

3

Van inhaled, opened the front door to his parents' house, and kept Elise's hand in his. The smell of cinnamon and vanilla filled the foyer. Laughter and happy voices bounced down the hallway like a much-anticipated invitation. Van guided Elise toward the kitchen, noting the same family pictures still hung on the walls. The same floorboards still squeaked under his feet, announcing their arrival. It was all so very familiar. The same and yet so very different. His mom wasn't humming in the kitchen while washing off the herbs she'd picked from her garden.

Instead, Gail turned from the stove and brushed her hands over a sunburst yellow apron. Her smile as wide and affectionate as his mother's had always been. Gail clapped her hands together. "You're here. I've kicked everyone out to the back porch to visit."

"Can we help with anything?" Elise asked.

"You can help by going out to the porch and visiting," Gail ordered. "It's rare to have all the Hollister men home together with no one working. We can't waste a minute of this time. Now out of the kitchen. I've got this handled."

Van's mom would've done the same to ensure her sons had as much time together as possible. It was hard not to appreciate Gail's thoughtfulness.

"I'm only here to get the honey butter for the biscuits Serena brought over." Seth stepped through the sliding glass doors, held up his hands, and grinned at Gail. His gaze landed briefly on Van and Elise's joined hands before his smile broadened. "Nice to see you, brother. And you too, Elise."

Seth's gaze drifted back to their joined hands to see if he was reconsidering letting it go. Van tightened his grip on Elise's hand and narrowed his gaze on his brother.

Gail handed Seth a ceramic butter dish and nudged him toward the sliding doors. "Let Nina know we have time for family pictures while we wait on the French toast to come out of the oven."

Van frowned. He'd only agreed to breakfast. "I should probably shower or something if we're taking pictures."

"Nonsense." Gail swiped her hand through the air. "I think informal pictures make the best portraits. Everyone is more relaxed. More like themselves."

"As long as you don't have broccoli or spinach in your teeth, it'll be fine." Seth laughed and stepped out onto the porch, then shouted, "Van's here with Elise, too. Now get your smiles ready because it's picture time."

"This should be fun." Elise tugged Van out onto the porch.

Twenty minutes later, Van's cheeks hurt, not from forcing his smile, but from his brothers and their continued antics to infuse what they dubbed *added flair* to the family pictures. Fortunately, Gail and his dad took it all in stride. Nina Thomas, Jared's girlfriend, simply continued capturing one photograph after another. Never pausing when Axel announced action shots with a football and proceeded to tackle Van in slow motion for frame-by-frame shots. Or when Seth declared it was time for everyone's funniest face. Or when Jared jumped on Axel's back and Seth on Van's for a quick game of chicken. Seth's teenage son, Matty, offered his own outlandish suggestions, earning the praise of the Hollister brothers. Even Elise and Serena, Seth's girlfriend, both grinning from the porch, called out ideas, which resulted in the brothers pulling the pair into the photographs, too. While Kimberly, Serena's teenage daughter, grabbed the camera so Nina could be included.

All in all, it was chaotic and more entertaining than Van could have imagined.

Finally, Nina lifted her camera away from her face and smiled. "That's a wrap for now. But be warned. My camera will be out all week."

Axel rubbed his stomach. "Please tell me it's time to eat. I'm starving."

The back gate opened. A blonde-haired woman and curly haired toddler walked through the backyard. Her bright smile was aimed at Axel as if he was the only one in the backyard. Penny Bell Carlson pressed a kiss on Axel's cheek. "Sorry, we're late. What did we miss?"

"You're right on time for breakfast. It's about to be served." Axel slipped his arm around her waist. "And Nina has already promised to take more family pictures with you guys later."

"Truck." The blond-haired little boy lifted his yellow toy truck toward Van and swayed in his sneakers as if finding his balance inside his excitement. "Up. Truck. Up."

Van swooped the little boy up into his arms, taking in the boy's impossibly round blue eyes, dimples, and his toy tow truck. "What do we have here?"

"Acks. Truck." The boy's blond curls bounced, his smile wobbled and widened.

"Van, this is Trey." Penny looked slightly taken aback. Axel a bit bemused. Penny shook her head. "Sorry, Trey is usually really shy and reserved with people he doesn't know, except it seems here."

"Good to see you, Penny." Van adjusted the little boy in his arms and smiled. "It's the Hollister house. It's easy to be yourself around here."

Axel reached over and ruffled Trey's curls. "This house really does seem to bring out the best in people."

Penny reached for her son. Trey curled into Van and pressed his cheek against Van's shoulder. "Stay. Here."

Penny gaped.

"We're good, Penny." More than, Van realized. His grief was still there, but the bite was less sharp. Less intense. Thanks to his brothers and now an adorable little toddler. Van headed for the long bench where Elise already sat at the patio table. He settled Trey on his lap and grinned at Penny. "Trey and I are going to talk trucks."

"Then I'll steal Elise for a minute." Penny hugged Elise as if she was a long-time friend. "We have potential studio locations to discuss and mimosas to sip while doing it."

Axel dropped onto the bench across from Van. His gaze tracked Penny around the back patio. The smile his brother shared with Penny was small and private as if Axel and Penny knew the secret to happiness. Perhaps that was it. Van hadn't ever seen his brother so content. Or relaxed. And the reason wasn't a secret. Van said, "So I like the new look, Axel."

Axel ran his hands over his T-shirt then touched his cheek as if checking for a beard. "What are you talking about?"

"Love. It looks good on you. You wear it well." Van laughed at Axel's slow grin then added the salt and pepper shaker to the bed of Trey's truck. Trey giggled and vroomed his truck around the placemat.

"You should try it yourself, Van." Seth tapped his fist against Van's shoulder then sat at the end of the table. "You might like it."

Or Van might like to remain single. With his heart intact. Love required him to trust someone else with his heart. Not ever happening. Van avoided things that were sure to cause pain and love definitely topped that list. Van's gaze landed on Elise.

She sipped her mimosa and grinned at him over the rim of the glass then walked toward him. Van's heartbeat picked up. Van acknowledged his attraction to Elise, then ordered his heart to stand down. After all, he had a short leave in Sea Glass Bay. And no time for entanglements.

Elise settled onto the bench beside him and greeted Trey.

Her hand brushed over Van's arm. Her laughter swirled inside him, tempting him to reconsider those entanglements.

Thankfully Gail appeared before Van could scoot closer to Elise and test that connection. Gail leaned between Van and Elise and set a large casserole dish on the table. "I hope you all brought your appetites."

"We won't need to eat for the rest of the day after this feast." Clay placed another casserole disk on the opposite end of the table.

Gail moved beside Clay and picked up her champagne flute. "First a toast. We're so grateful you all are here with us."

Clay took Gail's free hand and lifted his own glass. "I'd like to toast family. Whether you've been with us for years or you're new, we hope you feel our love and know that you're always welcome at our table and in our house."

"To family." Glasses lifted and clinked together around the table.

Van tapped his glass against Trey's plastic cup, then the pair shared a plate of fresh fruit and French toast. The powdered sugar snowfall Van created over the French toast earned cheers from the little boy. The conversations flowed as steadily and easily as the hot maple syrup.

Two slices of French toast remained in the casserole dish when Axel set his fork on his plate and said, "I can't eat another bite."

Jared nodded and tossed his napkin on his plate. "Me either."

Murmurs of agreement circled around the table. Clay rested his arm on Gail's chair and tapped his glass against hers. "Compliments to the chef."

"I was thrilled to cook for everyone." Gail reached for her phone. Her smile faded.

"Everything okay?" Clay asked.

"The wedding planner needs to change the rehearsal time to the morning on Friday." Gail set her phone face down on the table. Her voice lacked its usual cheer. "It shouldn't be a problem since we don't have a rehearsal dinner planned."

Axel rubbed his chin. "Shouldn't you have a rehearsal dinner?"

"Isn't that a key part of every wedding?" Jared frowned.

"It's typically the groom's responsibility." Clay's eyebrows pulled together.

"But we talked about this," Gail rushed on. "We both decided not to have too many things going on before the ceremony. That way we would just concentrate on our wedding day."

"But the boys are right." Clay's voice was earnest. "I've changed my mind. We should have a rehearsal dinner. It's supposed to be my part of the weekend."

"Meeting me at the end of the aisle on Saturday is enough." Gail squeezed Clay's arm.

Her sincerity squeezed inside Van. He ignored it. And could've sworn he heard his mom's quiet laughter. *Van, my son, you could move mountains with your stubbornness alone.*

Elise tapped her knee against Van's leg and lifted her eyebrows at Van. Then she whispered, "You should do it for them."

That wasn't happening. Van quickly gathered the empty plates closest to him and stacked them. Then he transferred Trey to Axel, picked up the plate stack and escaped inside. Elise never missed a beat and trailed after him, carrying more dirty dishes. They stood side by side at the farm-style kitchen sink where Van had often found his mom, who'd claimed that spot gave her the best view of her garden. He stared out the window now and noted the lack of weeds in the growing garden and the rose bushes—his mom's favorite—in full bloom. As if his mother still tended to her backyard oasis. Still something about the vibrant plants soothed him as if in those plants his mom lived on. "I can't give Gail and my dad a rehearsal dinner."

"But your dad and Gail want one." Elise shifted toward him. "A rehearsal dinner is an important part of the wedding weekend."

Yet Van wasn't certain he even wanted to take part in the wedding weekend. He'd shown up like his brother had ordered. But no one could make him participate.

"Elise is right." Seth carried a casserole dish into the kitchen and set it on the island. "They need a rehearsal dinner."

"It would mean a lot to Gail and Dad." Jared walked inside, pulled a pitcher from the refrigerator, and refilled several mimosa flutes.

"And Van, if you took the lead on the rehearsal dinner, it would show them both that they have your support." Seth tore a piece off the praline monkey bread and eyed Van. His challenge clear in his steady gaze.

Van leaned against the counter and stared at his brother. Seth had already been living at the Hollister's when Van had moved in. Seth had looked Van in the eye and then warned him not to mess things up, or else. Of course, Van had challenged Seth on the details of the *or else*. Seth had not backed down or minced words. In an instant, Van had discovered he liked Seth and a bond had been formed. Always frank with each other, Van said, "But I don't support the wedding."

Elise scrambled to close the sliding glass doors to the porch and frowned at Van. "You don't really mean that, do you?"

Van lifted one shoulder and crossed his arms over his chest.

"Van means it right now." Seth popped the bite of bread into his mouth and chewed. Then he grinned at Elise and added, "Van just needs time. Our brother has always needed extra time to assess a situation, collect facts, and gather evidence."

Nothing wrong with that particular tactic. It served him well in his line of work.

"Then it's all the more reason for Van to put together the rehearsal dinner." Elise crossed over to Van and touched his arm. "One week with Gail and your dad and you'll understand they're really good together."

Like we are. Van stepped away from Elise. He should've walked away this morning at the beach. Not gotten any closer to Elise. Because the closer she was, the more Van realized it wasn't enough. He wanted to hold her. Make her proud of him. Prove he was someone she could …. Van squeezed the back of his neck and pinched off that thought. He'd returned as requested. He wasn't there for anything else.

He turned and looked at his brothers. "Fine. I'll organize the rehearsal dinner." He held up his hands to stop their comments. "And I'm not doing it because I approve of the marriage. I'm only doing it because it's the right thing to do."

Seth glanced at Elise and raised his eyebrows. "He'll come around eventually."

"Come on then." Jared opened the porch doors. "Let's go tell everyone."

Elise grabbed Van's hand and squeezed. "I'll help too. Whatever you need."

He needed to remember she wasn't his. Wasn't ever going to be his. He needed to let go of her hand and remember all the reasons he wasn't built for love. "Thanks, but I should be good. It's just a dinner."

Gail pressed her hands to her cheeks and hugged Clay before Elise could respond. Then Clay hugged Van. "Thank you, Son."

Son. The one word full of emotion sank deep inside Van and pushed against his guilt. Van knew Clay was disappointed Van hadn't returned for his mom's funeral, even though Van had his reasons. And a direct order from his mom not to come back. Now, Van fought to support his father's second marriage. And it was one more reason he wasn't a very good son. Van wanted his father to be proud of him, yet he had no idea how to do that. So he simply returned his dad's hug.

The kitchen put to rights and a flag football game complete, Van walked Elise out.

She turned on the porch and stepped into Van's arms. "It's good to see you, Van."

"You too." Van wrapped his arms around her waist and pulled her close. Closer than a friend. Closer than he ever let anyone. One beat. Then another. With Elise in his arms, everything felt right. Except that was all wrong. Van released her, retreated a step, and clasped his hands behind his back.

Elise skipped down the stairs, waved one last time from the sidewalk and then walked away.

Van watched her until she disappeared around the curve in the street. Then he vowed to keep his hands and his heart to himself for the next seven days. How hard could that be?

4

The next afternoon, Elise stepped outside the commercial building nestled between the Bouncing Cherry Boutique and the bookstore, Bookmarked at the Bay.

"I'm telling you, Elise. This unit is ideal for a yoga studio." Penny locked up the front door of the vacant unit. "And you can't beat the location here in downtown either."

Elise held onto her smile. But her own studio had only ever been a dream. One she'd dared not imagine becoming real.

Penny spun around and waved. Her gaze fixed over Elise's shoulder. "Hey Van."

Elise turned. Van crossed the street toward them. He looked better than he had yesterday. More rested. Less lost. His gaze landed on Elise and stuck. His smile warmed her from the inside out. She collected the feeling and the moment, and recognized Van was one more thing that would only ever be temporary. Then reminded herself that remaining in the present was the safest place for her. Because futures with yoga studios and men like Van weren't for cancer survivors on borrowed time like her.

"This is great. Now Elise, you can talk things over with Van." Penny pointed at Van and arched her eyebrows. "And Van, you can tell Elise that she needs a yoga studio. If not for herself, then for all her clients, the current ones and the ones she'll get when she opens her own studio."

"I promise I'll consider it and get back to you." It would still be a no. Elise adjusted her purse on her shoulder and her disappointment. But it was better this way.

"Perfect." Penny pulled out her cell phone. "I'll call the landlord now and see about negotiating the rent lower. Talk soon."

Phone pressed to her ear, Penny hurried down the sidewalk, without the slightest wobble in her high heels. As for Elise, everything inside her wobbled. Penny presented a space, a business plan, and a five-year commitment. Elise's head spun even more.

"Your own yoga studio. That's impressive." Van peered in the front window. "Looks like it has good natural light."

"Yeah." Elise started walking. No destination in mind. She just needed to move. Work the apprehension and the temptation out of her limbs. "It's better than I could've hoped." Not that she subscribed to hope much these days. Still ... her own studio would be amazing.

"And the size?" Van caught up to her. "Enough room for your classes?"

"More than enough." Elise tucked her hands into the pockets of her sundress. If she closed her eyes, she could picture the entire space from the front mirrored wall to the open shelving for guests and the river rock water fountain in the reception area. The back wall would be a living wall she'd create with help from her friend, Leah Martin, the owner of the Flower Girl Shop. The space would be clean with earth tones. Inspiring and inviting. A place people would want to come back to again and again.

"What's wrong with the space?" Van's question disrupted her vision.

"Nothing." The unease was there in her voice. She'd need to soundproof and sand the floors, but she knew Sully Vaughn, Sea Glass Bay's resident handyman and jack-of-all-trades, would offer her a good deal. "There's nothing wrong with the space."

"Then what's the problem?" He slowed on the sidewalk and looked at her. "A yoga studio sounds like the next step."

"The owner wants a five-year commitment on the lease," Elise said.

Van nodded. "You're worried you might outgrow the space."

"Something like that." His ready confidence in her success warmed and touched her.

Yet it was her own future, not the building, that stirred a disquiet inside Elise. And making a long-term commitment of any kind quite frankly scared her. She'd beaten cancer once. There was no guarantee it wouldn't return. It was best if she lived in the present. One day at a time. Never thinking too far ahead and keeping her dreams—and her heart—on pause.

Elise started walking again, but that restless feeling trailed her. She reached for a distraction rather than the comfort of Van's hand. She asked, "How are the plans for the rehearsal dinner coming along?"

"I've got two locations, Tank's Bar and Grille and Lollapa-Pizza," Van said.

"Lollapa-Pizza," Elise repeated. "Besides, the bachelor party was held at Tank's."

"It was one of my parent's favorite places," Van said, considering. "My mom always ordered their white sauce pizza with the fresh mushroom medley and prosciutto."

Elise set her hand on Van's arm and tugged him toward the alley that offered a shortcut to the pier. She kept her voice neutral. "But it's not about your mom this time around."

"But it's supposed to be." Van curved his fingers around hers and stopped in the alley. "It was always supposed to be about my mom."

She ached for his pain and his loss. Her parents lived in Oregon, too far to see often, but she spoke to her mom almost every day. She'd be lost without them. "I know. And I'm so sorry."

His grip tightened. "Now you're going to tell me that I have to let go, my mother is gone, and I need to move on like everyone else."

Elise reached up and set her other palm against his cheek. "You loved your mom, Van. You don't ever move on from missing someone you loved like that." And if she loved Van like that, she knew she'd never move on either.

"What do you do then?" His clear, grave gaze searched her face as if she was the answer.

"You hold that love in here." She lowered her hand, pressed her palm over his heart. "Remember the good and gain strength from the memories. And you honor your mom by living the life she always wanted for you."

"Mom always told me: *Breath deep, Van. Always smile.*" A tenderness smoothed across his face. "Then she'd hug me and add, *I promise it'll be worth it, but you have to make the choice. Always choose joy with a heaped serving of laughter.*"

"I like that," Elise said. "So what are you going to choose?"

"Not pizza." His smile was wry.

She squeezed his hand then pulled out her cell phone and dialed Rigatoni's. The receptionist at the Italian restaurant confirmed what she'd already guessed. "They're fully booked Friday night."

Van rubbed his chin. "There's still Tank's Bar and Grille. They do serve the best lime and chili grilled fish tacos."

"One of my favorites," Elise said.

"But it's not *your* rehearsal dinner." Laughter wrapped around Van's dry words. "Yes, I'm paying attention."

"Right." Elise chuckled then considered him. "I have a client who might be able to help us."

"Us," Van said.

"Unless you'd rather plan this on your own." Elise arched an eyebrow at him.

"I choose you and any help you're willing to give me," Van said, simply and sincerely.

I'd choose you too. If she could. If she could risk her heart and bet on a future. And not have her love become a burden. She edged away from Van and concentrated on her phone. "Let me make that call and see what kind of help I have to offer."

When it came to her heart, there was nothing more she could offer.

5

"Welcome to Seven Sea Horse Bed and Breakfast." The B&B owner, Stella Sanders, stood all of five feet and hugged with the strength of a linebacker. She motioned Elise and Van inside. "Come in. Come in. I've got mint green tea smoothies mixed up and sour cream cherry scones fresh out of the oven. They're my secret energy refueling combination on my day off."

Van stood inside the opulent foyer with a massive curved staircase and peered into an equally stunning library straight from an English country house manor. The rich-wood built-ins filled with books climbed to the top of the double height room and wooden ladders offered assistance to those searching the highest shelves. Across the foyer, vintage loveseats and antique settees waited near a grand marble fireplace for guests to relax. Stella guided them through the first floor. If the front of the house was a nod to the home's history, the kitchen and back half were a celebration of all things modern.

The stainless-steel commercial appliances in the chef's kitchen gleamed, and the dining room tables, already fully set for a meal in the all-glass sunroom, only required guests. Van imagined a guest would need more than one day to explore the house and property fully. Van said, "I hope we aren't interrupting your day off."

"Not at all." Stella waved her hand. The dozen or so silver bangles on her arm moved in a slow, graceful slide, matching the melodic rhythm in her voice. "Elise is responsible for my inner peace. We've been on quite the journey together, haven't we, dear?"

"Stella was my first client here in Sea Glass Bay," Elise explained. She took two tall glasses from a kitchen cabinet. "I stayed here for almost six months when I first arrived in town."

That explained Elise's ease and comfort inside the house. She moved as if she belonged there.

"And we haven't missed our weekly sessions in all that time." Stella speared her arms to the sides. "Together, we've transformed this house and ourselves."

"Stella is personally responsible for referring most of my clients to me," Elise said. "I'm forever grateful to her."

"And me to her." There was a protective glint in Stella's bold gaze.

"I'll get the smoothies and the scones." Elise opened the refrigerator and pulled out a pitcher. "Stella, show Van the backyard. It's really quite romantic."

Stella linked her arm around Van's and escorted him out onto a large-covered patio. There was a full-sized L-shaped couch near an outdoor fireplace and several round tables for more private seating. The backyard opened into lush green grass that gave way to an ocean view. Stella pointed to the path that led to an infinity edge pool and another one that led to a garden maze. Then she motioned to one of the glass-topped tables. "Let's sit and you can tell me about yourself."

It wasn't a request. Van pulled out a chair for Stella then sat across from her. "I'm former Sheriff Hollister's son."

"I know Clay and Gail quite well." Stella slipped on a pair of rhinestone studded eyeglasses as if she wanted to observe Van closer. "And I was fortunate to meet Leda before she passed. A wonderful, giving woman who touched everyone she encountered, including me."

"I still miss her as much as I did two years ago." Van blinked, surprised at his own admission, and struggled not to cross his arms over his chest. The eccentric, but charming Stella Sanders would get nothing more personal from him.

"The deeper the grief, the stronger the love." Stella reached across the table and set her hand on top of Van's clenched ones. "Honor the grief but don't forget to live in all the love Leda left behind. That's where you'll find your own peace."

Van wasn't certain he'd ever known peace. At least not the kind Stella referenced. He'd experienced moments over the years. With the Hollister's and his brothers. And then again with Elise. But the feeling never lasted. He'd accepted that the same as he'd accepted the inevitable shuffling from one foster family to another growing up. "These days I find my work brings me a certain peace of mind."

Elise carried a tray over to the table and smiled. "Van is military intelligence, Stella. He makes the world safer for those of us living in it."

"That's admirable." Stella handed Van a tall glass from the tray. "But while you're looking out for us, who is looking out for you?"

"I have a team." Van stirred the straw around in the glass. "Remarkable women and men who share the same dedication and focus as me."

"And your heart." Stella pressed her palm over her chest. "Who's protecting that?"

I am. Like always. Van cleared his throat and sipped the smoothie.

"You'll have to excuse Stella." Elise sat in the chair beside Van. The frustration threading through her words was dulled by her amusement. "Stella believes everything centers around a love story, even though I've tried to convince her otherwise."

"Love is the core." Stella's sage grin reached into her sparkling gray eyes. Her eyebrows arched over her eyeglass frames. "After all, love is why you are here right now."

Van curved his fingers around his glass and regarded Stella. Ready to match his pragmatic side against her romantic flair. "I'm not sure how love changes the fact that we don't have a location for the rehearsal dinner this Friday night." Better to cut to the chase, to curtail more explorations of his heart.

"I have the location. Right here." Stella announced, waved her arm toward the lush grounds then tipped her head at Van. "But what I don't have is the love story."

"Is that a requirement?" Van asked.

"Absolutely." Stella's voice was firm. "The rehearsal dinner is a celebration of the couple and their love connection. What is Gail and Clay's love story?"

Van had no idea. In truth he hadn't wanted to learn it. Hadn't wanted to ask any details about his dad's relationship with his mom's best friend. As if even asking was some kind of betrayal to his mom's memory. "I know that Gail has always been around."

"Now, she's your dad's fiancée and this moment is about them." Stella regarded Van, her voice considerate and gentle as if she understood his struggle. "How do we properly celebrate them if we don't know Gail and Clay as a couple?"

"I thought the rehearsal dinner was just that." Van scratched the back of his head. "A simple dinner with close friends and family the night before the wedding."

Elise nodded beside him.

"It's also a chance for you as the host to show the couple what they mean to you." Stella touched a diamond and opal ring on her finger. "To make it personal and meaningful."

Van studied Stella. "And if we make it meaningful, can we host the dinner here?"

"Of course." Stella lifted her smoothie glass in a toast as if they'd completed an important business deal. "Once you know their story, we'll have a theme, and we can create the menu and the entire evening around that."

"Well, here's to a good love story then." Elise lifted her glass and tapped it against Stella's.

Van joined the toast and searched for his smile.

He considered making a story up, then discarded the idea. Stella most likely already knew Gail and Clay's story. And for some reason, the bed and breakfast owner wanted Van to learn it, too. So be it. He'd get the story to appease Stella and host the rehearsal dinner.

After all, it wasn't like a first date story about his dad and Gail would change his mind about the wedding. He didn't want his dad to move on. Wasn't ready for his mom to be nothing more than a memory. And he wasn't about to apologize for that, even if it was a love story for the ages.

6

The next morning, Van and Elise stood inside the Wide Awake Café. Van had joined Elise's sunrise yoga flow class and they'd decided on breakfast at the café. He waited for their order and watched his brother, his sheriff's hat pulled low on his head, walk inside. Serena, the owner of the café, greeted Seth with a kiss and large coffee. Seth's mood instantly lifted, and he joined Van and Elise near the pick-up counter.

"We have a location for the rehearsal dinner. It's going to be at the Seven Sea Horse Bed and Breakfast." Van accepted an iced-coffee and straw from Serena. "Now we need a theme."

"Why can't it be just a dinner?" Seth pushed the rim of his hat up on his forehead and eyed Van.

"That's what I said, too." Van shook his head. "But Stella request-ed that we personalize it for Gail and Dad."

Serena leaned on the counter. "What about a photo board? Like a montage. I saw that once in a magazine with the pictures attached to a strand of lights."

"We could ask Nina for help," Elise suggested.

"But it's still not a theme." Van frowned.

"What about recreating their first date," Serena suggested.

"That's good." Seth grinned and kissed Serena again.

Van nodded. "What was their first date?"

204

"Not sure." Seth rubbed his cheek. His eyes narrowed. "They did a whole bunch of things together around town. One day they were friends and the next day they were Dad and Gail, the couple."

"This isn't helping." Van stared at his brother.

"It's all I've got." Seth checked his phone. "And now I'm needed at the station." He paused at the doors to the café and glanced at Van. "You know, all you have to do is ask Gail and Dad. I'm sure they'd love to share their first date story with you."

But Van wasn't certain he'd love to hear it.

Elise picked up her breakfast wrap from the counter and grinned at Van. "Seth is right. You need to ask them."

"Want to come with me?" Van held the café door open for her.

"I'd like to, but I have private sessions booked until this afternoon." Elise smiled and touched his arm as if she understood his hesitation. "Text me later and we can grab takeout from Tank's, take it to the beach to watch the sunset and you can share what you learned."

"Will do." He would rather just head to the beach. Skip right to an evening alone with Elise. But he wasn't building his own love story. He was leaving after the wedding and returning to his life. What could he really offer Elise aside from sporadic visits and unnecessary worry? He was better alone.

Ten minutes later, Van ran into Gail on the front porch of his parents' house.

Gail closed the door and smiled. "Van, you're just in time. You can join your father and me. We're going to look at houses."

Van worked indifference around his words. "I have some emails from work to catch up on."

"You're supposed to be on leave." Gail arched an eyebrow at him. "Unfortunately, you can't stay here. A realtor is showing the house to potential buyers in ten minutes, and we need to be out. First, we need to get your dad. He brought an extra tent down to the beach for the kids' camp this afternoon."

Van definitely wasn't interested in watching strangers traipse through their house. He didn't want to discover that what he saw as charming quirks about the older house, they found off-putting. There was something special about the house that he knew strangers would never understand. And something no matter where he'd traveled too, he hadn't discovered again. Van followed Gail off the porch.

"This will be good." Gail slipped on a pair of sunglasses. "You might be able to help us decide what kind of home we should get."

Van knew a perfectly good one. It was behind them. "What are the options?"

"Your dad wants one of those townhomes on the cliffs." Gail frowned.

Van had seen the brand-new townhomes on his drive into Sea Glass Bay. "And you don't?"

"Don't get me wrong." Gail's hands fluttered in front of her as if she scrambled for a suitable argument. "The views look spectacular. But I'm worried there won't be enough space for everyone."

Confusion eased into Van's words. "But we don't live at home anymore."

"I promised your mom, Van." Gail paused on the sidewalk and turned toward him. Her voice was earnest and tinged with sadness. "I promised to help keep the family traditions going. That includes the weekly family dinners. I won't have enough room in a townhouse for all of you. It just doesn't feel right."

He hadn't considered that Gail had made promises to his mom, too—heartfelt ones from the sound of it. Even more, ones from the resolve on her face she fully intended to keep. He wasn't the only one who'd still suffered from the loss of Leda Hollister. Van cleared his throat. "What does Dad say?"

"That we can host outside." Gail waved her hands as if shaking off her frustration and started walking again. "But what happens when it rains? Family dinners. Holiday gatherings. Those are weatherproof, Van."

Van smiled at his mom's often used term. *Family always gathers together, Van. Rain or shine. No excuse.* And from the time Van had moved in, Gail had been a part of those gatherings and their family. "Why are you selling the Hollister house?"

"That's been quite the debate." Gail shook her head. Amusement skimmed over her words. "It comes down to us not being as young as we think we are."

Van considered her explanation. It wasn't about simply moving on, starting a new chapter, and leaving his mother's memories behind as if Leda hadn't mattered. Something inside Van softened and loosened that tight knot of grief he'd been carrying around.

"It's a large house with even more land to take care of," Gail added. "It's a five-bedroom house better suited for a young family to fill and add their own memories to. It's ready for the next generation."

Van wanted to argue. Wanted to convince them not to sell the house. But it wasn't as if he was going to be there to help with the upkeep and maintenance. He understood the inevitable aging that would come. And if he was honest, he wanted both his dad and Gail around well into their golden years. Finally, he said, "I get it."

"I know it'll be hard to let go, but we'll do it together. As a family." Gail turned and waved to Clay on the beach then shouted, "I've brought reinforcements."

Clay jogged over to them, kissed Gail softly and considered Van.

"Van agrees with me," Gail rushed on. "Van thinks we need a house, not a condo or townhouse."

"I'm neutral." Van backed up a pace. "But I can tell you that the Hollister's do like their space. We like to spread out."

"Well, we're visiting all kinds of places today." Clay wiped his hand across his forehead. "And I bet I can sway my son to my side."

Gail never hesitated and held out her hand. "I'll take that bet. When Van chooses the house I like, I get the extra bedroom for a craft room."

Van opened his mouth.

"And if my son picks out a bedroom in the townhouse, then I get to turn the extra room into a man cave complete with the largest big screen TV we can find." Clay smiled at Gail and shook her hand.

"Deal," Gail declared.

"I'm just along for the ride," Van interjected. "I'll keep my opinions to myself."

"Haven't known a Hollister who could ever do that." Clay laughed. "Guess there's a first time for everything."

"Let's get house hunting." Gail linked one arm around Clay's and the other around Van's. "Today is going to be an adventure. I can feel it already."

Four houses, three townhouses and one condominium crossed off the list, the slightly defeated trio stopped at the Deep Sea

Diner for what Gail called a late lunch and ice cream pick-me-up. Their real estate agent had returned to his office to refine their property search.

"Don't worry." Clay rubbed Gail's arm. "We'll find something that fits our budget without draining our entire retirement accounts. And something that doesn't need to be bulldozed to the foundation and completely rebuilt."

"What about the condominium with more cockroaches than mold?" Gail shuddered.

Van chuckled. "That was bad, but that last place was awkward with all the random stairs and doors leading no place."

"And it was ugly." Gail frowned when both Clay and Van burst out laughing. She pointed her finger at Clay. "I'm not hosting our family in an ugly house, Clay. And the energy was bad in there, too."

"Agreed." Clay dropped the maraschino cherry from his chocolate cookie and cream shake onto Gail's strawberry shake. Then he picked up her hand and kissed the backs of her fingers. "We will find a place we want to call our home. I promise."

The tenderness in his dad's gaze and the love in the simple, casual gesture was difficult to ignore. Even more difficult to deny. Van blurted, "Dad, where was your first date with Gail?"

Clay tucked Gail's hand in his and regarded Van. Amusement curved around his words. "Are you looking for date ideas for you and Elise, Son?"

No. He was looking for a love story.

"Oh. That's sweet." Gail beamed at Van. "There's a new dance class being offered by the community center. It's at night under the stars on the pier. You could take Elise there."

Van couldn't take Elise dancing on the pier, even if it sounded slightly appealing. Because Elise and he weren't dating. And he didn't even know if Elise liked dancing. Or what her idea of an ideal first date would be. Not that he intended to ask her out. He dipped a French fry in his ketchup and concentrated on his dad. "I was just curious about you guys. I never asked before."

"Our first date was an impromptu bike ride and picnic," Gail said.

Clay frowned at her. "Our first date was movie night on the beach."

Van gaped at the pair. "You don't know what your first date was?"

"It's all in how you look at it." Gail chuckled.

"Is it?" Clay asked. "The movie marathon on the beach was the first time I officially asked you out. And the first time we shared a kiss."

Gail blushed.

Van had already shared a kiss with Elise. Would she consider that their first date?

"One afternoon, I talked your dad into renting bikes and riding out on the trails to find the perfect, undiscovered picnic spot." Gail wiped a napkin across her mouth but failed to cover her wide smile.

"It was a disaster." Clay shook his head. His soft laughter spilled over the table. "My pants got caught in the bike chain, ripped and the chain fell off. Then the picnic basket slipped off and spilled all over the trail. And finally, a pop-up rainstorm soaked us."

"And it was the day I fell head over heels for your dad." Gail set her head on Clay's shoulder. "He held the picnic blanket over my head to keep me from getting wet while he got drenched. Then he gave me the fresh berries and the only part of our lunch not covered in mud and dirt."

His father had always been thoughtful and considerate—Clay Hollister was a good man. And Van always strived to be more like his dad. Van opened himself up to the conversation and grinned. "Well, Dad, when did you fall for Gail?"

"I should tell you it was that first date on the beach under the stars because that's the romantic version." Clay slanted his warm gaze at Gail. "But it was really on that bike ride when Gail put my bike chain back on. She never complained or teased me. Just fixed the bike, kissed my cheek, and reminded me to enjoy the ride, even the bumpy parts."

Van sat back in the booth. *Choose joy, Van.* There was so much joy between his dad and Gail. And Van realized for him, too, in being back in Sea Glass Bay. With his family.

"So there you have it, Van." Gail straightened and picked up her club sandwich. "We have our first date, which shouldn't be confused with when we first fell for each other."

"It's a story of first dates and first falls," Clay added. "But it was worth it since it all led here."

"And where is that?" Van asked.

"To something I never imagined possible after your mom passed." Clay's voice was pensive. Happiness and gratitude swirled through his gaze and drifted into his surprised smile. "A second chance at love."

And Van realized his dad deserved that and so much more. "I'm happy for you both."

Clay tipped his milkshake glass at Van. "Well, I'm pleased to see you with Elise."

"We're only friends," Van countered and attempted to extinguish that gleam of speculation in his dad and Gail's gazes.

"That's all your dad and I were, too." Gail chuckled.

"Until our hearts changed the rules," Clay added. "And we had no choice but to fall."

Van's heart wasn't changing. And he definitely wasn't falling. Not in love. And not for Elise. He had the love story he'd come for. That was more than enough. He glanced out the window and grinned. "Looks like your realtor is coming back already. Time to continue that house hunt."

7

Elise stretched her legs out on the beach blanket Van had brought with him and watched the sun sink into the ocean. She was relaxed. And the most content she'd been in a long while. Work had been good, but her company right now was even better. "I could watch the sunset right here every night and not ever get bored or tired of it."

"I'd be right here with you." Van finished his fish taco from Tank's and then added, "There's something about a sunset on the beach."

There was something about sitting with Van at the beach. At his family's house. Something that tempted her to let her mind wander beyond the moment. That tempted her to consider something unnervingly close to a future. With Van.

Elise brushed the extra salt from a tortilla chip. If only her growing feelings were as easily brushed aside. But her heart was supposed to be set on pause "So Stella liked the idea of recreating Gail and Clay's first dates for the rehearsal dinner."

"She already texted me the backyard picnic menu with my grocery list." Van glanced at his phone and chuckled. "And the supply list for the décor just came through now. I know what I'll be doing the next few days."

"I saw Nina at my afternoon class," Elise said. "She agreed to help with the photo montage."

"Sounds like it's all coming together," Van said. "I owe you for calling Stella."

"I was happy to help," Elise said. "And now that the rehearsal dinner is taken care of, I want to know about your most memorable first date?"

Van's squinted and his lips flattened together. "Do first date fails count?"

"I don't see why not." Elise had a few of those herself. "What's one of your worst?"

"I asked Tori Schultz out on a first date after we met at a friend's BBQ. I let her pick what we did. It was close to Christmas. She wanted to ice skate. I agreed then carried a Christmas tree home for her and helped her decorate her entire place." He paused and picked up a tortilla chip.

"That sounds more romantic than awful." Elise had dragged her Christmas trees into her rental cottage alone the past few years. She liked her single life, but there were times sharing moments with someone would be nice.

"It wasn't bad." Van reached for another chip. "At least I thought we had a good time. Until I got home that night, and Tori texted to tell me that she'd just gotten back together with her ex-boyfriend."

Elise's mouth dropped open. "I hope she got coal in her stocking from Santa."

"It's all fair in the dating game world." Van laughed. "How about your first date fail?"

"I met a guy, Derrick Landry, on one of those dating apps," Elise said.

Van groaned beside her. "Say no more."

"My friends and Stella talked me into it." Elise shook her head. "I chose to meet him at Rigatoni's. My friend, Mandy Witt, is a client and a bartender there."

"Good choice." Van nodded. "Always appropriate to have a back-up in place."

"Well, we sat at the bar, and I introduced Derrick to Mandy." Elise dunked a chip in the guacamole. "But we never made it to dinner. I got sick and had to leave. And Derrick ended up leaving with Mandy when she got off work that night."

"He didn't take you home?" Irritation shifted across Van's face. "Make sure you were all right?"

Elise set her hand on his arm, appreciating his anger on her behalf. "It wasn't his fault. I'd already called a cab because I was terrified of throwing up in his new car. It was like two days old at that point."

"He should've insisted," Van argued. "You're more important than some polished leather."

And Elise fell just a little bit more for her soldier. "It doesn't matter. Mandy and Derrick were meant to be. I was a bridesmaid in their wedding this past February."

"So they stole your happy ending." Van arched an eyebrow at her.

"We wouldn't have worked," Elise said. "He's too much like my ex."

"How's that?"

"Derrick and my ex like new, fancy things. Trips to five-star private European resorts and constantly being on the go," Elise explained. "They're both good at their jobs, successful and can afford it."

"What do you like?" Van watched her.

You. "Takeout on the beach. Midnight strolls," Elise said. "Drinking from the wine bottle, not a crystal glass."

Van smiled. "Sounds perfect."

It had been that one night with him on the same beach they sat on now. "So do you date now?"

"It's hard to find the time. There's a lot of travel in my job and it can be unpredictable." He stared out at the ocean. "I haven't met anyone willing to be that flexible and understanding."

Then he hadn't been looking in the right place. Not that she wanted him to look at her. But if she loved him, she'd take the moments he could give her. Cherish them like precious jewels. Too bad her heart was on lockdown.

He glanced at her. "What about your current dating status?"

"I find I don't have much inclination lately." At least not until Van came home. Elise slid a tortilla chip in the guacamole dip and added, "I had the husband and the marriage once before. I'm not looking for a do-over."

Van brushed his hands together and leaned his arms on his raised knees. "But did you have love?"

213

"In the beginning," she admitted. "Then came the diagnosis no one expects or wants. He stayed with me through it all. But we were different people at the end, and we wanted different things. We'd changed."

Van slanted his gaze toward Elise and asked, "Isn't love supposed to sustain through all that, including the growing and changing?"

"I suppose it does if it's the right kind," Elise said.

"How do you know if you have that?" His voice barely lifted above the crash of the waves on the shore.

It feels like now. With you. Elise scooped a piece of ice out of her drink cup and popped it in her suddenly too-dry throat. She added two more ice pieces before she located her voice. "I'm probably not the person to ask."

"That makes two of us. Love and I prefer to keep our distance from each other." Van straightened as if pulling himself away from that confession and out of the conversation. A slow grin tipped one corner of his mouth into his cheek and captured her full attention.

And Elise suddenly didn't want to keep her distance from Van.

"You are, however, the person to ask about this last taco." His grin broadened into a teeth-revealing smile. "Do you want it?"

Elise's deep laughter filled her long exhale. "Help yourself."

As for Elise, she helped herself to more guacamole and reset the pause button on her heart. After all, it was one sunset on the beach with a friend, not the start of something more.

8

*V*an walked through the backyard of the Seven Sea Horse Bed and Breakfast and marveled at the transformation. A half-dozen picnic blankets, each with its own picnic basket covered the lawn in the front of the outdoor movie screen. Fairy lights framed the entire area, adding a soft glow. Even the bikes had been bedazzled in white—one marked for the groom, one for the bride. Van and Axel had added cans they'd attached with strings to the bikes.

The past two days Van had spent scouring stores along the coast for everything to recreate Gail and his dad's first date experience had been worth it. And he had his family to thank for helping him pull it all together that afternoon.

Now, it was less than twenty minutes until Gail and his dad were set to arrive. Stella and Serena were in the kitchen finalizing the last of the food preparation. Nina and Jared turned on the string lights for the photo montage they'd hung and high-fived.

Serena and Seth strode into the backyard, each carrying large shopping bags.

Seth handed his bags to Van. "I have got to tell you, these pillows are made for a pillow fight."

"They're for lounging and cuddling, not fighting." Serena laughed and dropped her bag beside Van's feet. "We still have more to get from the car."

"I'll get the rest." Seth grinned and raised both eyebrows. "But just so we are all clear, if Axel or Jared start a pillow fight tonight, I'm honor bound to join in."

Serena gave Seth a playful shove and spun when Axel and Penny arrived, carrying more pillows.

Axel tossed a plastic wrapped pillow at Seth. "You know what these are good for?"

"Don't say it." Serena held up her hands. "This is a rehearsal dinner, not a children's sleepover."

Axel aimed his half-grin at Serena and shrugged. "I don't know what you're talking about. I was going to say these pillows will be great for movie watching tonight."

Serena laughed and shook her head then pointed at Seth and Axel. "Come on, you two. We have more pillows in the car."

Penny spun around when Elise called her name from across the yard. Van adjusted one of the blankets and watched Elise walk toward them. She wore a flowy sky-blue sundress that floated around her knees. Her hair fell in soft waves down her back. Van wasn't certain she'd ever looked prettier. Except last night, her face framed by the setting sun—he'd been captivated then, too. There was something about her that drew Van to her. Something that made his heart sigh. Something that settled a sense of happiness into his very core. The more time he spent with her, the more he wondered how he was ever going to let her go.

But there was time enough to deal with all that another night. They had the evening together and he intended to make the most of it. Van grinned and picked up one of the new pillows. Penny's stern voice pulled his attention back to the two women.

"No. Don't say it. I don't want to hear it. Today is about celebrating." Penny set her hands on Elise's shoulders and shook her head. "You're going to meet me at my office Monday morning and we'll discuss things then."

Van edged closer, yet the evening breeze swept Elise's response out toward the ocean. Penny and Elise shared a quick hug before Penny walked over to greet Nina and Jared.

Van concentrated on pulling the tags off the new pillows. "What doesn't Penny want to hear?"

"That I'm not signing the lease on the rental space." Elise removed two pillows from one of the shopping bags, took off the plastic wrapping and avoided looking at him.

"Why not?" Van watched her. "I thought it was almost perfect."

"It is." She arranged the fluffy colorful pillows on the nearest blanket. Her movements were relaxed.

Yet he caught the faintest hint of regret and longing in her voice. Van stepped closer to her. "What's the problem then?"

She stilled. Her words dipped toward whisper soft. "It's nothing." But her fingers trembled against the bold purple pillow.

Van touched her shoulder. "It doesn't sound like nothing."

"I can't sign a five-year lease." She rose, faced him, and crossed her arms over her chest.

Van searched her face. Noted the disquiet in her gaze. And the distance. He hated that. "Have you asked Penny about a three-year lease?"

"I can't sign any lease." Her words were firm. Unyielding.

That distance between them spread even though neither one had moved. "Why not?"

"It's nothing." Elise grabbed another pillow, shook her head then cleared her throat. "We should finish setting up. Everyone will be here soon."

Van didn't care about the others. He cared about Elise and the distress slashing across her face. He stepped in front of her, set his hand on the pillow she hugged against her chest and captured her attention. "Elise, you're upset. It's not nothing."

Her gaze drifted over his shoulder. Her bottom lip trembled.

Concern pooled inside Van like high tide flooding the reef. He wanted to reach for her, pull her into his embrace, but was worried she'd bolt. Her shoulders were too stiff. Her stance slightly askew. He worked a calm he wasn't feeling into his voice. "Elise, what's going on?"

Her gaze snapped back to his. Anguish washed through her words. "You want to know? Here it is: I can't sign a long-term lease for the same reason I can't fall in love with you."

Fall in love. With him. Van inhaled, sharp and quick and managed to keep his balance. Barely. "You love me?"

"No." Her brows slammed together. Her words were urgent. Almost desperate. "I can't love you."

Van rammed his own heart aside. "Can't or won't love me?"

"Both." Elise's fingers dug into the pillow and crumpled the faux fur. "Don't you get it? I can't love you and I can't sign a lease because I might not be here."

His concern plummeted into dread. The deep, mind-numbing kind. He knew what she was thinking. He just didn't want to get it. Didn't want to hear it. He wanted to argue. "We can go wherever you want."

"It's not that." Her hold on the pillow loosened. Resignation wrapped around her words. "I'm a cancer survivor with no guarantee it won't come back. No guarantee I can beat it twice."

Van wanted to shout. Curse. Rage against the unfairness of it all.

"I have to live in the present," Elise added.

"Alone and never planning a future." Van held her gaze. "That's no way to live, Elise."

"Don't talk to me about living, Van." Elise raised her chin and leveled her clear, steady gaze on him. "It's not like you're living either."

Van absorbed her anger like a well-aimed punch. He welcomed it. Better that than be defeated. "What does that mean?"

"You've been so busy hiding out in your grief for the past two years, you abandoned your own family," she charged.

Her words rammed harder against his chest. Van's throat closed.

But she never let up. "Did it ever occur to you that your family might've needed you? That they might've needed your support, too."

Van opened and closed his mouth. He wanted to block the truth. Wanted to cut and run. He was good at that, he supposed. He locked his knees, held his ground.

"Or that you needed your family just as much." Elise exhaled as if she'd exhausted her ire.

Van scrubbed his hand over his face and across his neck. "My work requires a lot of travel."

"Even so, you could've made time for what's important. For *who* is important." Elise tossed the pillow on the blanket with the others and wiped her hands together as if she was finished. With him and the conversation. She added, "Your mom passed, Van, but you still have an entire family that loves and needs you."

"But not you," he said quietly.

"We always knew we only had this one week and then we'd have to say goodbye." That distance returned to her voice. To her eyes.

How he hated that. He searched her face. Searched inside himself. All he felt was empty. All he saw was the truth. "Is this goodbye then?"

Her chin dipped down. "There's nothing else it can be."

"They're here." Stella's boisterous voice rang from the patio. She waved her arms, motioning everyone onto the porch and smiled. "Let the party begin."

Van watched Elise turn and join the others.

He ran his hands over his polo shirt and dress shorts and detached himself from the pain. From the heartache. Elise was right. It was always going to be a goodbye. He'd always known that.

And now he just had to accept it.

*J*ust after midnight, Van stood inside his childhood bedroom, the bunkbeds long since replaced by a queen-size bed, the mess of a teenage boy long since traded for clean white walls and plush carpet. Despite the updates, that undercurrent of comfort remained, in every room and every space.

He stared at a framed picture of his brothers and him at his high school graduation. They all had the same cheek-to-cheek grins full of hope and optimism. That same night, Leda and Clay Hollister had presented Van with his formal adoption papers. Turning Van from a foster kid without roots into a Hollister with a family. A family who understood his desire to join the military. And in turn they'd wanted Van to understand he always had a place to come back to.

Van turned at the knock on his door.

His dad stood in the open doorway and regarded Van. "Want to talk about it?"

"What makes you think there's something to talk about?" Van countered then shook his head. Just like that he was a teenager again; denying his parents knew anything about him and even less about his feelings.

His dad walked over to the closet, opened the door, and pulled something off the highest shelf. "Don't suppose you remember this?"

Van gaped at the familiar dark blue-and-tan backpack in his dad's grip. Surprise filled his words. "That's my old go-bag. I can't believe you still have it."

"That's your mom's doing." Clay shut the closet door and lifted the backpack. "Did you know your mom would replace the expired snacks you stashed in here? And she'd wash and refold the clothes once a month?"

"That sounds exactly like something mom would do." Van touched his chest as if he could capture the love and gratitude he still felt for his parents.

By the time Van was thirteen, he had slept in over twenty different empty beds in group homes, shelters, and foster houses, and he'd been simply waiting to age out of the system. That backpack was all Van had carried from one foster location to the next. He always had it prepared and ready to grab quickly. Then his luck had changed, and he'd landed at the Hollister's the summer before his freshman year in high school. Still, he'd kept that backpack packed and within easy reach those first few years with the Hollister's. His parents had known and understood.

"Your mom asked me to give it to you when you came home." Clay cleared his throat and added, "She told me I would know when you needed it."

Van ran his hand over his head and squeezed the back of his neck. He was leaving in two days. Heading back to his life. He wasn't sure what an old go-bag could give him.

His dad set the backpack on the end of the bed near Van. "I thought I'd give it to you when you left on Sunday, but something tells me you need it now."

It was just a go-bag. A relic from his old life. Van lifted it up to prove it was nothing to fear. "It's heavier than I remember."

The smallest smile shifted across his dad's face, there and gone just as quickly. He said, "That's your mom's doing again."

Van set the backpack down and unzipped it. He pulled out a sweatshirt and unrolled it, revealing a Sea Glass Bay logo. A notecard dropped onto the bed. He picked it up. His breath stalled in his lungs.

Printed in his mom's familiar cursive was the full address for the Hollister house, and a note again written in his mom's handwriting: *So you don't ever forget where your home is.*

The notecard was dated the same month and year that Van had moved into the Hollister's house. Into his first real home.

Clay cleared his throat again. "It wasn't luck, Van. We knew from the day you came to live here that you belonged in our family. And your mom wanted you to always know that too."

Van wiped at his eyes and noticed a binder of sorts inside the backpack. He pulled it out and realized it was a photo album. One that contained pictures from that same year he had moved in, and all the way through his time in the army and every trip home. Van flipped through the pages. Years of his life with his family captured for him to know where he belonged.

"Your mom started it." His dad's voice was thoughtful. "And Gail and I have been adding to it."

Inside the front cover his mother had written: *Van, in case your memories become a little less sharp.* Van turned the pages, to the current photographs. The ones without his mom. But he could see his mom's smile in Seth's. Almost hear her laughter in Axel's tipped back head. And feel her kindness in Jared's arm resting around his shoulders. There was his family. And there in those pages was so much love. Leda Hollister was still there within his brothers and in him. *Home. Roots. Family.* How it all mattered. He sent a silent thank you to his mom and looked at the man he wanted to be like one day. He paused, hesitated, then said quietly. "Dad, I don't want to go. I don't want to run this time."

Clay brushed his knuckles against his eye. "What are you saying, Van?"

"This is home." Van hugged the photo album against his chest. "It will always be my home. With you. My brothers. And now Gail, too."

"It's all your mom ever wanted." Clay's voice was gruff and emotion stained. "All we ever wanted was to give you a home."

"She did that. All of you did." All this time he had roots and yet hadn't been tending to them. That had to change. Van shook his head, regret tinging his words. "I just wish I hadn't stayed away for so long. That I'd realized sooner what this place means to me."

222

"Well, you're home now." Clay hugged him. "It's what you do next that matters."

"I love my work, Dad." Van zipped up the go-bag. "I'm committed to my team."

"I'd expect nothing less." Clay squeezed Van's shoulder. "And when you leave again for work, we'll all worry. That's what family does."

Van nodded then followed his gut and went on impulse. He said, "Dad, I want to buy this house. Would that be okay?"

Because the more Van turned over the idea, the more he liked it. The more it became less a whim and more of a must.

Clay blinked and studied Van. "You're serious?"

"I want a place to come home to. Even more, I need you and my family to come back to. I know that now." Van scrubbed his hands over his face. All that time searching and looking for what had been right in Sea Glass Bay all along: the place he belonged. The home that gave him a chance to find himself again. The family that helped him reset and strengthen his foundation.

"Are you sure?" Clay asked.

"Yeah." Van's smile stretched from cheek to cheek like the one in that photograph from years ago. "For the first time in a long while, everything feels right. And it feels even better knowing this house will stay in the family. See the next generation of Hollister's grow up right here."

"Next generation?" Clay arched an eyebrow at him. His gaze bright and joy filled. "Something else feeling right, too?"

Van laughed. And that joy filled him, too. "Yeah. Looks like Seth was right again."

"About what?" Clay asked.

"What it's always about, Dad." Van hugged his dad and laughed again. "Love."

10

When the last kitchen counter in the bed and breakfast was wiped clean and the freshly washed dishes put away, Elise wandered out onto the patio. Stella had turned the fireplace on for ambiance. The lights strung around the back yard were turned off and the giant movie screen blank. The backyard was quiet and still. Yet Elise was restless, and her inner calm seemed far out of reach. She stared at the flames in the gas fireplace and concentrated on her breathing.

Stella handed Elise a glass of red wine. "Your old room is ready upstairs."

"You didn't have to." Elise sipped her wine and turned her back to the fire.

"I insist you stay." Stella sat, anchored her bare feet on the edge of the fireplace then shook a bottle of glittery silver nail polish. "We have things to discuss."

Elise sipped her wine and eyed her friend over the rim of her glass. "Is this about the rental space?"

"We can certainly start there." Stella unscrewed the nail polish that Elise and she had chosen earlier to accent the strappy sandals Stella planned to wear to the wedding tomorrow.

Elise didn't want to think about the wedding. If she thought about the wedding, she'd think about Van. And if she did that, she'd hurt even more. She sat in one of the cushioned chairs beside Stella. "You think I should open a yoga studio in town."

"I think you should do what feels right in your gut." Stella brushed on the nail polish. Her movements as unrushed and easygoing as her words.

But they were talking about the future. Elise's future. The one Van wanted her to consider. That restlessness spiked. Elise set her arms on her knees to keep her legs from shaking up and down. "The space is everything I want in a studio."

"Then what's stopping you?" Stella waved her hand over her freshly painted toenails.

"I'm scared," Elise admitted.

Stella nodded. "Understandable. It's a risk."

"It's more than that." Elise swirled the wine around in her glass and considered her words. "It's like I'm poking at fate somehow. Making plans I have no business making. Like I should leave well enough alone and be grateful for what I have."

"You put your life on pause for cancer once before." Stella reached over and set her hand on Elise's knee. Her touch was light, her voice sincere. "Don't you think it might be time to press play again."

Elise cradled her wine glass and looked at her friend. Her confession scratched against her throat. "I don't know if I can." Or if she even knew how.

"Can I tell you a secret?" Stella asked.

"Please." *Please tell me what to do. Please tell me everything will be all right. Please tell me it's okay to risk.*

"We tempt fate every time we get out of bed in the morning." Stella's grin lifted her eyebrows. Her gaze was honest, her words candid and heartfelt. "But it's not how long we live, but how we choose to live that matters."

Choose joy. Leda Hollister's advice. If Elise chose joy, she'd chose Van. Again and again. After all, her heart belonged to him. She wouldn't deny that any longer, as much as she'd tried to hit the pause button whenever he was around. Yet that truth didn't set her free. "But I have a good life."

"You should have the *best* life, my dear." Stella finished her other foot and put the cap on the nail polish bottle. "The best life for you. Not one you settle into because then the cancer has won after all."

Elise had beaten cancer, according to her doctors and her follow-up tests. It hadn't won. She hadn't let it ... or had she? The treatments were over. Her recent checkups clear. But the fear—well, that she'd let in like an old friend. She'd accused Van of hiding and yet she'd been doing the same thing. She'd fought for a second chance, and it was past time to enjoy that victory. Anticipation, hope, positivity—she wrapped all those feelings around her lingering fear and smiled at Stella. "I'm going to open my own studio. Choose my dream."

"That's my girl." Stella sat back her own smile full of pride. "Now about those other things."

Elise lifted her hand like a crossing guard. Her own studio was no small step. And more than enough, wasn't it? Her heart raced, wanting its dream, too. "Please don't make this about Van and me."

"I don't need to." Stella tipped her wine glass at Elise, her words and grin all too insightful. "You did that all on your own."

"He's leaving," Elise argued.

"Because you didn't open your heart," Stella countered.

Stella made it sound as if it was all so simple. Could love be that clear-cut? That uncomplicated. She wanted it to be. So very much. "Van is leaving because he has a life *outside* Sea Glass Bay."

"Open your heart, dear," Stella urged. "And give Van a reason to come back home to you."

Back home to me. Those words curled through Elise and filled her. She wanted to be Van's reason. He was hers. Would her heart be enough? She didn't know, but she had to try. This was about her best life *with* Van in it. Scratch that: this was about *their* best lives. Together. "Stella, I'm going to need your help."

"Of course. You always have my help." Stella straightened in her chair. A gleam sparked in her gaze. "Now, what are we doing?"

Elise grinned. "Claiming a soldier's heart."

11

The next morning, Elise paced around the kitchen island in the bed and breakfast and second-guessed their plan and the purple-and-white floral sundress that Stella had insisted Elise put on, after declaring that Operation Snag a Soldier was too important not to dress up for. Elise adjusted the spaghetti strap on her shoulder and checked the clock on the oven.

There was still time. She could run upstairs, slip on her yoga pants and comfy wrap and center herself. Elise headed for the staircase.

The doorbell chimed like an alarm signaling her time was officially up. She slowed, smoothed her hands over her dress and veered toward the foyer. She pushed the loose spaghetti strap back up her shoulder, then reached for the door and her most serene expression.

"Van." Elise's fingers curled around the metal door handle like an anchor. He was close enough she could walk right into his arms. If only he'd open them to her. His hands were tucked inside the pockets of his short pockets. Everything about him was too contained. Too closed off. Worry skimmed over Elise.

"Stella texted me to pick up the picnic blankets." The baseball hat pulled low on Van's forehead shadowed his gaze, but not the reserve in his words. "Stella thought they might be welcome on the beach for the reception this evening."

"She had several errands to run and took the blankets with her to drop off." Elise tried to work her tone into apologetic, just like she and Stella had planned. "I guess you didn't get that text." No surprise since Stella hadn't sent one.

Van lifted his arm and motioned toward the curved driveway behind him. "Then I should probably ..."

"Come inside," Elise cut him off. The strap on her dress sagged off her shoulder again, but she refused to give up.

Van rubbed the back of his neck and hesitated on the welcome mat.

"I've got homemade bacon cinnamon rolls and caramel vanilla iced-coffee from Wide Awake Café," Elise rushed on. *And my heart to give you if you want it. Please tell me you want it.* "I was told those are your favorites."

"They are." A hint of a smile washed across his face. Then he sobered again. "Look, Elise."

"Van," Elise said at the same time. Then she rushed on, no backing down. "There are things I need to say. Do you mind?"

"Please." He motioned as if giving her the floor.

Elise clutched her hands together in front of her. She wanted to hold Van. Instead, she locked her gaze on his and confessed, "I know what I said last night. And I know how I feel about you. I can't guarantee a long life, but I can guarantee I want to spend whatever time I have with you. I want us to be together, Van. I don't know how that looks. Or what that means." Elise paused, exhaled around her nerves, and finally revealed her heart. Her whole heart. "What I'm trying to say is that I love you. I love you, Van. And I want to know if you could love me too."

Van had gone completely still. His chest barely rose as if he was even afraid to draw a deep breath.

Silence surged between them, broken only by the thud of Elise's heart in her ears. Elise touched her throat, but nothing eased the chill building inside her. "Van. Say something. Anything. Please."

Please. I'm falling here. I don't want to fall alone.

"I had the words. Had a whole plan worked out." He cleared his throat, rubbed his cheek as if putting himself back together. Another small smile flickered across his face. Awe and surprise worked around his words. "But it was for tonight, on our beach." He took a deep breath. "I have so much to tell you. So much I want to say to you also."

Elise bit her bottom lip. Fought the tears collecting in her eyes.

"I didn't realize until I came home how much I missed it." He reached up and brushed his fingers across her cheek. Tender. Gentle. "And then with you this week, I started to find myself again. With you, I discovered the man I want to be. The man my mom always saw in me. And the person I want to be for us."

Elise swayed. That chill started to recede.

"And now I'm just going to keep it simple, if that's okay with you." He stepped inside, moved right into her space. His other arm wrapped around her waist as if she was his anchor. His gaze was warm and intense and focused completely on her. As if she was his everything. His words came clear and sure. "Elise Harper, I love you, too. I've loved you since that night on the beach."

Her heart soared. It was all she wanted. All she needed. Elise threw her arms around his neck. He met her halfway for a kiss that joined two hearts. Promised love. And built a foundation she'd only dreamed about.

A car horn honked from the driveway. Elise pulled away, set her head on Van's shoulder, and laughed.

Stella waved from her sporty convertible, grinned at them, and called out, "Have you two finally found your love story then?"

Van's arm tightened around Elise as he pressed a kiss on her forehead. Happiness spilled through his words. "I believe we have."

"Definitely." Elise beamed.

"That's nice and about time, too." Stella got out of her sports car and made a *shooing* motion at them. "Now we all need to be getting ready. There's a beach wedding to get to, family to enjoy, and love to celebrate."

Elise slipped her hand into Van's. And for Elise and Van, a life to build. Together.

Epilogue

by Cari Lynn Webb

"You've inspired me, Clay." Stella Sanders slipped her sparkly sandals into the shoe-check station Gail and their wedding planner had designed for their sunset beach-wedding ceremony.

Clay handed the bed and breakfast owner and the couple's good friend a bottle of water and grinned. "You don't sound too happy about that realization, Stella."

"I see you and Gail together Clay, and I find myself entertaining the idea of love again." Stella's laughter twinkled around them, merry and bright like the sea glass sparkling on the sand. She shook her head. "I thought we were too old for love."

"I've discovered we're never too old for soul-deep happiness and peace," Clay admitted. "And we all deserve that, no matter our age."

Stella touched her sea-glass necklace and nodded. "I couldn't agree more."

Axel stepped up and offered his arm to Stella. "I saved you one of the best seats on the beach, Stella."

"You did good, Clay." Stella slipped her arm around Axel's. "Your sons will be true blessings to the families they marry into."

Axel straightened, pride filling his grin. Clay's gaze warmed and shifted to the two women already seated in the front row: Penny and Serena. The two women chatted with Seth and their laughter flowed easily between them. The Hollister family was expanding, and Clay was fairly certain there would be walks down the aisles soon for the women and his sons. It was all Leda had ever wanted, for Clay and their sons to lead full lives after she was gone. Love softened that pang inside his chest. The one he'd accepted would always be there for Leda.

But today was about looking forward. Just as Leda wanted. Nina captured a picture of Stella and Axel, then aimed her camera at Jared escorting Leah Martin and Hank DeLeon to their seats. Leah and Gail had designed the orchid and lily arrangements bursting at the end of each row. And the lush floral and green arch where his sons moved to stand. Jared tapped his watch on his wrist and motioned for Clay to join them.

Clay greeted more guests, ran his hands over his suit jacket, then made his way to the arch and his sons. Nina continued capturing moments on her camera while directing everyone into their positions. The wedding planner swept through, checked on the officiant and the groom, then drifted away to check on the bride.

Clay clasped his hands behind his back, smiled for Nina's camera, and waited for the pause between flashes. He slanted his gaze toward Seth. "Where's Van?"

A woman skipped down the aisle and dropped into the empty seat beside Penny. Elise smiled wide and gave them a two-thumbs up signal. Clay slipped a warning into his voice. "Seth. Where's Van?"

His oldest son gave Clay a mysterious smile and the same two thumbs up sign Elise had flashed.

Jared reached behind Seth and squeezed Clay's shoulder. "We got you, Dad. No need to be nervous."

"I'm not nervous," Clay whispered. He was exasperated and becoming slightly irritated. And on his wedding day. *Wedding. Day.*

Clay scrubbed his palm lightly over his face. He hadn't thought he'd ever be standing at the end of an aisle, waiting on a woman. One that had captured his heart completely and perfectly. He'd fallen in love again, and it wasn't time to concentrate on anything but that and the woman he would spend the rest of his life with. A slow smile built from inside him.

"It's time, Dad." Axel stepped in front of Clay and adjusted his father's bowtie. "You clean up good."

Clay chuckled. "You're not too bad yourself."

Axel grinned and took his place on the bride's side of the arch.

One of the local Irish band members set her bow against her fiddle. The first vibrant bars of the Irish wedding song flowed across the beach, harmonizing with the slow, gentle crash of the calm ocean waves. The airy, light notes of the flute joined in. Their guests stood and turned toward the end of the rose petal strewn aisle.

Clay's breath slowed and dissolved. His bride stood at the end of the aisle. She wore a stunning pale-green silk dress with ivory leaves and vines embroidered on the lace overlay and the most brilliant smile he'd ever seen. Tears pooled in Clay's eyes.

Clay's gaze shifted to the man escorting Gail down the aisle. *His son, Van.* In his full-dress Army uniform. The light from the setting sun caught on Van's medals and sparkled. And one of Clay's tears slipped free. Van's hand covered Gail's fingers resting on his arm and the pair started their walk toward Clay.

He was surrounded by his family. Love and gratitude flowed through him—so much it was hard to contain. A man shouldn't be so lucky in his life. So fortunate. He'd spend everyday making sure his family knew and felt his love for them.

Van handed Gail over to Clay and smiled. "Take good care of each other."

Clay cleared his throat and wrapped his fingers around Gail's. "I plan to."

Gail brushed at her damp cheek. "Me too."

"Even so, we will all be watching." Van grinned. "Just to make sure."

Van moved to stand beside Axel on the bride's side. Clay took Gail's hands in his and the officiant welcomed everyone to the uniting of two hearts. One family.

Clay wasn't certain how his life could get any fuller. But he was certainly looking forward to the adventure with his family beside him.